EVERYTHING HERE IS UNDER CONTROL

A NOVEL

EVERYTHING HERE IS UNDER CONTROL

A NOVEL

EMILY ADRIAN

BLACK
STONE
PUBLISHING

388 2562

Printed in the United States of America

First edition: 2020
ISBN 978-1-982639-64-8
Fiction / Women

1 3 5 7 9 10 8 6 4 2

CIP data for this book is available
from the Library of Congress

Blackstone Publishing
31 Mistletoe Rd.
Ashland, OR 97520

www.BlackstonePublishing.com

For Kate,
who tried to warn me

CHAPTER ONE

There was a point in Carrie's labor when she wouldn't stop asking if I was okay.

Carrie had declined drugs until she was six centimeters dilated and the contractions left her shaking so hard she couldn't steady her jaw. When she forfeited her fantasy of a natural birth, she did so completely; she wanted the drugs flowing through her system in an instant. But the anesthesiologist was with another patient, and then he was on his lunch break, and then he was with yet another patient. Moaning and periodically vomiting into the plastic tray her mother held beneath her chin, Carrie endured. In the few seconds between each contraction, she would wipe tears from her eyes and say, "Is Amanda okay?"

Crouched in the corner of the hospital room, I was too dizzy to stand and too ashamed to answer Carrie's question.

"Amanda's fine," said Mrs. Hart, her voice clipped. Carrie's mother hadn't wanted me in the room to begin with, and now she took no pleasure in having correctly predicted my uselessness.

She wanted me gone, but I was not going to leave. My goal was to return to Carrie's side. In another second.

"Don't worry about Amanda," murmured the nurse, strapping a fetal monitor around the globe of Carrie's abdomen. "Amanda's not the one having a baby tonight."

Later Carrie would say she had been sincerely worried about me. Driven insane by pain, it seemed possible to her that I had, coincidentally, been struck ill. That I needed medical attention. That the nurse's indifference toward me would facilitate my swift and untimely death.

No, I was just freaking out.

Carrie's pain shocked me for two reasons. For starters, I believed we were prepared. We had read all the books and attended a six-week childbirth class in a church basement. With our eyes wide open we watched both the vaginal delivery video and the C-section video. Neither of us passed out—which was more than we could say for one husband in the class, a man whose habit was to surreptitiously eat Skittles out of his pocket while the instructor defined *mucous plug* and *episiotomy*. Carrie and I both cried at the videos' conclusions. The blue-faced babies covered in wax and jam, the moms with their naked elation.

The second reason was that I had once watched Carrie attempt to hurdle a shopping cart in the Walmart parking lot and land on her face. Peeling herself from the pavement, horror movie blood gushing from her nose, she regarded the boy who had issued the dare and said, "My bad."

In the delivery room Carrie moaned like she was already half dead, but her pain remained theoretical to me. I couldn't share it. I couldn't make it stop. A small and stingy part of me even suspected her of exaggerating. Of writhing and wailing because birth was, among other things, a little bit boring. The child in me—the child even younger than the one I was—wanted to gripe, "C'mon, Carrie, cut it out."

But if Carrie could have labored quietly, with a stoic grimace on her face, she would have.

The anesthesiologist remained MIA. Carrie asked the nurse to check the progress of her cervix.

"We checked an hour ago," the nurse argued.

"I just feel like I need to push," Carrie said.

"Can you describe the sensation? Does it feel like you have to poop?"

Through gnashing teeth, Carrie said, "It *feels* like I need to push a baby out of my vagina."

I laughed in my corner.

"You!" Carrie shouted. "If you're dying, then go get some help already. If you're just being pathetic, then get your ass over here."

I got my ass over there. Seeing my friend up close was a revelation. Moments ago her agony had rendered her strange to me, but now I realized she was more herself than ever. Carrie was in charge; she was pissed off; she was unapologetic. She was alone in this, but she wanted me near her. No one would have blamed her for banishing me from the room, either out of girlish embarrassment or an instinct to shield me from my own future suffering, but the two of us knew what no one else would admit: Carrie could handle this.

The nurse confirmed that Carrie had dilated from six centimeters to ten in under an hour and finally paged the obstetrician. He was a white man with square glasses and an equally square head, who entered the room with a Coke Zero in one hand and took his time assembling his collection of tools. As he removed the lower half of Carrie's bed, he said, "First baby, I hope?" and

Carrie clamped her eyes shut, as if the effort would make the doctor disappear. The wayward anesthesiologist wandered into the room, took one look at Carrie with her knees splayed, and reversed back into the hall.

I will hate those men forever.

For two hours I held Carrie's right leg while she pushed. When her doctor, nurse, and mother began counting in unison from the start of each contraction—urging Carrie to sustain the push—I studied the creases in her forehead and said, "Don't do that. She hates it." When her lips became so dry they cracked and bled, I smeared cherry-flavored Chapstick all over her mouth.

Between each contraction I offered her both a basin for puke and a drink of water. She had time to choose only one.

When she screamed for someone to *please, please* help her, I cried into the scaly flesh of her bent knee. I didn't think about her age (inadequate) or about the boy (same) whom she'd abandoned in the waiting room. I'd forgotten all about the baby. I thought, distinctly, *This girl is the love of my life.* If Carrie died, I would die too. Her mother had stopped shooting me looks and was standing on the other side of her with a concerned, haunted expression. Like she couldn't remember what year it was.

I watched Carrie's perineum tear open and spill blood onto the doctor's shoes. I watched Nina emerge sunny-side up with her full head of black hair. She was waving her arms, protesting the eviction, the arctic air of the delivery room. The doctor tried to hand the baby to the nurse, but I said, "No. Give her to Carrie," with such ferocity that no one argued.

With her daughter in her arms, Carrie laughed. "That was so fucking brutal." Radiating love, she stroked the pillow of Nina's cheek. For the first time I understood what it meant to be proud of another person. That I could already feel Carrie retreating from me didn't seem to matter. We were eighteen years old; one of us would snap at the other within the hour. So what? I was sure of two things I hadn't previously known: I would become a mother too, someday, and Carrie Hart would be in the room when it happened.

"I promise, nothing will ever be so bad again," Carrie told Nina.

Even now, over a decade later, I count this among the best days of my life.

CHAPTER TWO

By the time I untangle the baby from the straps of his car seat, he's screaming like I'm trying to murder him. His fire engine song exhausts me without actually winning my sympathy. Every once in a while, his sorrow is slow to build, beginning with wide eyes and a trembling lower lip. That's the move that melts my heart, but he has no idea.

Avoiding my own reflection, I slam the car door and carry him up the porch steps. I knock softly, as if—despite our mutual hysteria and the odors clinging to our clothes—Jack and I will be mistaken for polite.

Down the street, the setting sun makes the white houses glow amber. Cicadas drone, atonal and urgent. I grew up two blocks from here, and this neighborhood still looks the same: cracked slabs of sidewalk, bundles of coupons spilling from every mailbox. It makes me think of ding-dong ditching the neighbors, of lying down in the middle of the road to make a suicidal snow angel on a Tuesday night in January because our mom had kicked us out of the house. She needed to balance her checkbook. She needed, she told us, to hear herself think.

Jack will never know the pleasure of lying in the middle of the road. We live in Queens.

Bees emerge from a mess of lavender beneath the living room window and hover way too close to the baby's bald head. The veins visible at his temples still freak me out. It's alarming to think of his anatomy, delicate but complete. To realize I'm the one responsible for ensuring he grows into a full-size, weather-resistant human— and though I've googled it before, I can't remember what you're supposed to do if your baby gets stung by a bee.

I can't remember if I locked the car, or if it's even customary to lock your car in Deerling, Ohio.

I can't remember the last time I slept more than two consecutive hours.

This baby has driven me a little bit crazy. I once believed I was capable of understanding that an infant cries because he is an infant—because he was born, if not literally yesterday, then last week or last month or last spring—and not because he has specific designs on ruining his mother's life.

But I was wrong. I'm not capable.

From inside I hear footsteps, the first confirmation that anyone's home, and I consider turning on my heel. I should go to my mom's. No matter what I interrupt, Jaclyn will give the impression of being overjoyed to see me. For a moment I imagine myself trusting her joy, doing nothing to resist it, wrapping it like a blanket around my shoulders. But the baby makes quick getaways unrealistic. Even if I managed to strap Jack into his car seat in record time, Carrie would see the New York plates on the retreating car and know.

A teenager answers the door. We stare at each other, unblinking. After a while she says, "Greetings."

I should compliment her hair, formerly cloudlike but now pulled away from her face and secured in cornrows—definitely her mother's work. I should exclaim over her height, her upcoming birthday. Because Nina is not yet a teenager; she's two weeks from turning thirteen. Lately, as far as I'm concerned, people are either babies or not-babies. Nina might as well be college bound. She sleeps through the night—or, if she doesn't, she's secretive about her sobbing.

Nina's gaze lands on Jack. "What's all over his shirt?" she asks. It's her first time meeting him. Her arms hang loosely at her sides.

"Spit-up." It's overwhelming, Nina no longer being three. "Is Carrie here?"

Nina steps willingly aside as her mother appears in the doorway. The relief I expected to feel at the sight of her eludes me. Carrie's features are stitched tight with guarded confusion, her toned arms are covered in tattoos I've never seen, but she's fundamentally unchanged. I would recognize this woman with my eyes closed. We're like dogs born in the same litter, programmed to remember each other's scent.

"Why is he crying like that?" she asks.

I kiss the top of Jack's head. He's two and a half months old, but it's been years since Carrie and I welcomed unplanned visits from each other. "What do you mean? He's a baby."

"He sounds hungry."

"He ate an hour, maybe two hours ago. He was asleep on the highway, but he hates getting in and out of the bucket seat. It's super awkward. I'll be glad when he has some neck control." I'm shouting, ostensibly to be heard over Jack, but also because I need to shout.

I need to shout, to pull my own hair, to sink my teeth into something firm but yielding.

"If he was sleeping, why didn't you bring the whole car seat inside?"

She's a genius. "I didn't think of that. I'm not used to driving. In the city, we—"

Carrie reaches for Jack. I hand him over, and the relief is immediate. It's like climbing to the fifth floor of our apartment building and letting the grocery bags slide from my wrists.

"I gave birth," I announce. Nina has vanished into the recesses of the house, and I'm glad. Carrie may resent my arrival, but she's still the only person on earth whom I want to see right now.

"You did," she concedes.

We're Facebook friends, the connection forged in memory of our actual friendship, long dormant. Carrie has left congratulatory comments on the pictures I can't stop posting.

"I need help," I say. And the admission is cathartic.

Carrie Hart's body is familiar to me, from the shape of her eyebrows to her small and permanently arched toes, but her expression in this moment is impossible to read, overcompensating for all the years in which we intuited each other's every thought.

"Amanda," Carrie says, "how am I supposed to help you?"

Jack is curled against Carrie's chest, his screams reduced to hiccups. His pose, fetal, induces a surge of grief. Part of me wants to snatch him back, and part of me wants to abandon him with Carrie. I've been fantasizing about waiting rooms, long lines at the supermarket, gridlock traffic. Everything that used to make me miserable.

"You already are," I say.

* * *

"Take a shower," Carrie tells me, still holding my baby. "You smell like spoiled milk and . . . something else." When she wrinkles her nose I see the sixteen-year-old she used to be. I flash upon climbing into the passenger seat of her pickup truck, early morning, before school, her obvious disdain of the Victoria's Secret "Endless Love" body mist my mother gave me for Christmas in 2001.

Whatever happened to that truck? I want to ask her, but it's the wrong time.

"Jalapeño chips," is all I say.

Before turning down the hallway, I steal a look at the two of them. With one hand Carrie opens the refrigerator, removes a carton of orange juice, and pours herself a glass. Whenever I try to multitask with Jack in my arms, he protests, demanding 100 percent of my attention at all times. When Carrie does it, he's none the wiser.

I've realized that the handling of newborns is a language your body either retains or forgets forever. Gabe's mother trembled the first time we gave her Jack to hold. She cupped his head in her palm like he was made of ash.

Gabe's parents came to New York two weeks into Jack's life, when I was still so raw and weepy I could hardly look at anyone. They marveled at what they called Gabe's *involvement*. Imagine, Hank and Diane Feldman's own son changing diapers! Their own son with his special trick of bouncing the baby through the air, simulating the soothing sensation of riding an old elevator.

"You've got it made," Diane told me. "Hank was always at the office. Day or night, didn't matter, I was on my own."

She meant to shame me as I sat on the couch in my sweatpants, scrolling hungrily through the internet while Gabe tended to our infant. I was unmoved. I did pity Diane though. Gabe plus his two older brothers amounted to nine years of diaper changes, nine years of teething and temper tantrums. Hadn't Diane deserved a break?

Carrie's bathroom is stocked with hand soap and hand towels, the accoutrements of a level of adulthood to which Gabe and I still aspire. Ten times a day a single bar of Ivory travels between our sink and the edge of our tub. Occasionally one of us will cloak our annoyance in vague intention: "Whoever goes to the store next should buy some hand soap." But whoever goes to the store next will be daunted by the aisle of toiletries and cleaning supplies. Beneath the buzzing fluorescent lights, all of it will seem frivolous, exorbitantly priced. Three ninety-nine? For what—the plastic pump?

In Carrie's shower I'm happy, almost drunk on autonomy. I try to ignore the phantom baby who always cries behind the clamor of the water hitting the tiles. Even harder is ignoring the real baby—mine—who has woken up. Who is screaming now.

As we drove across the interminable state of Pennsylvania—Clinton signage gradually conceding to red barns branded, in white paint, TRUMP—I tried to desensitize myself to the sound of crying. I remembered that Jack had been fed, burped, and changed. That he was, by definition, okay. My zen would last for a minute or two, tops, before a switch would flip. With my heart racing, nerves fraying, I had to pull over. In the back seat I would hug him close to me, furious but unable to bear his fury.

Carrie has four different kinds of conditioner—the packaging sleek and sexy, splashed with niche terms like *keratin*—and about two squirts left in a bottle of generic shampoo. I skip the shampoo and massage something oily into my scalp. Since the birth my hair has been brittle, as dry as September grass. Rushing to rinse it, I'm not anxious so much as excited. To have gained entry into

Carrie's house thrills me. So she didn't wrap me in her arms, and maybe never will again, but she did reach for Jack. Automatically and without fear.

Doesn't that count for something?

After putting back on my stale clothes, I go to the kitchen, where Carrie calmly hands me my enraged baby. He shakes his head from side to side, clenched fist waving in front of his mouth. Sinking into a chair, I lift up my shirt and latch him onto my breast. There's a twinge of pain, a wave of shame, a sudden awareness of my own hunger—and then nothing. I'm at ease, feeding my kid in Carrie's kitchen. Like it's nothing new.

Carrie leans against the counter, holding her empty juice glass. "Where does Gabe think you are?"

"Here," I say, wishing she hadn't thought to ask.

"Here in my house?"

"Here in Deerling."

She waits.

"I'm sure he assumes I'm staying with my mom," I say.

"But you're leaving him to assume?"

I search her expression for signs of triumph or satisfaction. She looks only concerned. "I'll fill him in," I say.

"When?"

"Soon."

"Amanda." Carrie drops her chin, looking at me like she means business. "What happened?"

Nothing happened, except that Gabe and I were nice to each other for thirteen years. His weekday alarm was set to ring ten minutes before mine, allowing him to make coffee and eggs while I negotiated myself out of bed. On a Friday night a friend would text him after dark, hoping Gabe was up for grabbing a drink at the Deep End, and Gabe would frown at his phone and say to me, puzzled, "But I'm hanging out with *you*." Throughout my pregnancy we exchanged handwritten notes, compiled playlists for each other, and made out on the couch like teenagers. And then came the baby, with his ceaseless hunger, his cries so hot the windows fogged over. And suddenly I couldn't look at Gabe without seeing yet another creature wanting something.

When I don't answer her, Carrie says, "Did you guys get a second car?"

"No."

"So Gabe's stuck in New York."

"He's flying out after the last day of school. We'll drive home together and everything. We had a fight, but we're still . . . We'll be fine."

"Okay." She accepts my claim. And I guess it doesn't matter to her whether Gabe and I break up or stay together. What she wants is to know what I'm doing in her kitchen.

"I need some help," I say. "Gabe's at work until six every day. Taking care of the baby by myself is impossible. It's a two-person job."

She lifts her eyebrows and waits for me to realize what I've said. Hot-cheeked, I try to take it back. "I mean, it's either a job for two incompetent people or one extraordinarily competent person. Gabe and I fall into the first category, whereas you—"

"Right." Carrie turns her back to me, placing the glass in the sink. "So, are you pumping?"

I shake my head. "I rented an electric pump for the first few weeks, but I hated it. The sound it made was like a bullfrog dying."

Facing me again, Carrie watches Jack's hand as he reaches toward my neck, searching for jewelry or a lock of hair, anything he can grab and pull. "If you start pumping, I can give him a bottle sometimes while you catch up on sleep."

I lock eyes with Carrie. Her gaze is so neutral, so steady, I'm forced to look away.

"Okay," I say. "That would be good."

She nods, and it's settled.

We're staying.

* * *

Last night, back in New York, Jack wouldn't sleep. All of us collapsed into bed around ten. Jack woke up at 10:45, 11:51, and 12:38. Then, around 2:00 A.M., he woke up mad and stayed that way, refusing my breast, refusing his pacifier, refusing "Hotline Bling" and any other song with a bass line like a heartbeat. He didn't care to be swaddled, shushed, or swung. Instead he cried—his face scrunched and tomato red, his lung capacity limitless. I seethed with a kind of as-seen-on-TV anger, the kind that inspires aggrieved male characters to heave chairs across rooms. Last night, I did not feel like anyone's mother; I felt like a victim. My baby, who did not sleep and did not appear to love anything, was the perpetrator. But because Jack was tiny and I knew, in a purely theoretical way, that he was innocent, I took out my anger on Gabe.

"Wake up," I said to his offensively prone body. Gabe groaned and rolled over. Balancing Jack on one forearm, I pulled the covers from Gabe's shoulders and yelled at him. This time, he sat up straight and rubbed his eyes. "Is the baby okay?"

"He is. I'm not. I need you to take him. I need to sleep."

"Amanda . . ." Now that Gabe could see no one was on fire or unresponsive, he performed his annoyance, squinting at the time on his phone. "I have to be at work in four hours."

Before the baby was born, Gabe had decided he wouldn't use up all his sick days right away. We agreed he would cash them in one at a time, opting to stay home with me after especially challenging nights. We believed this plan bespoke foresight and restraint—back when we still believed some nights would be challenging and others would only be nights.

"And I have to take care of this baby all day, every day, forever. If I could go teach Faulkner to a bunch of teenagers instead, believe me, I would."

"You have no idea what you're talking about. You don't even have to get dressed."

"Can't. Can't get dressed."

We went on like this for a while. The more I cursed, the harder Jack cried. Eventually Gabe told me to calm down. I told him to take his fucking baby. He said to me, "You're the one who wanted this."

I would have strangled him if my hands had been free.

In fact, we both counted the days of my cycles. We both spontaneously and independently brought home presents for a baby who didn't yet exist, not even in embryonic form. Gabe's pick was a New York Public Library onesie, which Jack, with his phobia of long sleeves, wore exactly once. I indulged in a pair of charcoal-gray booties—thirty-four dollars from a boutique in Bushwick. I could have invoked Gabe's own anticipation, his own longing, but I didn't. It was easier to dismiss the evidence and believe this 3:00 a.m. version of Gabe, whose voice was shot and unfamiliar. I believed what he'd said and also what he wasn't saying: I was the one who wanted this; he was the one who didn't.

It's been my fear all along—even before we had Jack—that I tricked Gabe into making a life with me.

I took the baby into the living room. I lay with him on the couch while he screamed into my ear. Gabe sank promptly into a deep sleep; he was snoring by the time Jack released his last rattled sob. When I could safely transfer the baby to the vibrating chair on the coffee table, I located my phone and crept into the kitchen to call my mother.

She answered on the second ring, her voice clear and uncompromised by sleep. It used to take my mother days, sometimes weeks, to call me back. She was slow to acclimate to contemporary cell phone usage, didn't understand that the point was to be available at all times. But Jack's arrival did the trick. Now she requests photos of her grandson daily, is always prepared with heart-eyes and kissy-face emoji and, apparently, for a nocturnal emergency.

"Is he okay?" she asked.

I started to cry.

"Oh, honey." My mother's name is Jaclyn. We named the baby after her, my consolation prize for letting Gabe pass Feldman onto Jack. Minutes after he was born, when a nurse automatically labeled the plastic bassinet "Baby Flood," Gabe said with a lilt of panic, "That's not his name!" The nurse told him to relax; the sticker was not a legally binding document.

"Gabe is an asshole, it turns out."

She went quiet. Gabe would be a sore subject between us if we ever talked about him. Mom has never been able to forget, or forgive, the circumstances under which we first got together.

"What's going on?"

"He expects me to do this by myself. I don't think he even realizes he expects it, but since he's been back at work, I've become the default parent. When Gabe wants to take a shower he goes and takes one. If I want to take a shower—like, for instance, after days of Jack vomiting my own breast milk into my hair—I have to ask Gabe if it's okay. And sometimes, Mom, he has the nerve to say it's not."

"Well, honey, Gabe has a job."

Until recently I, too, had a job. I wore imitation silk blouses from H&M and skirts that were either too loose around my waist or too tight around my hips. Working as an office manager for a branding agency didn't typically impress people, but secretly, I was sometimes impressed with myself. Riding the subway to West Fifty-Eighth Street, depositing my coat in a break room with a view of Columbus Circle—these were elements of a routine that, to anyone from Deerling, Ohio, would have looked like success.

For years Gabe encouraged me to apply for a better position within the company, which hired new designers all the time. The candidates were mostly boys with skinny ties and large glasses. My task was to show them to the conference room and offer them coffee, which they invariably accepted, though it was past noon and they must have understood I would have to make a fresh pot. Gabe—who maintains an endearing belief that I am an artist, sticking my doodles to our refrigerator as if to encourage a small child—always wanted me to throw my own portfolio into the pool, but *portfolio* was a generous term for my life's work. My bosses didn't want to see faded sketches of my childhood best friend or the view from our bedroom window in Queens (air shaft, puddle, pigeon). All the company wanted was to hire a twenty-three-year-old with a degree in graphic design.

When I was pregnant with Jack but still hiding my bump beneath blazers and sweaters, a position opened up in project management. The job paid twice as much as I was making. The money meant more to me than having a career vaguely related to art, and I applied. During the interview, I sat in my boss's office—where I often sat, computer open on my lap, as he dictated his correspondence through wet mouthfuls of Caesar salad—and claimed I could do the job in my sleep. No training necessary. For years I had been booking travel and arranging meetings for the guys who already did the job. I knew everything about our company, our diverse roster of clients.

"And I'll still pick up your dry cleaning," I added desperately, inappropriately. "And I'll keep watering the plants. That ficus won't die on my watch!"

The following Monday, an email informed me that "after discussing the matter at length," the firm's partners had chosen someone with more experience—and also, when I had a free moment, could I call Connor and let him know he got the job?

Jack, by then, had started punching and kicking and turning somersaults in utero. Even through the thick material of my sweaters, his acrobatics were discernible to anyone who stared hard at my midsection. My intention had been to take three months of unpaid leave, but now I thought, *Why?* Daycare would nearly negate my salary. Gabe's job came with health insurance. The men for whom I worked defined me by the college degree I didn't have. One option was to quit right then and never come back. So I did.

Over the phone, I told my mom, "Staying home with a baby is harder than a job. You know it is."

"But Gabe has to show up on time. You're already where you need to be."

"I want him to share the responsibility. He shouldn't be squeezing the occasional hour of babysitting into his life; he should be scheduling the rest of his life around his son's never-ending needs and demands."

"Men don't usually do that," she said, placating but firm. My mother, normally a little bit scared of me, wielded more authority with each of these late-night phone calls. "May I make a suggestion?"

She was smoking. I could hear her lips opening and closing around the cigarette. I wished she would quit. I wished she would eat something besides Stove Top stuffing, coleslaw kits, and Skinny Cow ice cream sandwiches.

I wished she would use moisturizer and vote Democrat.

"You may," I said.

"Try loving Gabe less."

"Excuse me?"

"If you love him less, you'll lower your expectations of him, and then Gabe won't be able to disappoint you anymore."

Momentarily, Jaclyn's reasoning struck me as genius. I could accept that Gabe was not who I thought he was; I could subscribe to the belief that men are good for breadwinning and mowing the lawn and not much else.

Except that we don't have a lawn, and my relationship with Gabe has been the only consistently satisfying venture of my adult life.

"I can't love him less than I already do."

"Are you sure?" Jaclyn asked. "After you were born, I made a deliberate choice to love your father less. I remember the exact moment. I was trying to breastfeed you, but you were never any good at it. You kept arching your back, squirming and fussing. Your father stayed in the other room, not even offering to bring me a glass of water or an extra pillow. And I thought, *You know, I should really just love him less.*"

I took a moment to resent my dad, an activity that brought

automatic pleasure—as it aligned me with my mother—but an equal amount of guilt. Distracted by the dichotomy, I was slow to identify the flaw in Jaclyn's advice.

"You and Dad got divorced," I said.

"And he hasn't disappointed me in many years."

"Loving Gabe less won't solve the problem of this baby needing to be attached to my body at every fucking moment."

"That's not a problem, Amanda. That's motherhood."

As soon as we hung up, Jack realized I'd forsaken him and began to wail. *Watch*, I told my mother in my head, *Watch what happens next*, and I waited for Gabe to rise from our bed, scoop Jack into his arms and—with remorse in his averted eyes—tell me to go lie down. My plan was to forgive him instantly. Gabe was exhausted, overwhelmed. He' didn't have the option of spontaneously quitting his job or the kind of mother he could call, hysterical, in the earliest hours of the morning.

Jack cried, and Gabe stayed in the bedroom. I changed my mind; I would not forgive him. I was the one who had given birth. I had done enough. By the time Gabe's alarm went off at six thirty, the diaper bag was packed. All I had left to do was throw some clothes into a suitcase and gas up our mostly sedentary car.

He begged me not to go. Over and over he said he was sorry. He touched my face. He reached for Jack. He offered to call in sick and spend the day on baby duty. We already had plans to drive out to Ohio after his last day of teaching. We would see my mom then. There was no reason for me to go alone. Plus, Gabe claimed, he didn't want to miss a moment of his son's infancy, let alone a full two weeks.

"Really?" I asked. "Because you seemed perfectly happy to miss last night."

I was proud of my cruelty. My tendency is to be passive, to end fights with an earnest apology almost as soon as they start, Gabe's hand in mine. Of course I've fantasized about winning, but my desire to prove him wrong rarely outmeasures my need to be in Gabe's good graces.

Yesterday morning he thought I was bluffing, but I wasn't. As he pleaded with me, I was already calculating how many times I would have to stop the car to nurse Jack, whether we would need to stay the night somewhere in rural Pennsylvania.

"Don't do this, Amanda. Give me the baby and go get some sleep."

I didn't give him the baby, and I still haven't slept. I told Gabe I would see him in July. The sound of our padlocked door clanking shut filled me with an exhilarating sense of power, which was almost immediately consumed by regret.

Once a decade, often enough to constitute a pattern, I do something unforgivable to the person I love most. My transgressions fold into one another, so that as I was leaving him, I was leaving her all over again.

CHAPTER THREE

The fraught animal sound of Jack wailing drives me to bite my own arm. Afterward, teeth marks linger on my purpling flesh. That's how Carrie finds me: hissing obscenities in my baby's direction and bruising fast.

Somehow, it's 3:00 A.M. again.

"Sorry," I say, teetering between shame and indifference. It's not the first time Carrie has caught me in a compromising act.

She shakes her head, dismissing my apology, and takes Jack. I love her for the confidence with which she seizes him, never offering or asking permission. What I've learned since giving birth is that few people are truly helpful. Unwilling to risk fucking up, most people *want* to help but require clear instructions, live tutorials—which is the opposite of helpful. Carrie does what needs doing. In her sturdy arms, Jack has already calmed down.

Passing him to Gabe sometimes has the same effect. Maybe it's because neither of them smells like breast milk, that drug the baby craves always but can only stomach at two-hour intervals.

I grab the kettle from the stove and fill it with tap water. "I guess he'll figure out I'm an asshole pretty soon."

Carrie looks amused. "What?"

"The swearing. The insults."

"Oh, don't worry about it. You won't always feel like saying terrible things to your baby."

"When will I stop?"

"In, like, another two months."

"I don't remember you ever saying terrible things to Nina."

"Oh, god." Carrie grimaces. Her memories appear to cause her physical pain. "Let's not even go there."

I can't come up with anything lucid to say. We stand in silence. The cuffs of Carrie's sweatpants hit below her knees, showing off webs of tattoos covering both her calves. Some are sharp and saturated, while others have already begun to fade. Her hair is wrapped in silk for the night. Staring at the scarf, teal and gold, my first thought is I've never seen it before.

My second thought is I'm losing my mind.

Carrie nods at the kettle. "Grab it before it whistles?"

She cups a hand over Jack's ear. My baby eyes me reproachfully as I slide the kettle to the back burner. The moment he's attached to someone else, I remember how lovely he is. With his curled fists and velvet cheeks, his scalp that inexplicably smells like cream and cinnamon. My need for him is physical, the way I once needed to cling to my own mother's leg or how, as a teenager, I couldn't keep my hands away from my hair. If I could, I would exist exclusively in those rare moments when Jack is returned to my arms.

The hours after he was born were the worst of my life. Two pediatricians whisked him off to the NICU, and every time I asked the roomful of remaining nurses and doctors what was wrong with my baby, they seemed to answer in another language. A resident stitched me back together under the supervision of an OB—who commented, casually, "It's not your best work, but it'll do"—while I, shocked and hollow and in no less pain than before, looked up at Gabe and said, "I haven't even met him yet. I only came here so I could meet him."

We were apart for two hours. All I ever understood about his time in the NICU was that someone there had taught him how to breathe.

In the aftermath of childbirth, women tend to announce their private thoughts. I don't know why, but Carrie did it, and I did it too. Holding Jack for the first time, looking into the ice-blue eyes that have already darkened, I said, "Oh, we're going to be fine."

I couldn't have imagined feeling a fraction of the frustration I now feel toward him nightly.

The problem is I am a person with only two hands, one boob that works better than the other, overactive tear ducts, injuries in dark places, and feet that no longer fit into my shoes. And I need to sleep. My need for sleep occurs to me sometimes as a revelation, the way when I was a child it would periodically dawn on me that what my parents needed was money.

When we both have tea—mine in my hands, Carrie's growing cold on the counter—I finally think to say, "I hope we didn't wake up Nina."

"Nina's not home."

"Where is she?" The possibility of Nina being anywhere without Carrie is for me a novelty.

"Sleeping over at a friend's house. I said no, earlier, but then you showed up . . . and, well."

"You renegotiated? Is that wise?"

I realize I'm still swaying from side to side, dancing along with Carrie and Jack. To stop myself, I sink into a chair. Jack's cheek is deflating against Carrie's shoulder, his eyelids at half-mast.

"Nina demands constant renegotiation. It feels like I never stop bargaining with her."

"Are things not good between you guys?"

I'm conscious of having phrased the question like I'm asking Carrie about a coworker, or a lover.

"She thinks I'm evil incarnate."

"What happened?"

"Nothing. It's just the usual preteen stuff. When I'm home, I'm *breathing down her neck*. When I'm working, I'm guilty of neglecting her on, like, a criminal level. I occasionally require her to eat a vegetable, or a damn egg. Yesterday I wouldn't let her get a pair of camo jeans from the juniors section at Walmart, and she *still* hasn't forgiven me."

"Were the jeans expensive or something?"

"They were camo," Carrie repeats. "Camouflage jeans."

I blink at her.

"Camouflage is for ill-adjusted white boys who pose with the corpses of the animals they've just killed."

"I doubt she sees it that way."

"What other way is there?"

"I don't know. There are hipsters wandering around Brooklyn in Carhartt jackets. She probably just thought they looked cool."

Carrie shakes her head. Admittedly, I have a hard time picturing these pants on her daughter. If I try too hard to reconcile preteen Nina with the three-year-old I once carried on my hip through the aisles of the video rental store, beaming when people assumed she was mine, I know I'll be flooded with regret.

"Where's the sleepover?" I ask. In Deerling, a person's address tells you everything you need to know. The town is divided into four quadrants: the farmlands, the trailer parks, and a residential jumble bisected by train tracks in the conventional sense. Carrie and I grew up on the right side of them. My mother has since downgraded.

Carrie avoids my actual question and tells me, "She has this new friend."

"Go on."

Carrie heaves a sigh. It's a bottomless 3:00 A.M. sigh. "She's fourteen, and her name is Maxine."

"Max for short?"

"Never. Always Maxine."

"What's her deal?" I'm thirty-one years old, a card-carrying member of our neighborhood's grocery co-op, and thrilled to be gossiping about some small-town teenage girl. This is the most enthralled I've been in months.

"No deal. She's perfectly sweet. I mean, she keeps asking me to tattoo her, which is annoying."

"What does she want?"

Carrie gives me a blank stare.

"Like, for her tattoo."

"I haven't asked. I'm not tattooing her. It's illegal."

"Do you ever do it, though? Tattoo kids who you know are lying about their age?"

"Of course not, Amanda. I could get my license revoked."

I've insulted her. By implying she's strapped for cash or somehow less than professional. It's not what I meant. I was thinking about Carrie and me, the kind of mischief we used to concoct for ourselves. Back then, I couldn't believe I would ever become an adult.

Now I can't believe I'm supposed to stay one forever.

"Sorry," I say.

"My concern about Maxine is I'm not sure her family's the best influence on Nina. They're filthy rich."

"Come on, this is Deerling. No one's filthy rich."

"They won the lottery."

"What do you mean?" I ask, assuming family money or stock market success.

"I mean they literally won the Powerball jackpot."

"No."

"And then they bought all that land adjacent to the wildlife preserve and built, like, a *Cribs*-style mansion on it. Tennis courts. A circular driveway. A pool edged with actual palm trees."

I shudder. "That's spooky. Palm trees in Ohio." Jack is asleep, but Carrie knows better than to test her luck by sitting down. She continues to sway. It's tempting to sneak out of the room and crawl into bed, but talking to Carrie is an addictive pleasure. Given the chance, I'll stay here until dawn.

"Well, Nina's obsessed with them. She says Maxine's parents have traveled. Maxine's parents know about cheese made from animals other than cows. Maxine's parents treat them like adults."

"Big deal. It's 2016. Any redneck can invest in some spread-able goat cheese."

When Carrie resists laughing, I tell myself it's because she doesn't want to startle the baby.

"My daughter thinks I hate her best friend," she says.

"Do you?"

Carrie presses her lips into a line. "No. But I see through her."

"You see through her," I repeat.

"Sure. She's one of those kids who wants to feel important and admired, so she's found a younger girl willing to look up to her, mythologize her, whatever. She's, you know, poetic. She has song lyrics scribbled all over her backpack. She's chatty and charming."

"Some girls can't help being chatty and charming. You never could."

Rolling her eyes, she says, "I wasn't like that. I think you're remembering yourself."

"No . . . Carrie, I worshipped you."

"Why?" She sounds disgusted.

"I don't know. All the usual reasons. Because you were gorgeous and talented. And when boys took you to the drive-in, you stuck to your usual order of three coneys with extra onions."

Carrie wrinkles her nose. "Those are terrible reasons."

I shrug.

Jack makes a sleepy, satisfied chuffing sound. Carrie brushes her lips against his forehead. It's so easy for her to love him. She knows what a baby is, and how briefly he will inhabit this hot-water-bottle form before becoming a person. To me, Jack's personhood is still notional. When I think about his future, more than excitement or curiosity, I feel hope. A desperate kind of hope that makes me wish I were religious so I could pray for his safety.

"I don't think you worshipped me," Carrie says. "I think that's a convenient way to remember things. As if I had some kind of power over you."

"All right. I'm sorry."

"I'm just saying, the admiration was mutual. I think we actually had a remarkably healthy friendship. I'm still waiting to feel as comfortable with another person as I did with you when we were kids."

Gabe has a theory that no one has more than five friends. You may think you have twenty, but you're kidding yourself. No more than five individuals are genuinely pleased to attend your birthday party. No more than five will visit you in the hospital, let you borrow their family's house upstate, or remember the results of your last visit to the allergist.

By Gabe's definition, Carrie and I are not friends. But I do think about her every day. Often I have trouble convincing myself we are not the same person, living out alternate versions of one life.

Did I worship her?

Not exactly. As a kid, I loved her and loathed her with a kind of recklessness typically reserved for loving and loathing oneself.

We've been taking turns letting our guards down. The moment one of us veers toward sincerity, the other's hackles go up. To tell Carrie what she wants to hear now would mean betraying Gabe. And however it looks, that's not what I'm trying to do.

I stay silent too long. Resentment radiates from Carrie.

"I'm glad you were comfortable," I say.

"You weren't?"

"I was. Mostly."

"Was there something else I should have done? To make things easier for you?"

I'm too tired for this. "I'm not a comfortable person, like, in general?"

She exhales through her nose. "Right."

I offer to take the baby back. Slowly, Carrie uses her whole body to lower Jack into my arms. The deadweight of him is so satisfying. He's the most substantial thing I've ever made.

I stand up, yawning. Carrie's looking at me like I owe her something—and it's true, I do, but it's almost beside the point. She and I both understand why I drove from New York to Deerling—five hundred miles with a baby in the back seat, both of us crying more often than not—and turned up on her doorstep utterly unannounced.

Carrie Hart is the best mother I know.

* * *

Gabe is a model father. When he's home, he tends to our son with a patience that is not willed or performed but innate. A patience of which he seems completely unaware. On our best Saturdays—when Jack has slept an extra hour or when one of Gabe's colleagues has had bagels delivered to our apartment door—I watch him whisper sweetness into our son's ear, and I'm charmed, contented. The sight of them together is sexy in a way that has nothing to do with the act itself and everything to do with the smug, animal satisfaction of having made a healthy baby with a good man.

If you ask Gabe's parents—and if they were a few drinks in and feeling honest—they would specify that he's a little *too* good. Overachieving, or even overcompensating for something (me). Mr. and Mrs. Feldman, along with all of our friends in New York—who ask us about parenthood as if it's an exotic destination where they haven't yet vacationed—note how often Gabe goes beyond the minimum dad duties. He carries Jack out of the room for diaper changes without passive-aggressively presenting the baby for me to sniff. He holds Jack face-out, so that the baby is seated in the crook of his right elbow, for hours at a time. He talks to the baby in a voice that is half Raffi, half Grover, even though the baby is too young to laugh and can only gaze at his dad with solemn appreciation.

Meanwhile, I keep a mental list of all the things Gabe doesn't do.

Gabe has never

- trimmed the baby's fingernails,
- checked the baby's temperature,
- wiped away the cheese that forms in the rarely exposed creases of the baby's neck,
- put socks on the baby's feet,
- refilled the plastic dispenser with a fresh stack of wipes,
- scheduled the baby's next checkup, or
- turned the baby onto his front for ten supervised minutes of "tummy time"—a ritual that is both ineffably crucial to the baby's development and, judging by the baby's screams, absolute torture.

Even more than I want to sit in a dark movie theater for 110 minutes—even more than I want to eat a medium-rare hamburger the size of my face—I want Gabe to do these things. Not because these things are so vital, but because I can't opt out of a single task. I am the baby's servant and his playmate. His transportation vehicle and his home. His bed, his food source, his mother.

And nobody ever tells me I'm a good one.

At Jack's two-month appointment, he was mad even before the needles. He didn't like being naked on the cold metal scale; he didn't like having his tongue depressed, his testicles prodded, his reflexes affirmed. The doctor, a scruffy resident, asked if our baby was always so fussy, if he was "super colicky." Gabe's cheek twitched and dimpled, a sure sign he was offended, but his response was an even-keeled, "Not at all."

My job was to hold Jack as still as possible, even as he reeled and writhed. We were flanked by two nurses, each young and ponytailed and wielding her syringe with an obvious lack of confidence.

A poke in each of his thighs. Jack locked eyes with me. His mouth rubber-banded into a shocked, silent O. By the time he found his voice, I was crying too. I pressed his cheek to mine, and our hot tears mingled. The clinic evoked the hospital, a place to which I'd never wanted to return.

The doctor and I were the same age. I could tell. We might have shared a middle school gym class or a dormitory floor in college. If you cut open our trunks, we'd have the same number of rings. He furrowed his unibrow at me and, shouting to be heard over Jack, asked, "How's everything going at home, Mom? Do you have all the support you need?"

It's a disorienting phenomenon about which no one thinks to warn you: starting the moment you get pregnant, doctors never bother to learn your name. They seem to relish referring to you exclusively by your new role; perhaps they imagine you relish it, too.

Grimacing, I nodded at Gabe. My entire support system.

"And you're doing okay, emotionally? Any fatigue, anxiety, guilt? Feeling overwhelmed?"

Yes to all of it. What new mother could honestly answer no? Still, I must have shaken my head. I was bouncing and swaying, dying to strap Jack into his carrier and rush homeward. The motion of the subway would put him to sleep. It always did.

The doctor asked, "Have you harmed your baby or imagined yourself harming your baby?"

They were such radically different questions—why had he asked them back-to-back, in almost the same breath?

I have imagined Jack getting hurt in every way. Falling tree limbs, aggressive dogs, pots of water boiling over. Earthquakes and lightning storms and crosstown buses. Once, years ago, Gabe and I were driving between Deerling and New York and we passed the immediate aftermath of a collision. The paramedics had just arrived at the scene where an entire family—Mom, Dad, baby boy—had been ejected from their minivan and now lay prostrate, bleeding out onto the interstate. I had suppressed the memory until recently, when Gabe brought it up. I was eight months pregnant. We were shopping for a car seat.

Now the image crosses my mind daily.

I have imagined losing my temper. Shaking my baby or dropping him onto the floor and walking away. In the earliest, sleepless days I feared myself as much as I feared the weather, the highway, or miscellaneous acts of God. Over and over I realized the worst thing, the soul-destroying thing, would be if I hurt my son. To hurt him would be to erase every decent thing I'd ever done, reducing my life to one uncalculated yet unforgivable act of violence.

When I find myself at my wit's end—3:00 A.M., always 3:00 A.M.—I think *the worst thing* until I catch my breath. Until I am back in my own skin. Until I am kissing his soft cheeks.

I found I couldn't answer the doctor's question, and Gabe intervened. With his hand on my back, he said, "Amanda is an amazing mother."

The doctor made eye contact with Gabe and nodded. "I'm sure she is," he said, and looked down at his pager. Their exchange had nothing to do with me. It was one man confirming to another: *Everything here is under control.*

Later, back in our apartment, the table strewn with gift wrap from the packages that wouldn't stop arriving, I ranted about the scruffy doctor.

"What was the point of those questions? If I'm not head-over-heels in love with my infant at every moment, I require medication? If I'm not euphoric, I'm unhinged? Since when is ambivalence a crime?"

I trusted Gabe to take my side. In our old life, one of us was always ranting, gesticulating wildly with a drink in hand. Drops of red wine formed constellations on the ceiling of our apartment. I pointed upward, slyly, whenever a dinner guest witnessed one of Gabe's impassioned speeches. But I was always on his side, and he was always on mine.

We had no reason not to agree on everything.

"I don't think that's what he meant," Gabe said. Jack was asleep in his vibrating chair atop the kitchen counter. His lips were adorably pursed. "I think he was just running through common symptoms of postpartum depression."

"Which are also common symptoms of having *recently had a baby*!"

Gabe shrugged. He seemed profoundly bored with me and only slightly more captivated by something on the internet. It could have been an email detailing school-wide budget cuts, or passive-aggression from his mother, or a hospital bill we couldn't pay. I imagined grabbing his phone and chucking it across the room—but I didn't do it.

"Do you think I'm depressed?" I asked him.

"I don't think you're happy," he said.

"I didn't have a baby because I thought it would make me happy."

Gabe turned up his hand as if I'd said something laughably illogical. *I didn't order this pizza because I was hungry.*

"Really?" he asked. "Then why'd you have one?"

I don't remember. All I know is that I cannot un-have him, and I have never, for a single moment, wished I could.

CHAPTER FOUR

When Nina comes home the next day, I'm breastfeeding Jack in the kitchen and drinking one of Carrie's beers. I am briefly terrified to be alone with her.

"Getting your baby drunk?" Nina asks. Her eyes are shadowed with post-sleepover exhaustion. Her purple skinny jeans are stained with something—pizza grease or nacho cheese.

Caught off guard, I can't decide between putting my boob away and grabbing a receiving blanket to drape over it and the baby. I decide to do nothing, to fight sarcasm with sarcasm. "You want one?"

"A baby or a beer?"

"A beer."

"Um, I'm twelve?"

"If Jack's old enough, you must be."

"No thanks. The mother would kill me."

I smile. "Speaking of Carrie, what time does she get home?"

Nina glances at the clock on the microwave. "Depends. Sometimes six, sometimes later."

"Like, how late?"

She squeezes her shoulders, an exaggerated shrug. "Eight? Nine?"

"Does that happen a lot?"

"Yeah, like if someone's come from far away."

Carrie owns her own tattoo studio in Mansfield, the closest town with a main drag and a movie theater. She inherited the shop from her mentor, a woman who ran it for thirty years until she died of lung cancer.

Carrie is famous for her tattoos. The Instagram account to which she posts pictures of her finished pieces has over two hundred thousand followers. Sometimes the tattoos get republished on Facebook or on Buzzfeed listicles of *Fifty Tattoos You Wish You Had*. I always recognize Carrie's work when I see it. She's known for inking—on strangers' biceps, shoulders, or ribcages—particular characters of her own invention: a wild-eyed fox, a somber Hitchcockian gentleman. One character of whom the internet is especially fond resembles me. She has my asymmetrical eyebrows, my round nostrils and pursed lips.

The explanation is simple: there were entire summers when all Carrie and I did was draw each other.

With one hand pinning Jack to my breast, I use the other to wrestle my phone from my back pocket. I want to text Carrie to ask if there's something I can pick up for dinner. The screen displays our most recent exchange. It's from two and a half months ago—a message I barely remember sending, followed by a response I'm sure I never read.

April 2, 2016, 2:34 A.M.

Me: I'm in labor.

36

Carrie: You've got this! I love you.

Carrie and I have not regularly texted each other since the earliest years of our twenties, before phones were smart or punishing enough to preserve the conversation in one continuous archive, time-stamped and searchable. In the throes of active labor, hours I spent cursing my own mother's name—after Jaclyn's doctor extracted me via emergency C-section, she waited a mere eighteen months before squeezing out my brother, claiming the traditional method was *relaxing* by comparison—I, apparently, felt Carrie's absence. Did I assume her number had stayed the same, as mine had, or did I imagine I was shooting a plea out into the void?

Texting her again will force her to review the exchange, to remember my silence. What happened was I stopped checking my notifications at about six centimeters. And later, after Gabe sent around a postpartum shot of me with Jack—I looked gaunt, delirious—there were so many messages, all of them seemingly meant for someone else. Someone who could see straight.

Still, Carrie's text hadn't been compulsory. It had been generous. The longer I stare at it, the more I worry her lukewarm reception of me and Jack on her front porch had less to do with ancient history than with this message, isolated and suspended at the top of the screen when it could have been long-buried in baby pictures, my frantic questions, and Carrie's calm answers.

I drop the phone on the table.

"Do you guys eat dinner together?" I ask Nina.

"Yeah. Mom brings something home."

"That's so nice."

Nina looks skeptical. "What's nice about it?"

"I don't know. When Carrie and I were your age, we never ate with our parents except on, like, federal holidays. Or Sundays."

Nina considers this. I wonder how much she understands about my history with her mother. "My mom would never let me skip dinner. She's super uptight."

Before I can check myself, I'm agreeing. Carrie Hart is a lover of rules and rituals. An author of pro-con lists. Probably it's unfair to classify a woman who leaves her child alone until eight or nine in the evening as *uptight*—in New York, the term would be *negligent*, or perhaps *criminal*—but from personal experience I know Carrie's deep-seated caution can feel oppressive to a kid.

Nina eyes me critically. My agreement was too automatic—and who am I, anyway, to insult her mother? She takes a breath, briefly withholding her complaints about Carrie, and then, for whatever reason—maybe I strike her as passively receptive, trapped in this chair with this baby at my breast—she releases them.

"I just *can't* with her right now. She wants to know *everything*. Every piece of homework I have, every grade I get, all my teachers' names. If a friend invites me to do something, Mom wants to talk to their parents first—even if it's, like, bowling. I mean, *bowling*. What does she think is going to happen at Leonard's Lanes?"

"Well . . ."

Some of the more sinister events of my girlhood transpired at Leonard's Lanes, but before I can phrase a delicate objection, Nina rolls her eyes. "Everyone knows Leonard's a perv. We get our shoes and ask for lane twenty-two, far, far away from that creep."

"Good thinking."

It fascinates me, Nina's ability to have a conversation. Will Jack ever be so sentient?

"And even if something bad happens someday, what's texting me every ten minutes going to do? Like, I'll write back 'I'm fine' . . . 'I'm fine' . . . until suddenly I'm like, 'Being murdered, actually. Send help!'"

Jack has fallen asleep, lightly mouthing me. I try to avoid exposing myself as I yank up the triangular panel of my nursing bra. I mostly fail, and Nina's eyes widen. I refrain from saying something inappropriate about the life stages of the nipple. Mine, once bottle-cap sized, now resemble coasters.

"And what's really frustrating," she says, recovering from the shock, "is how she assumes Maxine is, like, bad news."

"Why does she think that?"

"I don't know. Because Maxine's parents are rich? Because when we're over there, her mom's not breathing down our necks the whole time? Because she has a nose ring?"

I had a nose ring. I obtained it during a school field trip to a long-defunct reformatory in Mansfield, now a popular wedding venue, a ready-made prison film set, and a place to take a hundred teenagers. The tour was not intended to educate so much as reward the sophomore class for selling more magazine subscriptions during our annual fundraiser than the freshmen, juniors, and seniors. Because Carrie's parents had not allowed her to go door-to-door, neither of us had sold a single subscription, and I convinced her we were not obligated to endure the prize. We sneaked away from our group and walked to the town's commercial strip, equal parts sleepy and seedy. She squeezed my hand while a man with a tarantula tattooed on his neck pierced a hole in my left nostril. It lasted half a year, until I got a job at Arby's and my manager made me remove the ring. The piercing healed, leaving a scar that looks like a permanent pimple.

"Is Maxine a good friend?" I ask Nina. "Do you guys watch out for each other?"

Nina looks me in the eye. "She's the best."

I nod, appearing to take Nina at her word. Privately I acknowledge it must be petrifying raising an adolescent in this town with firsthand knowledge of how adolescents in this town operate. Even I am tempted to present Nina with a list of things she's not allowed to do: no joyriding the unpatrolled roads of Amish country; no hanging around boys who like to put bullet holes through Budweiser cans; no hitchhiking; no ATVs; no breaking into singed, abandoned buildings; no talking to anyone who tries to tell you the Civil War was fought over "states' rights."

If I pretend Nina is someone else's daughter—whom I never held against my chest, whose silky, newborn skin I didn't slather in lavender-scented lotion—I understand that a list of forbidden activities becomes, in the hands of a teenager, a list of good ideas.

But I don't regret the years Carrie and I spent risking life and limb. How do you strip a kid of her essential fearlessness? Would you want to, if you could?

Jack stirs in my lap, and I think, *Yes. Duh.*

I tell Nina, "It's scary for your mom to have such a grown-up daughter, you know? It might take a second, but eventually she'll realize she can trust you."

I believe Nina is not her mother. More crucially, I am certain Nina is not me. At her age I would never have looked an adult in the eye and spoken with any amount of candor.

"She thinks I'm a baby," Nina says.

"She doesn't think you're a baby. She thinks you're *her* baby. I know this sounds super weird, but when you have a kid, you feel like you have to protect them from the entire world forever."

Nina regards Jack. He's lying across my thighs, his arms splayed. "Baby Jack versus everybody," she says, reaching out to touch his downy head. I hold my breath, hoping he won't wake up. He doesn't.

For the first time since he was born, I feel like I might be able to accomplish something unrelated to his livelihood. I can prove to Nina that her mother is a good one. My official stance will be that Carrie's *not* uptight. Not paranoid, or obsessive, or lame. I'll convince Nina her mom is the reason cars don't crash and front doors remain locked. When it rains, Nina reaches into the depths of her JanSport, finds the umbrella Carrie planted there, and stays dry until the storm passes. Without her mother, Nina would not be free. She would be screwed.

When I succeed in making this point, Carrie will forgive me. She will forgive me, at least, for knocking on her door.

"I take it back," I say. "Your mom's not uptight."

Nina raises an eyebrow.

"You know, when we were young, Carrie Hart was the coolest girl in Deerling. Nothing fazed her."

Nina looks torn between dismissing this information outright and accepting it as a gift. She starts to smile, but at the final moment her lips veer into a sneer. "But then she got pregnant."

"Yes," I concede.

"She was only five years older than I am now."

"Yes."

Nina lifts her chin. She's a beautiful kid. She has Carrie's warm brown skin and curly hair so thick that elastics snap in their effort to contain it. Only if you were to examine her blue-flecked eyes would you ever guess her dad was white.

"Not so cool anymore," Nina says.

* * *

Carrie brings home Chinese food. We eat in shifts, passing Jack back and forth between us. I refer longingly to the vibrating infant chair I left behind in New York. In our regular life, Jack has three parents—one of them is that chair. Its polka-dot hammock is the only physical space, with the exception of my arms, in which Jack is completely at ease. I ordered it from Amazon two weeks after he was born. The package arrived while Gabe was at work. Though illustrated, the assembly instructions were in Portuguese. I attempted to lay Jack on a couch cushion while I fiddled with the screws, the buckles, parts A through K. He screamed inconsolably; I wept and condemned the Fisher-Price Company. Remembering this scene causes residual rage to pinprick my palms.

After Nina shuts herself inside her room, I say to Carrie, "Your kid is perfect."

Half an egg roll hanging out of her mouth, Carrie shoots me a wary look. "Who, Nina?"

"Yeah. That one."

"She's definitely not. Our girl has some serious flaws."

"Perfect flaws."

Carrie grins as she grabs a beer from inside the refrigerator door. She offers one to me, and I accept, and now it's my first two-drink day in over a year. Since before I got pregnant.

"I've been trying to decide if I should get her out of this town," Carrie says.

I wait.

"The studio's become reasonably profitable. And I have enough of a following now, I think I could move somewhere more central and still have steady work. But there are no guarantees, obviously. People always assume I've done so well in *spite* of my location, but I worry the shop's success is *because* of it. There's no competition out here. And besides, I don't know how Nina would feel about leaving. She's so attached to this Maxine person."

With her eyes on the ceiling, Carrie sips her beer.

"Where would you go?" I ask.

"I'm not even sure. I'd have to be able to afford a house, and studio space. But somewhere slightly more evolved would be nice."

"Hey, Deerling's evolving. Did I spy a microbrewery behind the Buffalo Wild Wings?"

"The beer's flat."

"Damn."

"My parents are frequent customers though. Reminds them of home."

Carrie's parents met in Cleveland when they were both thirty-five, both already once divorced. They moved here when Carrie was six and Mr. Hart accepted a tenure-track job teaching theology at the local Christian college. That her parents took some amount of pleasure in small-town life was obvious. Her dad enjoyed his detached garage, where he spent Saturdays tinkering with antique engines and building sturdy patio furniture. Each new family who moved to Country Club Drive—grandly named for its proximity to Deerling's rinky-dink golf course—received a pair of cherry-stained Adirondack chairs as a welcome gift. The chairs flanked front doors or fire pits, defining Carrie's street as one where people not only sat outside, in plain view of their neighbors, but talked to one another as they did so. Her mom always had a gaggle of church friends, women who delivered Pyrex containers of chicken soup to anyone who so much as sneezed during Sunday service. Rosalind Hart was a public librarian for over twenty years; she led story time twice a week and knew the name of every child between the ages of zero and eighteen. To say she was beloved is an understatement.

"Are your parents good?" I ask.

"Yeah. My dad and Nina are like this." Carrie crosses her fingers. "Another reason not to leave."

"He hasn't retired yet?"

"No. He's too attached to his students."

My mom used to say of Carrie's father, "He sure makes yours look bad." Mine moved to South Bend when I was in fourth grade, my brother in third. He still calls us on our birthdays to ask a series of rapid-fire questions about our jobs, our relationships, our apartments. As if the speed and volume of the interrogation will mask his indifference.

Lately, I understand that parenthood is an all-or-nothing venture. I don't know if this revelation softens or hardens my attitude toward my father.

"And your mom?" Carrie asks, stiffening. "Is she getting close to retirement?"

Carrie's reluctance to mention my mother pierces me with shame. Carrie has a habit of defining people by the worst things they've ever said.

"Nope. I'm not even sure she's heard of it."

Jack spits out his pacifier and screeches at the ceiling fan. Excited by his excitement, I kiss his cheeks and murmur, "You like that? You like the spinny fan? It goes around and around and around . . ."

Carrie is fidgeting in her chair, peering down the neck of her empty beer bottle. "The thing about moving is, I want to move *toward* something. I don't want to pack up our lives and take

Nina away from everything she's ever known just for, like, my own self-esteem."

Clutching Jack beneath his armpits, I count the fan's rotations and hold perfectly still. "New York," I say, aware of Carrie watching me, "is expensive. Insanely so."

She tosses her bottle into the recycling bin beside the fridge. The clatter of glass on glass startles Jack from his ceiling-fan reverie. Carrie and I both cringe, expecting him to cry, but his scandalized expression slowly fades.

"New York never crossed my mind," Carrie says.

* * *

Later, when Jack and I are doing our 3:00 A.M. laps between the living room and the kitchen, we find a shopping list left on the counter:

- *Bread*
- *Turkey for sandwiches*
- *Diet Dr Pepper*
- *Raisin Bran*
- *Chair for Jack?*

Carrie's handwriting is so familiar to me. Forty years could pass, and I would still recognize the shape of that question mark.

The Walmart in town is open twenty-four hours a day, 365 days a year. I can remember it closing exactly once in my life, during a power outage. My mom and I were among the aspiring shoppers circling the parking lot like fish in a bowl, confused by the number of empty spots, the dark oblivion beyond the supercenter's glass doors. "What are we going to *do*?" Jaclyn lamented, laughing at herself but genuinely unsure.

Jack may cry in the car, but at least I'll have an excuse to ignore him.

Deerling is deserted until we get closer to 71, where an exit sign directs long-haul truckers to our fine dining options. The drive has put Jack to sleep. Outside Walmart I am delighted to find a shopping cart rigged with a contraption that allows you to dock an infant car seat where you would normally place a more substantial child.

Before deciding a doctor would deliver our baby at Mount Sinai, Gabe and I met with a Brooklyn-based midwife who implored me to spend the first weeks of my son's life at home—ideally, topless and in bed. "Let other people bring you food and wash your dishes. Your baby's first few weeks will set the stage for the rest of his life."

Walmart offers an alternative approach to new motherhood: Why should expelling a human being from your body mean missing out on this month's rollbacks?

Disheveled employees stocking the shelves are annoyed with me for reaching around them to grab the Raisin Bran, the Diet Dr Pepper. I get it. The perk of the nightshift should be no moms in pajamas, no sour-smelling children. One shelf-stocker, a middle aged woman with a haircut from the past, frowns at Jack and says, "He should be in bed."

"Tell me about it," I say.

Upon closer examination of my infant's furrowed brow, the woman concedes, "He's cute though."

Is Jack cute? Toddlers are cute. Puppies, kittens, bright-eyed creatures that scamper are cute. At ten weeks old, Jack is something else entirely. His movements are still stiff and erratic. His hands are pruned like an old man's. When he sucks his lower lip and fixes his watery gaze on mine, the rest of the world recedes, irrelevant to our intimacy.

Jack isn't cute, I don't think.

Jack is a marvel.

We get everything on Carrie's list, plus beer to replenish her supply. Almost involuntarily I find myself pushing the cart toward juniors' apparel. The pants Nina wants are on display, front and center. Their camouflage pattern is more impressionistic than Carrie implied—a woodsy blur of green and beige, no distinct twigs or leaves. Remembering the size Carrie wore in middle school, I throw a pair into the cart. The pants are seventeen dollars. They will make Nina exceedingly happy, and Carrie only a little bit mad.

At the register, a blue-smocked cashier asks to see my ID. He holds my New York State driver's license gingerly, as if it's a photograph he doesn't want to smudge. His badge labels him a Proud Walmart Associate. His age is somewhere between thirty and sixty-five.

"What brings you to Ohio?" he asks, passing my license back to me.

"Family," I say.

CHAPTER FIVE

A couple of weeks after Carrie gave birth, she said to me, "You know how everyone thinks when you have sex you, like, lose your innocence?"

Newborn Nina was with Carrie's mom. With our single hour of freedom, on a late July day without a breeze, we went to the dump. It was our old haunt, and not an actual dump but a network of seldom-used trails crisscrossing a retired landfill. The property, all rolling fields and wooded hilltops, was and remains beautiful; only on the wettest days does an odor expose the land's unsavory past.

I flinched when Carrie mentioned sex. Although it had formerly been our favorite topic, we'd stopped discussing sex when Carrie started having it and I continued not having it. To bring it up now felt gratuitous, almost cruel.

"I guess so," I said. My resentment mingled with irritation; we were walking so slowly. I had watched Nina emerge from Carrie's body but didn't yet understand how long the discomfort lasted— how, weeks later, it could feel like the floor of your pelvis was in danger of collapsing. Sliding forward across a chair or a mattress could make you howl in pain.

"That's not how it was for me. Sex was just, like, another thing. On the same level as my first kiss or getting my driver's license or whatever."

My resentment surged.

"But I think I might have lost my innocence when I gave birth. I knew it would hurt, but I didn't know how much I would *suffer*."

I had already begun the process of forgetting Carrie's labor. The experience had been traumatic for both of us, but for me the details were caving under the cultural consensus that birth is no big deal. It happens every day. On television women squint and pant until their husbands say, *You've got this*, or, *You are the strongest woman I know*, and they are inspired, finally, to push like they mean it.

Carrie and I had been getting on each other's nerves. In a few weeks we were planning to become roommates—though, as it was, I'd hardly slept in my own bed since Nina's birth.

"Isn't suffering, like, Birth 101?" I argued. "Isn't it on the first page of the Bible? *In sorrow thou shalt . . .* push out a thousand babies?"

Initially, Carrie looked bewildered. Then she laughed. "True. It's like labor is the first thing people needed an explanation for. That's how bad it is. For a while, about halfway through, I really thought I might die."

I remembered. She had made the announcement to the RN, her mother, and me. *I really think I might die.* Carrie had gasped for breath then, but now she spoke placidly. At some point she had stopped looking to me for acknowledgment or approval.

"You were never going to die," was all I said.

I didn't think about this conversation—or about the light bathing the field, catching the coppery undertones of Carrie's skin—for years. By the time her words came back to me, I was pregnant and smug.

Maybe it's your prerogative as a first-time expectant mother to assume you, uniquely, have an advantage over all the women who have ever complained about childbirth. Because you took prenatal classes or herbal supplements or weekly drop-in yoga. Because your own mom described contractions as "bad period cramps" and you've always resembled her physically—you two have the same calves and elbows and detached earlobes. Of course, afterward, you'll admit it was hard—you might even say "the hardest thing I've ever done"—but only so other women don't feel bad that *you* were built for this.

Pregnancy could have been my excuse to finally call Carrie after years of silence. Several times, tempted to ask about heartburn remedies, whether she'd gambled on shellfish or dared to soak in bathwater above body temperature, I almost did. But I couldn't gauge whether my questions would offend her. Or burden her. Forced to compare her own pregnancy—the chaotic end of her childhood—to mine, a natural development in my grown-up life, would Carrie grieve? Would she envy me?

Did I want her to?

I was delusional enough to imagine not only my pregnancy but my own impending birth in opposition to Carrie's. The delivery would be tidy. Straightforward and sweet, like in those movies.

It hurts to have been so stupid.

Now when I remember being in labor, my mind glosses over the good parts. The hours I spent at home, lurching around our apartment in Gabe's old bathrobe, letting him apply counterpressure to my lower back and feed me bites of a chicken salad sandwich. The pain was astounding, but I had never felt stronger or more productive. All my wildest fantasies about myself were coming true. For a long time, Gabe and I laughed between my contractions.

What stands out is a moment thirty hours into the whole endeavor: A darkened hospital room. An RN with tight curls and breasts straining against the fabric of her scrubs, instructing me to calm down.

"Help me," I kept saying.

"We can't help you, Amanda." The most generic of therapists, Linda, the labor nurse. "Only you can help you."

"You have to help me. It's your job."

"My job is to make sure your baby gets here safely."

The truth was I had forgotten about Jack, whom my body was treating like the last squeeze of toothpaste at the end of the tube. All I remembered was that afternoon at the dump, the boredom and the jealousy with which I'd dismissed Carrie's suffering. She had tried to warn me.

"Forget the baby," I told the nurse. "I'm the one who's dying."

* * *

April 2, 2016, 2:34 a.m.

Me: I'm in labor.

Carrie: You've got this! I love you.

June 19, 2016, 2:36 p.m.

Carrie: Hey, huge favor . . . can you pick up Nina and Maxine from the middle school?

I guess they missed the bus?

Me: Where should I take them?

Carrie: Home? I mean, Maxine can come to our place if she wants.

Me: Sure. No problem.

* * *

Once Jack is strapped into his car seat, solemnly sucking his pacifier, I sprint back inside the house for a trash bag. The Subaru is so filthy it qualifies as an actual garbage receptacle. Any passenger who attempted to position her feet amid the granola-bar wrappers, flattened coffee cups, and mateless baby socks would be met with resistance from the organism that is the mess itself. Kicking around the floor mats are tangles of receiving blankets, crisp and sour with old breast milk; bloated diapers balled and Velcroed; half-empty water bottles; and the scattered contents of a toolbox Gabe purchased on a whim, and which was upended from the back seat during a near collision with an erratic Uber driver in Brooklyn Heights. I throw everything into the bag, the bag into the trunk.

I'm relieved to discover I still have the capacity for embarrassment.

The backroad to the middle school is potholed and lacking in landmarks, but I could drive it with my eyes closed. My body anticipates the twists and dips of the road moments before each appears. It's like singing along to a song I didn't know I had memorized.

Officially, New York is home. I would never go on record with another answer. But sometimes, in winter, the wind whipping across the East River and wet pellets of snow cutting horizontally through the air, I miss Ohio. I miss the whitewashed houses sharing sprawling backyards without defined property lines. The stacks of firewood, the faded hammocks, the Weber grills. The way every residential neighborhood yields to an open expanse of grass—fields that belong to the county but are quietly tended by old men astride their John Deeres.

The men in this part of the state love to mow, would mow all day if their wives would let them.

When Gabe took me to New York with him, I was eager to let the conventions and cadences of Deerling drain from my blood. I was ready to mock Middle America, to talk casually about flyover states. I wanted to eat in restaurants where no item was described as *smothered*. And I did. I do. The city is the choice I'll make again and again, but it remains a foreign language in which I am only technically fluent. The truth is some frozen part of me thaws out here, where I can decode every look, every gesture. I know that when your neighbor says *good morning*, you say it back. Never *hello* or *hi* or *hey-how's-it-going*; that would be rude. Deerling's soundtrack is the one my ears still expect: Screen doors slamming.

Trampolines squeaking. Siblings squabbling in the street. Tornado test sirens blaring on the first Wednesday of every month.

A few years ago, I was listening to NPR and I heard the words *Deerling, Ohio*. I was sitting in my parked car, waiting for the minute at which it would become legal to repark on the opposite side of our street in Queens, and I gasped. It was the same feeling that prompts people to go wild when a rock star addresses the crowd by the name of its city. The satisfying confirmation that someone so famous—so seemingly larger than life—navigates the same world as you.

The next words I heard were her name, and I stopped breathing. My first thought, irrationally, was that she had died.

My shock settled into relief, then rapt attention as the interviewer finished introducing her. The Subaru filled with Carrie's voice. Her tone was friendly, unhurried, confident. "I never went to art school," she said. "It never really seemed like an option, I guess. I had my daughter when I was eighteen. I'd always been creative, but after she was born I started drawing obsessively. Of course I was dead tired, and I didn't technically have the time, but I couldn't quit. I had the sense that if I stopped making art right then, I'd stop forever."

THE HOST: (in her inquisitive warble) *And you began posting your work online?*

CARRIE: *Yeah, I had a blog. I was literally just taking photos of my sketches with this old point-and-shoot digital camera and putting stuff online as a way of connecting with people. As anyone who's had a baby can attest, motherhood can be really, really lonely. For some of us, the internet is the only balm for that loneliness, right? And then what happened was people started asking if they could buy my stuff. And I was like,* absolutely, you can do that.

She sold each drawing for five dollars plus shipping. Her medium was black ink with occasional splashes of whiteout on recycled scraps of cardboard or newspaper. She took commissions, allotting herself a half hour to complete each piece. By the time Nina was a year old, Carrie was squeezing two or three drawings into each nap. Every other day she would drive with the baby to the post office and wait in line, struggling to keep Nina from crumpling the sealed envelopes between her frantic fists.

> CARRIE: *And then, one day, someone emailed me to ask if they could get one of my drawings as a tattoo.*
>
> THE HOST: *Can you describe the drawing?*
>
> CARRIE: *It was an early version of one of my characters, a sort of scowling teenage girl.*
>
> THE HOST: *Did you say* yes?
>
> CARRIE: *I did. And then, as my blog gained more and more traffic, I kept getting the same request . . . and it really started to bug me that some other artist somewhere had earned hundreds of dollars recreating my work. And at the same time, people would send me pictures of the finished tattoos and I was like . . .* damn, that's cool.

Carrie's blog gained in popularity. Tattoos became a staple of mainstream hipster aesthetics. By the time her daughter was two, Carrie knew of a dozen people who'd had her work permanently etched into their skin.

In every case, their skin was white.

> CARRIE: *It was definitely something I noticed. At the time I was starting to think about getting tattooed myself, but every*

artist within driving distance of where I lived had portfolios featuring only white skin. Even when I was totally in love with a person's work, I had no confidence they could, or even would, be willing to create something equally beautiful on me.

THE HOST: *Are there challenges associated with tattooing darker skin?*

CARRIE: *Sort of. Black skin is more likely to scar, so you have to be extra careful with your needle. And obviously, certain shades of ink won't show up as well. But looking around, especially in the Midwest, and especially back then, you'd think dark skin was* impossible *to tattoo. I couldn't find anyone who was doing it. And even if these white artists weren't outright refusing to tattoo black people, none of the work ended up online.*

THE HOST: *Did you set out to specialize in tattooing people of color?*

CARRIE: *I wouldn't say that.*

THE HOST: *What would you say?*

CARRIE: *That I fell in love with an art form. That as a black woman, I wasn't interested in working exclusively with white skin.*

Limited by time and money and motherhood, Carrie traveled no farther than Mansfield, Ohio, to learn her trade. At twenty-one years old, she walked into the curtained tattoo parlor that had been festering on a far-flung corner of Mansfield's downtown for decades and asked the owner, Shirley Hayes, for an apprenticeship. (I held my breath, but Carrie didn't mention having been there before.)

CARRIE: *I was lucky the only shop I knew of happened to be owned by a woman. I can imagine how the whole thing would've gone down if I'd approached a man with the same request. I mean . . . I was a kid, a girl, a mom. The odds this would work out in my favor were low.*

THE HOST: *But they did.*

CARRIE: *Shirley was definitely skeptical, but she agreed to train me. The first tattoo I ever did was on myself.*

THE HOST: *And was it . . . your first?*

CARRIE: (laughing) *Yeah, my first tattoo was my first tattoo.*

THE HOST: *And how long ago was that?*

CARRIE: *It's been about seven years.*

It had been at least as long since I'd seen Carrie. I listened to her describe the sleeves on both her arms—flowers, birds, and ivy starting at her wrists and curling around her biceps, grazing her shoulders. The interviewer read aloud the URL of Carrie's website, where listeners could check out her portfolio and see examples of the work for which she was now famous: "intricate, striking designs on skin of every shade."

Smooth jazz signaled the end of the program. I was glued to the driver's seat, stunned. Half our neighbors had already moved their cars to the opposite side of the street. Ahead of me was the task I'd been trying to avoid: parallel parking between a minivan and a sausage delivery truck.

My eyes burned.

I had known about Carrie's blog and her apprenticeship and her blossoming fame—but only now did I understand these events as installments in a triumphant narrative. I should have called her. I had the perfect excuse: *I heard you on NPR and realized I don't know the first thing about your life.* But, as always, I refrained. I worried she hated me, of course. I worried my own name on the radio would compel her to turn it off. That if I illustrated a children's book, she wouldn't buy it; if I died under newsworthy circumstances, she wouldn't tell a soul she had known me. But most of all, I feared the call would mean nothing to Carrie. Confused, she would answer, the only thought in her head: *But why?*

I couldn't face her indifference, not even the remote possibility of it.

Pulling up to the middle school, I scan the ragtag assortment of kids dawdling outside the entrance. Nina and Maxine are sitting cross-legged at the base of the flagpole, their knees touching. I honk my horn. Nina squints in my direction, shielding her eyes from the sun. She's wearing the camouflage skinny jeans that appeared, neatly folded, at the foot of her bed while she was brushing her teeth this morning. By the time she found the gift, I had made myself scarce, but from the guest room I overheard her lavishing gratitude on Carrie. "Thankyouthankyouthankyou," Nina had trilled.

Carrie's confusion was briefly evident in her silence, before she said softly, "You're welcome."

Maxine wears her bleached hair in short pigtails and an oversize denim jacket with something scribbled in Sharpie down the sleeve. In one hand she clutches a box of Little Debbie Cosmic Brownies.

"So this is Amanda, the *famous* Amanda," Maxine says, climbing into the back seat.

Nina takes the passenger side. I learned recently that modern-day kids are supposed to ride in the back until they're thirteen. Nina is still twelve, but the rule strikes me as so far-fetched that I can't bring myself to mention it. Instructing a seventh grader to ride in the back, with shotgun unclaimed, sounds about as effective as asking a golden retriever to take the wheel.

The girls are giggling. I must have grown up at some point;

being the butt of an inside joke doesn't bother me at all. It's practically an honor.

"Yup, and next to you is baby Jack. He's almost three months."

Maxine peers into the car seat. "Hello, baby Jack. Would you like a brownie?"

I reach back. "He's a little young, but I'll take one."

Maxine peels off the wrapper before placing the brownie in my palm. I eat the whole thing in three bites. It tastes like a chocolate gummy bear, and I immediately want another.

"Where to?" I ask the girls.

Nina turns toward Maxine. "Your house?"

Maxine groans. "My house is boring. Let's have an adventure."

Nervously, Nina fixes her gaze on me.

"Um . . ." Jack is going on forty-five straight minutes of contentment. A new record. I rack my brain for errands that could be construed as adventures. I desperately need a new nursing bra—the one I brought to Ohio has given up its fight against my ever-expanding and shrinking boobs—but Walmart won't register on the girls' adventure-meter. I could use a drink, but while the neon glow of Harvey's Pub might delight them, the field trip would probably get me evicted from Carrie's house.

"You guys want to visit my mom?" I ask.

My heart protests. It's as if I've jumped onto someone else's treadmill mid workout. I love my mother, but she and I have a relationship best maintained at a distance. When I visit, she interprets my every move—my offers to make spaghetti Bolognese instead of ordering from Pizza Hut, the Fitbit I gave her one Christmas, my habit of emptying all the ashtrays overflowing in her tiny kitchen—as slights against her, her home, my entire childhood. She doesn't outright accuse me of antagonizing her, never gives me the chance to assert my gratitude, my humility. Instead she plays the victim. She hisses apologies and retreats to the yard for long periods of time, returning with her eyes swollen, the fingers of her right hand bloodless from the cold.

I'm dying to see Jack in her arms, but the longing is hard to reconcile with my guilt. I should have invited her to New York after he was born. So what if she didn't have the money? So what if she's daunted by air travel? I could have wired her the cash and talked her through the whole thing.

I call her between three and five times a week, demanding an explanation for the impossibility of motherhood, and I have never introduced Jaclyn to her own grandson.

There's a chance she already knows I'm in town. Carrie may have told her own mother, and Rosalind may have encountered Jaclyn at the bank or the Amish-run farmers market. Even more likely is that Gabe has called, hoping to bypass my cell. Whenever I see his name on the screen, I invent a reason why I can't pick up. Because I'm about to shower, or because Jack needs his diaper changed, or because it's my turn to do the dishes. I text Gabe the reason.

It's not that I don't want to talk. I crave his voice—specifically, the casual tenor in which he tells me, almost daily, "I have a theory"—as much as ever. I can't silence his calls without first taking a deep breath to forestall my own tears.

The problem is I'm mad at him, and I don't know how to stop being mad at him. No more than I know how to *love him less*.

If Gabe has called my mom—assuming, as he must, that my mom's place is where I am—I can imagine how Jaclyn navigated the situation. With her nose for deception and general sense of loyalty, she would have covered for me. There's no doubt.

Nina is skeptical, even as Maxine shouts "Yes!" and pumps her fist in the air.

"You sure?" I ask. "I mean, she's just an old lady in a trailer park."

"Positive," Maxine says. "Old people are hilarious."

It's tempting to correct myself. Jaclyn Flood is many things, but old is an exaggeration.

As we drive to the opposite end of town, Maxine hovers over Jack and narrates every development: "His eyes are closing. They're half closed. Now they're kind of twitching. Now he's smiling? Like, smiling and then frowning? Oh my god! No offense, Amanda, but your infant here is a little bit creepy."

I'm about to murmur in agreement, but Nina chastises her friend. "Don't say that. He's an innocent baby."

I watch carefully for breaks in the roadside brush so I don't miss the turnoff for Green Acres Mobile Home Park. After my brother left for Ohio State, my mom sold our house and paid for her trailer in cash. "It's not like the parks down by the train tracks," she assured me over the phone. "The lots are plenty big, and there are rules about not using sheets for curtains, keeping your grass nice and short . . . that kind of thing."

Where does your mother live? I asked myself after we'd hung up, so I could practice answering: *In the nicest trailer park in Deerling County.*

I feel something like shame as I signal for the next left. Green Acres is crowded with assets worth more than the mobile homes themselves—boats and Fords and Harley Davidsons. Wide satellite dishes hint at thousands of channels. The wind smacks against starched American flags. Two lots down from my mom's place, nestled in the overgrown grass, is a MAKE AMERICA GREAT AGAIN sign.

I'm relieved by the lack of signage in Jaclyn's own yard.

Freeing Jack from the car seat, I hug him close. As Nina and

Maxine survey the scene, I try to gauge their reaction. The patriotic clutter must look more or less ordinary to them. Green Acres is shabby, sure, but in rural Ohio even the daughter of Powerball winners has caught drive-by glimpses of real poverty. This isn't it.

Their gazes have landed on my mother's plywood porch. To the right of the front door sits a stone statue of a Siamese cat. Strung around the cat's neck, a notecard says, HI BRIAN!

My embarrassment blooms. My mom is not one for hijinks or cheekiness, but the kind of men who periodically attract her attention are prone to both.

We knock. My fervent wish is that she's alone.

"Is this where you used to live?" Maxine asks.

"No." My mom raised us in a two-bedroom house that the original owner ordered from a Sears catalog circa 1945. My brother and I slept in bunk beds until I hit puberty, at which point my mom gave me her room and finished the attic for herself. The roof was always mossy. The screen doors never latched, storms sending them slapping against the vinyl siding of the house. Shag carpets, fraught plumbing, never enough air. My friends in New York would barely be able to perceive the difference between my childhood home and Jaclyn's current setup, but to me, the difference is everything.

I haven't driven past the property since she sold it.

When my mother throws open the door, she takes a step backward and gasps. Her voice, when she finds it, comes out hushed and reverent. She reminds me of someone spotting a deer in the woods.

"Look at him."

She reaches to touch the baby's head, but her fingers flutter south. She strokes his hand.

"Amanda," she says, without taking her eyes off the baby. My name is an admonishment or a blessing. I don't know which. "Well," she says, composing herself a little, enough to acknowledge both Nina and Maxine. "Who are . . . what are . . . ?" She laughs and wipes her hands on her jeans. She's wearing her hair in a low ponytail, a white tank top with lace edging the straps. She's skinny. She wasn't always.

I once googled *Ohio mom*, hoping, I guess, for a screen full of comforting faces. Hundreds of mugshots stared back at me. Horrified, I showed Gabe, who theorized that plugging any state into the formula would yield similar results. We googled *California mom*. "Ha!" I exclaimed, before realizing the rows of yellow-haired women clutching their yellow-haired sons were actually the same woman and that she had been kidnapped.

My mom says my name again.

"This is Nina and her friend, Maxine," I tell her.

Mom's eyebrows jump. "Nina Hart?" As if she's never seen Carrie's daughter around town.

"That's right." I place a protective hand on Nina's back. No longer secure, the baby squirms.

"Hi," squeaks Nina. Maxine looks stunned. Maybe I should have mentioned that we would be introducing Jack to my mom for the first time.

Jaclyn leads us inside. "I wasn't expecting you until the twenty-ninth," she says. "Where's Gabe?"

The baby has begun to fuss. His staccato shrieks will turn to wails if I don't feed him within seven minutes.

"Back home. He's flying out at the end of next week. You'll see him then."

"You drove here by yourself?"

"Me and Jack."

From the fridge, Mom selects three sweating cans of store-brand pop. She delivers them to the table and urges us to sit. Compared to the dust and decay of our apartment in Queens, her trailer feels clean, almost modern, if not exactly spacious.

A few scratches mar the kitchen table's layer of white paint. Upon closer inspection I realize it's the same table that served as a makeshift desk in my childhood bedroom. I used to doodle on its surface, carve sullen song lyrics into the wood. I remember etching, in deranged capital letters, a line from a Tori Amos song about bleeding. I had thought the singer was threatening her lover with suicide. Only now does it dawn on me that Tori was singing about uterine lining. She was threatening a boy with a baby.

Did my mother ever lean over my desk to read my carvings? Not once was I tempted to search Jaclyn's sock drawer or peer beneath her bed; back then, I would have assumed she was equally uninterested in my own secrets.

Obviously, she read my desk. And probably my diary, and probably the notes folded into paper footballs and piled on my night-stand. Was she mortified for me? Concerned? Sickened with dread?

And as she slapped paint over my adolescent angst, did she celebrate?

I'm waiting for her to ask where I'm staying and how long I've been in town without stopping by, but she cuts straight to the chase.

"Why would you come without Gabe?"

I jiggle the baby, who's rooting against my shirt. I look into Jaclyn's eyes. She must know. She had me when she was twenty-one, my brother when she was twenty-three. On Saturdays she worked overtime at the DMV. My dad sat on the couch and periodically hollered at us to come change the channel. We called this babysitting.

Jack's hunger has become urgent. More than ever, I wish for

an alternative to lifting up my shirt. I'm embarrassed by the map of blue veins beneath my white skin, my doughy stomach ravaged by stretch marks. My mother won't scrutinize me; I know that. Still, I feel as if I'm about to present her with an injury or a self-inflicted scar—damage done to the perfect body she gave me.

Jack is thrashing, giving me no choice. I hunch my shoulders and shift toward the wall while he latches on. "We were bored," I say. "Gabe has so much grading to do this time of year. Jack and I were ready for a vacation."

Nina snorts. "Some vacation," she says.

A Siamese cat jumps onto the table, tail taut, motor running. It's a beautiful specimen of a cat, with lush fur and long whiskers.

I've never seen this animal before in my life.

Maxine, who has been trying hard not to look at my boob, is delighted by the distraction. "Who's this?"

"This is Van," my mother answers. Without asking, I know the cat's last name is Morrison.

"What's his story?" I ask.

Jaclyn blinks at me.

"For example, why did you have Van's likeness carved in stone?"

"Also, who's Brian?" Nina asks.

Wearily, my mother strokes the cat's back. Van arches his spine and purrs. "Brian lives next door with a handful of other young men. Brothers, I think."

Nina and Maxine exchange a look pertaining to some inside joke or secret code. They do this often, like cops or girls in a bar.

"M-A-G-A?" I ask.

Mom feigns ignorance. "What's that?"

I shake my head. She continues, "Brian has a nephew who visits on weekends. He keeps a sandbox behind his trailer."

My laughter shakes my chest, compelling Jack to nurse with renewed force.

Nina says, "What's so funny?"

"Well, to a cat, a sandbox looks a lot like a litter box," Mom explains.

"Ohhh," the girls chorus.

"Did you leave some surprises for Brian?" I ask the cat, who is head-butting the baby, who is too milk-drunk to care.

"He did indeed." The pride my mother takes in this cat, this neighborhood rivalry, disorients me. The version of Jaclyn with which I'm familiar is nonconfrontational, forgiving to a fault. "Brian pounded on the door and asked me, 'Did someone tell you you could have a cat here?' And I said, 'Well, Brian, no one told me I couldn't.' Brian goes, 'Funny, I was under the impression this was a no-pets park,' and I say, 'The beagle on the corner didn't mention anything.' And Brian goes, 'I don't know nothing about a beagle, but I know cat poo carries all kinds of nasty diseases, and I know what I'll do if I catch your cat in my nephew's sandbox again.'"

The girls look upset by my mother's story. Maybe by the word *poo*, specifically, or by my mother's exaggeration of Brian's north Ohio accent, which turns *catch* into *kee-atch*. Jack has pulled off my breast and is staring at the ceiling light. I scratch Van behind the ear. "Think you can dodge a few bullets, buddy?"

"We're not worried," Jaclyn says. She pulls the cat into her lap and focuses on Nina. "You look *just* like Carrie."

"Mom," I warn.

"Well, she does."

Nina is unfazed. "I get that a lot."

"What about you?" Mom shifts toward Maxine. "Do people say you look like your mom or your dad?"

She shrugs. "No one ever really says, either way."

"Trust me, there was a time in your life when it was all anyone talked about," I say.

"Well, let's see." My mom, emboldened by the subject of Brian et al., ejects Van Morrison from her lap and takes the baby from me. He gazes up at her with astonishment. Frequently, Jack resembles an alien stumbling from the wreckage of his spaceship, eyes roving, asking, *What planet is this?*

"He looks like Gabe," my mother admits.

"That's the consensus." They have the same full lips, broad forehead, and pointy ears. I didn't think it would bother me, my son sharing none of my features, but it does.

The baby grows restless. My mother takes him on a tour of her trailer, struggling to interest him in the gold-framed photos of me as a child, the water pouring from the bathroom faucet, the buttons of the remote control. He allows himself to be briefly distracted by a team picture of the 2001 girls bowling team and by Jaclyn's dramatically whispered tale of the time I bowled a 240, leading Deerling to victory against a rival school.

Jack loses it when asked to admire the Ronald Reagan calendar hanging above the kitchen trashcan. My mother—who was fifteen when the man took office—replaces the calendar with a current version each year. Ronald is number one on her list of celebrity guests, dead or alive, whom she would invite to a dinner party. Fantasy dinner party is one of my mother's favorite games— though, to my knowledge, she has never thrown a dinner party.

"We should probably go," I say.

Nina and Maxine are quick to jump to their feet. Reluctantly, my mother hands over my miserable baby and walks us to the door.

The girls are halfway to the car, shuffling over the gravel and singing a Taylor Swift song in a restless, soulless way. My mother palms the top of Jack's head and stoops to kiss the tears from his flushed cheeks. "He's beautiful," she says. "Good job."

She's not going to mention the pain I've caused her, delaying this moment for ten long weeks.

"How many times has Gabe called you?" I ask.

"Zero times. Why would he call me?"

"He thinks I'm staying here."

"Now, why would your daddy think a thing like that?" Mom tickles the baby's bare feet.

"We're kind of fighting."

Her eyes darken. "You walked out on him, didn't you?"

"I guess."

She exhales my name.

Bouncing my knees to keep Jack happy, I stare at her, unapologetic.

"You walked away? You took his baby from him?"

"*His* baby? Mom, we'll be apart for two weeks. We talk every day."

Technically, we text, and only about the baby. I send him pictures of our son, and Gabe replies, "He's huge!" I send footage of Jack lying on Carrie's living room rug, kicking his legs and hooting like a barn owl, and Gabe replies with a row of heart-eye emojis.

I listen to the videos carefully before I send them, turning up the volume, checking for Carrie or Nina's voice in the background.

"You have to make things right with him," Mom says.

"Aren't you the one who told me to love him less?"

"He's not supposed to *notice* you loving him less."

I laugh. "How could he not notice?"

My mother stares past me toward the overgrown grass of Brian's lot. Her forehead is creased, and she's squeezing the fingers of her right hand repeatedly. If I were to lift her hand to my lips and kiss her knuckles—a dramatically tender gesture I performed often as a child—I know her skin would smell like tobacco. She won't light a cigarette in Jack's presence. The deprivation must hurt.

Her fear is real. Something about her inability to express it—or her inability to even keep trying—freaks me out.

Leaving New York without Gabe was the closest I could come to quitting. And I wanted, in that moment, to quit. As abruptly and unceremoniously as I quit my job at Arby's, informing my manager, "I'd rather not," and leaving through the emergency exit. Most things, when it comes down to it, can be quit. Work, school, friendship, marriage. Even fatherhood allows for resignation; a judge will determine the fee. But there is no way to quit motherhood—not without going to prison or getting kidnapped—and so I went through the motions. I screamed at Gabe; I packed a bag; I gassed up the car.

I left, even as he begged me not to.

I'm mad at Gabe for all the usual reasons. All the myopic assumptions men make every day: that he works harder than me, that he is fundamentally smarter than me, that helping to take care of his own child—far more than his father ever did for his mother—is enough. That the pitch of his voice signals sanity, his dry eyes the proof he's not hysterical. It all sounds so trite—until the person who swore never to desert you is standing in his boxer briefs telling you to *calm down*.

But I'm also mad at Gabe for a reason I can barely admit, even to myself. When he took me from Ohio, he took me from Carrie. She wasn't with me when I gave birth, and she wasn't with me at 3:00 A.M. The blame is so misplaced as to be unforgivable. I know that. I'll never lay it on him. Instead, I'll hope he can forgive the rest: the impromptu road trip, the "Take the fucking baby," the "I didn't have a baby because I thought it would make me happy."

The way my face tightens with dread every time Jack starts to cry.

"Mom," I say, "please don't worry."

Nina and Maxine have loaded themselves into the Subaru. I can see Carrie's daughter through the windshield, her seatbelt already buckled. She's checking her reflection in the rearview mirror.

"How can I not worry? You need stability. Now more than ever."

When I was eighteen and I told her I was choosing a boy over college, Jaclyn said, "If your plan is to rely on him, you better be damn sure it's going to work." What she wants to tell me now is that if I get dumped, I'm on my own. Jaclyn is not my *safety net*, a term my friends will sometimes use in oblique reference to their own parents. There is no guest room, no savings account, no disposable cash for disposable diapers.

Gabe's name is on Jack's birth certificate. Legally, the diapers are his problem too.

Inside the car, the girls appear to be wrestling. It takes me a second to realize Maxine is endeavoring to honk the horn while Nina flails to prevent her.

"Gabe and I are fine. We're the picture of stability. I got pregnant on purpose, you know."

Mom frowns. She thinks I'm comparing my pregnancy to both of hers.

"If you're so stable," my mother says, "then prove it to him."

Jack starts to cry, and I feel myself wince.

* * *

When I was twenty-five, I both wanted a baby and wanted never to have a baby.

When quizzed by friends or Gabe's nosy sisters-in-law, my

official answer was yes. I wanted to belong to a family comprising the man I loved and two or three children who would grow up and ensure that neither Gabe nor I died alone. Motherhood was expected of me, and motherhood was what I had always, vaguely, imagined for myself.

Then there was the night of the bachelor party on Staten Island, where Gabe imbibed buck-a-shuck oysters that slid innocuously down his throat but left him weak, wan, and fearful. A fellow partygoer buckled him into a cab for the bank-breaking ride to Queens and wished him luck. Gabe made it home, where he took to the bathroom floor and proceeded to vomit seventeen times before daybreak. Neither an athlete nor a risk-taker, Gabe's life had and has since been nearly painless, but that night, I worried. He perspired into a bath towel folded beneath his head, pulled his bony knees to his bare chest, and shut his eyes against the world.

My thoughts turned toward what Gabe calls "negative fantasy," which is when you imagine, in painstaking detail, the last thing you would ever want to happen.

If he died, would I forget him? Would I remember him feature by feature, as I do my father, or require a photograph to assemble his face in my mind? Would his personality be reduced to a collection of stale anecdotes repeated by me and his loud brothers, his voice a cliché I described in my diary at the age of nineteen?

Even if Gabe survived a lifetime of bachelor parties, even if he outlived me, did I not want to see his smile alight on our child's face? Was I going to deprive myself of that pleasure? These questions began to keep me up at night. And competing with our imaginary offspring was my desire to preserve our life exactly as it was. To sustain our happiness, our comfort in each other— neither of which had come easily or guiltlessly.

We wanted it both ways. Maybe everyone wants it both ways, and the only way to have it both ways is to retire one version of your life and prepare for the other. We were twenty-eight. We made up our minds. Suddenly, I had never wanted anything more than a baby. It seems improbable, almost magical, how badly I wanted to become pregnant even before I knew it was Jack I would be pregnant with.

Having him is the most deliberate thing I've ever done.

In our old life, Gabe and I never even left the bathroom door open when we peed. Now I was giving him daily updates on the consistency of my cervical mucus. It was supposed to be clear and as thick as egg whites. It was supposed to stretch between two fingers, like a long string of melted cheese. Making breakfast before work, he cracked an egg into a bowl and lifted his eyebrows lasciviously. It was a joke, the idea that tracking my cycle and scheduling intercourse could be sexy. But it also wasn't a joke.

It was also sexy.

We would lie in bed at odd hours—5:00 A.M., before we had to get ready for work, or midafternoon on a Sunday—and talk about the human life we may or may not have initiated. We would calculate his or her due date, first birthday, high school graduation. Gabe claimed he wouldn't want to find out the gender in advance of the birth. "There are so few surprises left in life," he argued, but I refused to entertain the idea, which struck me as archaic, reminiscent of a time when the surprise was only a good one if the baby had a penis.

My preference was to know the gender at the earliest possible moment and to pick out names even sooner. Given the option, I would have skipped pregnancy altogether and become a mother overnight. Having a baby was, I felt certain, the last step to becoming a full-fledged adult and to leaving my own childhood behind.

The first time Gabe's sperm fertilized my egg, it didn't take. A week after I watched two pink lines appear in the plastic window of a Dollar Tree pregnancy test—a week after I wordlessly dropped the test in Gabe's lap and braced myself for his joy—I started to bleed. The drops became gushes, which became sinister clots, falling out of me in the shower and staining the water swirling around my feet.

The pain was not categorically worse than the most painful cramps I'd ever had, but it was different. Sharper. More breathtaking. When it peaked, I was fresh out of the shower, still wearing a towel. Gabe was on his way out the door. It was Saturday and we had no food in the apartment. He heard me gasp, and the sound made him hesitate.

"Is it okay for me to go?" he asked.

I almost said no. I almost made him stay home, for no other reason than to bear witness to the end of my brief pregnancy. But I felt brave. Both the pain and the blood seemed appropriate; anything milder wouldn't have done the situation justice. Looking back, I regret my so-called bravery. I should have made him stay—Gabe ought to have worried about me as I had worried about him, decimated by bargain seafood—if only to delay our inevitable separation. Motherhood would bring a kind of agony through which Gabe would not be able to reach me, pain with which I would be entirely alone—but it didn't have to start yet! If I could go back, I would tell Gabe to forget the groceries, order takeout. I would demand that we be together, before the word *together* lost its meaning.

Curled crescent on the bed, I bled and cried. Gabe came

home. We filed our taxes. I drank a beer and ate half a package of sour gummy worms purchased from the same Dollar Tree that had supplied the off-brand pregnancy test that had convinced us we would soon be someone's parents.

And then it happened again.

It happened three times in six months.

The sequence of events was always the same. Around day twenty-four of my cycle, I would pee on a stick and the longed-for second line would appear, barely. Faintly. A near mirage. The next day, a repeat test might show a line of equal or even slightly more compelling visibility, but after another day and another test, the line would have vanished. Soon, blood.

The technical term for this process was chemical pregnancy, not miscarriage. Sperm met egg, but uterus rejected the almost-embryo.

What Gabe and I never said aloud but both understood: A chemical pregnancy was the fault of my body, not his.

* * *

I can't do it.

I can't whisper-sing Fleetwood Mac into his ear. I can't press him against my chest and trot in brisk circles around Carrie's coffee table. I can't bounce him, or stroke him, or pretend to eat his toes. I can't stay awake another minute.

Would it be acceptable to storm into Carrie's bedroom, thrust this screaming infant into her arms, and go collapse on the cool concrete floor of the basement, beside the washing machine?

Maybe it wouldn't be so bad, being kidnapped. Not at first. I'm interested in the part where you get to ride around in the trunk of some lunatic's Chevy Malibu. That part would last at least thirty, maybe even forty-five, minutes.

With my last shred of patience, I lower the baby to the couch. His screams intensify. I step into the hallway so I don't have to watch his eyes roam the room. I ball my fists and press my forehead against the wall. The baby has undone me, and this is a problem. I am the problem and Gabe is the solution. It was his body who helped make this child's body—the tireless vocal cords and scrunched, red face. Gabe was complicit in this. He's liable.

Gabe has been taking care of me since we were eighteen. Our first year in New York, I lived in his dorm room. We slept on the university's narrow plastic mattress, tangled in each other's limbs. I wasn't a student, but no one ever said anything. I looked the part. Gabe never let me pay for food, or concert tickets, or the bottles of wine we bought from a convenience store called Family Mart, where you could still rent movies from a wire rack near the Twinkies and where they never asked to see anyone's ID. When we both had colds, it was Gabe who braved the walk to Duane Reade, sparing my sinuses the wind's assault. His parents called on Sundays; he would pull on his jacket and go pace circles in Washington Square Park so I wouldn't have to hear Mrs. Feldman's strident disbelief at what we'd done.

He was nurturing. Selfless, for a teenager. It's no wonder I wanted to have his baby.

I miss him.

What *have* I done?

The crying stops, and I turn a hopeful ear toward the living room. Maybe the baby has cried himself to sleep. Maybe he'll sleep through the night forevermore. Maybe I've unwittingly Ferberized him.

Jack unleashes a ceaseless wail. Like the milk steamer on an espresso machine or a cat about to attack. I dart into the room. The couch is unoccupied, and Jack is on the floor.

What have I done?

I gather him in my arms, sobbing, "I'm sorry, I'm sorry, I'm sorry," and demanding to know if he's okay. My voice is raw, ravaged, resentful. This baby has never rolled over in his life. Harnessing the force of his own rage, he must have flung himself from the couch just to stick it to me.

His cries yield to sad little gasps. If I've succeeded at anything it's at lowering his standards; Jack is relieved to be back in my arms, at a safe distance from the rug. My own sobs fill the silence. I hate myself. I have always hated myself, and now, because I let my son fall from a height of nineteen inches, I always will.

Some flicker of movement or intake of breath causes me to look over my shoulder. Carrie is hovering in the doorway, watching.

"What the fuck?" I ask her. "How long have you been up?"

"The whole time? I'm a light sleeper, and he's . . . loud."

"Why didn't you help me?" My anger is too much. It's intimate.

"What could I have done?"

"Taken the baby? He always stops crying when you hold him."

Carrie rubs at her eyes. "Maybe I didn't feel like taking your baby, Amanda. Maybe I just had to pee."

"That's fine. So you sneak into the bathroom and back into bed. You don't stand there silently gawking at us!"

"I'm sorry. I was . . . I was trying to remember how that feels."

"To almost kill your baby?"

"No. Just . . . to be alone, in that moment."

"How did you do this?" I snap. "How did you take care of a baby by yourself? You were a teenager, for fuck's sake."

I am bouncing up and down. Jack is clinging to my shoulder, enjoying the ride, his tumble and his anguish long forgotten. With my question I have given Carrie all the power, all the authority. And she knows it.

"I told myself I was no better than my worst moments," she says.

"And that worked?" I ask.

"Eventually."

One of these nights, Carrie is going to stop pretending to forgive me. "I'm sorry I woke you up."

"You don't need to worry about waking me up."

My laughter is unhinged. "Okay, great. I'll stop worrying about it. He'll scream and scream, and I'll do nothing."

"That would be fine."

"Yeah, sure. Of course. Everything will be fine." The edges of my voice are ragged with hysteria.

Carrie backs away from me. The bathroom door clicks shut. Lately Gabe has been disengaging from our fights with the same abruptness. What's it going to take for someone to notice I am not okay?

Jack tightens his grip on my shirt sleeve.

"You could sleep," I tell him. "You could close your eyes and go to sleep."

But his eyes, fixed on mine, have never been wider.

* * *

I am worried the baby is developing a flat spot on the back of his head.

I am worried the baby will scratch his corneas with his tiny fingernails, which I am too scared to trim.

I am worried the baby will stop breathing in his sleep.

I am worried I will spill hot coffee on the baby.

I am worried the baby will remember me saying to him at four in the morning, "You belong in a mental institution."

I am worried the baby will soon realize I cannot sing at all.

I am worried the baby will go tumbling out of his stroller and onto the cracked, uneven sidewalk in front of Carrie's house.

I am worried Gabe will leave.

I am worried I will never want to have sex again.

I am worried the baby has already damaged his own hearing, screaming his throat raw.

I am worried the nauseating knot of scar tissue at the base of my vagina will never go away.

I am worried I will pull the blankets over the baby's head.

I am worried I will crash the car and kill us both.

I am worried the baby does not love me.

I am worried the baby will never love anyone but me.

CHAPTER SIX

On Saturday morning, Carrie and Nina get into a fight. From the guest room, where I'm trapped in a diapering-nursing-diapering loop, I hear Nina begging for permission to spend the day at Maxine's house. Carrie denies the request on the grounds that this would be the sixth consecutive Saturday Nina has spent at Maxine's house and pretty soon they're going to start charging her rent. Nina insists this Saturday, for unaccountable reasons, is crucial, that Carrie is being a control freak, that if she's allowed to go this one time, she'll stay home for the next fourteen Saturdays or until she dies of boredom—whichever comes first.

With a maniacal shriek, Carrie aborts the argument. "No!" she says. "No, no, and please don't ask me again."

A second later, Carrie throws open the door to the guest room.

"Hey," I protest, hunched over a bare-bottomed Jack, "I could be naked in here."

"I took my chances. Are you getting baby poop on my linens?"

"I mean, probably."

She nods. "Want to go grocery shopping?"

The last thing I'm going to tell Carrie in this moment is no.

At Walmart we take turns pushing the cart and carrying Jack. Dayshift employees, more chipper than their nocturnal counterparts, stop and ask us how old he is, how he's sleeping at night, how much he weighed at birth. Other moms—their children performing cartwheels in the cereal aisle or begging to visit the toy section—regard us with suspicion.

Every time I reach for a modestly sized bottle of laundry detergent or a single roll of paper towels, Carrie redirects me to the jumbo version. (*Jumbo* is a term I'd forgotten about; I don't think the concept exists in New York.) We get more food than it has ever occurred to me to buy at once. The total is $168, and Carrie doesn't stop me from retrieving my debit card to pay for half.

Loading up the trunk of the car, I'm thrilled by how easily we've obtained enough groceries to last a fortnight. No one has to schlep an overstuffed backpack through the snow or stand with a half dozen tote bags clenched between her feet on a crowded subway train. We don't have to choose between buying milk and orange juice; we can have both, plus a six-pack of sparkling water infused with natural pomegranate flavor. At Carrie's encouragement I have purchased ninety-four disposable diapers. If I don't use them all before the end of my trip, she'll give them to her neighbors, who have twin girls.

"I love Ohio," I say, buckling my seatbelt.

"You hate Ohio," Carrie reminds me.

"That too."

As kids, she and I were constantly doing things together that we could have accomplished alone. Our homework, our chores. It was typical for one of us to read magazines in a waiting room while the other had a cavity filled. As we're driving home, I try to thank Carrie for taking me shopping, and my voice catches.

"Are you *crying*?" Carrie asks.

"No."

Jack is already passed out in his car seat. If I bring the whole thing into the house, maybe I can park him next to the bed and take a nap.

"Sheesh," Carrie says, accelerating through a yellow light. "Hormonal, much?"

* * *

It's the gold standard of naps. We sleep through the rest of the morning and into the afternoon. When Jack does finally wake up, it's with a few mild squawks. I pat the mattress blindly before remembering he's still in his car seat on the floor. Normally we sleep together, our breathing synced. My lips against his forehead or his mouth on my breast. The risk of the blankets smothering him has never seemed as real to me as the risk of letting too much space get between us.

He kicks his legs as I lift him from his car seat.

"Are you so, so happy?" I ask him. "Should we go to Walmart every day from now on? Is it the most stimulating place in the world?"

He smiles at me for the first time. It's sloppy and asymmetrical, but I know my child's grin when I see it. I spend the next ten minutes squealing at him, trying to capture his smile with my phone. Though his mouth widens frequently, his joy eludes the camera, and I end up with fifty photos of my baby looking stunned, perplexed, or gassy.

We exit the bedroom and try to find Carrie, but the house

feels empty. The groceries have been put away, the lights turned off. I knock on Nina's closed door.

"Yeah?" she says.

I let myself into the room. Nina is flat on her bed, holding her phone inches from her face. "Any idea where your mom went?"

"Picnic."

"Carrie went on a *picnic*?" Jack reacts to my raised voice, looking up at me like I'm about to reveal the punch line to a ghost story.

"Such a hypocrite, right?"

I blink. It takes me a second to remember Nina's fight with her mother. And while it does seem unreasonable that Carrie would hold Nina hostage at home while picnicking elsewhere, I accept that the nuances of the conflict are lost on me.

"With *whom*?"

Nina lets her phone fall to the mattress. "With Tyler."

I hear the name Tyler less and less since I left the Midwest, but it always makes me think of the first boy I ever kissed, during our eighth-grade graduation dance. The song was "Hero" by Enrique Iglesias. I spent its four minutes and eleven seconds concerned that pit stains were seeping through my dress, the ensuing summer listening to the same song on a Discman and hoping to catch Tyler performing ollies in the school parking lot.

I kissed him three times total. Tyler Cox of Deerling, Ohio.

"Wait," I say to Nina, my heart suddenly pounding. "Tyler *Cox*?"

She smirks. Tyler's own coping method—on the advice of his older brother, Damien—had been to own the surname, to replace the *x* with a *c-k-s*, no matter how many detentions the trick earned him. "Yes."

My jaw falls open. "Christ. No wonder she didn't tell me."

"What's the big deal?"

"Well, I kissed him first, for starters."

Nina rolls her eyes. "Aren't you basically married?"

"Um, yeah?"

"So, maybe it's time to let go of the past."

"Nina, if I knew how to do that, I wouldn't be here."

She looks pained, like I've said something about my own bodily fluids or mental health.

"Do you want to get out of here?" I ask, energized. Carrie going out with a fully grown Tyler Cox is a lot of things—ridiculous, primarily—but it's also, I suspect, a personal attack. "We could drive to Cleveland if you want. See a movie."

Propped up on her elbows, Nina frowns. "Won't he cry?"

In my agitation over Carrie and Tyler, I have forgotten about my infant son. With one hand cupped beneath his butt, I jiggle him up and down, as if to prove to Nina that I am a fully engaged parent. Nina, who, I'm sure, wants nothing more than for her own mother to disengage.

"Maybe not a movie," I admit. "And maybe not Cleveland."

In silence, she waits for me to revise my offer.

"Want to go to the drive-in?" I ask.

The fridge is brimming with fresh produce, the freezer with pizzas and pot pies. We have no reason to spend even a minimal amount of money on fast food, but after a second of deliberation, Nina swings her legs over the bed, pats her braids, and says, "Let's go."

Again she rides shotgun, and again I don't have the nerve to ask if she's allowed. She rides with the soles of her sneakers pressed against the glove compartment—something Carrie used to do too. Nina is alarmed to discover my car has no Bluetooth, no auxiliary input. Even the CD player is broken. Gabe and I bought ourselves a pre-owned 2005 Subaru so we'd have a cheap way to drive to Ohio and back a few times a year. In the weeks before Jack was born, we used it for trips to Ikea and to get to my final prenatal appointments. I had developed a fear of going into labor on the subway. I was worried about getting stuck underground and delivering on the sticky floor of the M train.

If I had understood how much time would pass between the first contraction and Jack's first breath, I could have commuted in peace.

"What do you guys do?" Nina asks. "Sing to yourself?"

"Sometimes. Or we listen to the radio."

She looks at me like I've suggested churning our own butter.

"Don't knock it till you try it," I say.

With an uncertain hand, she scans the stations. "Christian, Christian, country, Christian," she summarizes.

It's a side effect of growing up in rural Ohio, the ability to recognize a Christian rock song in three seconds flat. The production is canned, the vocals generic. The first discernible word is always *grace*.

"The options are better in New York," I tell her.

Solemnly, we listen to a song about a girl with *a body like a backhoe*.

"Is that even a good thing?" I ask, after a couple of verses. "Isn't a backhoe sort of . . . ungainly?"

"A body like a back *road*," Nina clarifies. "Not a back*hoe*."

When the chorus returns we both dissolve, and we're still laughing as we pull into a spot outside the Deerling Drive-in. FIRE DOGS, CONEYS, AND MORE! Almost instantly, a waitress a few years older than Nina mimes for me to roll down my window. She rotates her fist in the air, and I wonder if she knows the origin of that gesture, if she's ever been in a car without power windows.

"Hey, Neen," the girl says, leaning into the Subaru.

Nina shuts off the radio. "Hey."

"This your mom?" The girl's dyed black hair has been chopped into jagged layers. The shortest pieces graze her chin; the longest touch her shoulder blades.

"No," Nina answers quickly, without explaining who I am. "Could I get two coneys with extra onions? And a root beer?"

The girl scribbles Nina's order onto a sticky note. "And yourself?"

"I'll have the same, but with an average number of onions, please," I say.

"Coolness," she says and skips back toward the kitchen. Nothing about the Deerling Drive-in has changed in the last decade. Not even the prices. I remember my dad complaining that two bucks per hot dog was *about a buck too much.*

"That's Maxine's sister," Nina says. "Trinity."

I remain silent.

"I know," Nina says. "They sound like strippers."

"Why does Maxine's sister work at the drive-in? Aren't they rich?"

"The parents, not the kids."

My laughter is condescending. "That's not how that works."

Nina shrugs. "They get, like, no allowance. Neither of them ever has cash."

In the back, Jack is growing restless. I can hear him raking his tiny fingernails along the water-resistant interior of his car seat. I'm trying to become Nina's friend, her confidante, and I'm failing.

Trinity reappears and affixes an aluminum tray to the lowered window. Atop the tray she unfurls a red rubber mat and arranges our coneys in their paper boats, our root beers in their glass steins. She uses several packets of soda crackers to anchor a stack of napkins. The crackers are in case we feel our chili-cheese-onion hot dogs lack texture.

"Anything else?" Trinity chirps.

"This should do us." I hand her five folded singles. The tip amounts to half our bill. She accepts the money with wide eyes and skips toward another car. Is skipping written into this kid's job description?

"There," I say to Nina, "now Trinity has some extra pocket money."

Nina reaches over me for her food. "You're a little bit of an asshole."

"Yeah," I sigh. "I know."

What I want is for Nina to tell me her secrets, so that I can swiftly deliver them to Carrie. Because the central conflict between Carrie and her daughter seems to be a lack of information. As a mother, you go from tracking your kid's every bowel movement and checking her temperature at the first sign of discomfort to never knowing whom she's texting or in what dubious activities some other child's parents have allowed her to participate. Carrie doesn't want to make Nina miserable, she simply wants a full report on everything that's ever happened to her.

Moms: the original stalkers.

Jack is starting to fuss. There's something so painful about the moments before he cries, when my thoughts become skittish and hard to corral. With the time we have left—somewhere between twenty seconds and three minutes—I blurt out, "Hey, what were you and Maxine going to do today?"

Nina side-eyes me and says, "Nothing illegal."

"Well, that's a relief."

She wipes coney sauce from her upper lip. "We didn't have specific plans."

"I don't believe you."

Nina shrugs, as if my personal beliefs are none of her business. I am deeply familiar with the particular rise and fall of her shoulders, her impenetrable aloofness. It must be genetic.

Jack's whimpers escalate just as Trinity returns to collect our trash. "Aw," she says, noticing the baby for the first time. "Little cutie-pie. How old?"

"Almost three months," I say.

She tilts her head, clicks her tongue. "Beautiful."

As it turns out, I have missed girls like Trinity. In New York, even women my own age are often too self-conscious to comment on a baby. To heighten the pitch of their voices, drop to their knees and appeal to the toddlers, the puppies, the prideless among us.

Until I had Jack, I never told a stranger her screaming baby was beautiful.

I regret that.

* * *

Nina and I are driving home—I keep apologizing for Jack's interminable crying; she keeps saying, "It's just sad he's sad, is all"—and we're about to turn onto Center Street, when we are blocked by a police car, its lights silently flashing. My throat constricts until I remember I am not seventeen, not stoned, not breaking any laws. That I know of.

Also, I realize, the cop isn't patrolling. He's escorting a funeral procession.

First come the 4-H girls. I'd recognize them anywhere, with their long, crimped ponytails, their slumped shoulders in pink flannel. Six equestriennes lead the procession, each clutching a flag in her right hand. Two are American flags, two are Ohio state official, and two celebrate the football team of the local college I was once slated to attend, where Carrie's dad still teaches. The girls are somber and sweaty as their steeds stomp through the intersection. Next come the pickup trucks, new paint jobs shimmering in the sun. Most are driven by teenagers. All these lockjawed boys wear their sleeves pushed past their elbows and steer with one hand at twelve o'clock. Some have penned elegies onto their windshields: *Rest in Peace, Jared.*

One last ride for JJ.

I sigh dramatically, and I half expect Nina to reiterate her assessment from earlier: I'm an asshole. Yes, but it's a slow parade, and my baby's crying, and death is common out here. A Deerling High School graduation ceremony isn't over until the principal has paid homage to whichever kid wrapped his car around a tree in the week before finals.

The casket rides in the flatbed of an old Chevy. The casket is draped with a Confederate flag.

My skin crawls, but it's a familiar sensation. The scene in the street doesn't shock me as much as it should or as much as I wish it did. Maybe I am still seventeen. Maybe Nina is Carrie, the baby a fantasy. Maybe I never left this town.

There's a version of Deerling that exists only in my head and only at a distance of several hundred miles. It's the Deerling I invented whenever I was trapped in a Manhattan office building, 3:00 P.M., so far from the ground that I couldn't hear the rain hitting the pavement. What I wanted was to touch the velvety cheek of a horse or to climb behind the wheel of a car older than myself. What I wanted was my mother, but what I thought I wanted was to go home. Being here now is like getting back together with a boyfriend whose flaws time temporarily erased.

You meet on the sidewalk. He is handsome and smells great, but in the restaurant he condescends to the waitress and returns his food to the kitchen twice. *Oh*, you think, *it's you.*

When Carrie and I were kids, the high school's mascot was a rebel soldier. Every fall, at least one teacher took it upon herself to sheepishly explain that Deerling High was the offshoot of a larger school that had split in half. We were the south campus, therefore we had *southern pride*—despite residing in the northeastern quadrant of a union state and despite learning, in a cursory way, that slavery had been a mistake. By the midnineties, the school handbook officially banned "the wearing of any imagery known to ignite racial violence," but as of 2003, proud alumni still showed up to football games with the Confederate flag pinned to the backs of their motorcycle jackets.

Behind the unconventional hearse are two grown men straddling twin white stallions, each holding up one end of a banner.

The banner says, MAKE AMERICA GREAT AGAIN.

Stunned laughter climbs my throat. I turn to Nina, but she is leaning forward in the passenger seat, frantically snapping pictures of the procession through my dirt-streaked windshield.

"These aren't turning out. Can we open the sunroof?" Her finger has already found the switch. She unbuckles her seatbelt, preparing to stand. I throw out an arm to stop her.

"You can't, Nina. These people. They should be arrested."

"I won't let them see me. I'll be sneaky."

"But what if they do see you?"

"They're supposed to be mourning?"

"Clearly they're multitasking."

Nina shrugs and rises again. She's not going to listen to me. I exude none of Carrie's maternal authority; I am the hapless babysitter, easily convinced bedtime is two hours later than noted in the instructions stuck to the fridge.

I grab Nina's phone and push her back into her seat. Getting a good angle—capturing not only a flash of red but the full Southern Cross smoothed flat across the casket—almost requires climbing onto the roof of the car. By holding Nina's phone above my head and snapping blindly, I try to squeeze more context into the frame: the teenager behind the wheel, the patient horses, the sign above the Chinese restaurant on Center Street advertising both Peking duck and air conditioning in neon script. Nina is smacking my leg to convey urgency. Jack is screaming like a horror movie heroine midshower. One of the riders notices me protruding gopherish from my vehicle. His upper lip curls into a sneer.

Resisting the urge to stick out my tongue, I duck before he can shout or arrange his fingers into an objection.

A second cop car brings up the rear, and traffic is free to resume.

"Drive," Nina says.

I keep my foot on the brake. "What *was* that?"

"That was Jared Jenkins's funeral."

"Who's Jared Jenkins?"

"High schooler. Got into a wreck on 71 last weekend. No seatbelt. His brother's in my geometry class."

Finally, and for no discernible reason, Jack falls silent. "Why do you need pictures?"

A car behind us honks. I make a left onto Center Street.

"Because fuck white supremacy?" Nina is already flipping through the album, favoriting the few images that unambiguously feature both the casket and the banner. These she sends to Maxine.

"Obviously, but—"

"But what?"

I don't finish the thought, and I avoid Nina's gaze for the last few minutes of the drive. At her age, I never did anything in the spirit of "fuck white supremacy." Boys like the boy Jared Jenkins must have been—I'm remembering particular buzz cuts, particular belt buckles—were plentiful but seemed irrelevant. Always, I was more concerned with my future escape than with the present reality of Carrie sitting among those people in class.

Of course, I believed we would escape together.

In the driveway, I kill the engine. "You're *sure* it's legal? Taking pictures of a stranger's casket?"

Nina looks me in the eye, surprised and slightly chastened. Carrie may be the boss, but I'm starting to understand how calculating, how ambitious Nina can be. She knew the precise hour at which Jared's funeral procession would snake its way through downtown Deerling. It's why she wanted out of the house on this most crucial of Saturdays. It's why she agreed to eat chili-soaked hot dogs with me.

"It's legal," Nina says. "I swear."

"What are you going to do with them?"

"Tweet them."

"Nina, no."

The way she looks at me, it's like I drove the hearse myself. Nina waits for me to make my case. It's tempting to invoke JJ's mother, because her baby is gone. No one else's baby is gone. Probably, Mrs. Jenkins did not design the alt-right funeral but left the arrangements to her son's friends or to her own opportunistic brothers. Maybe she made a brokenhearted attempt to nix the flag and the banner, or maybe she was easily persuaded that Jared would have enjoyed the procession doubling as provocation.

Either way, does Mrs. Jenkins deserve what Nina has in mind?

I was around Nina's age when I decided I did not belong
here. All the evidence—school photos in which my bangs were
long and parted in the middle, my front tooth chipped into a
perfect circle—suggested I did, but I believed, baselessly, in my
own superiority. (Jaclyn did nothing to encourage or temper
my arrogance; when I referred to my future earnings, my house
with a TV in every bedroom, she sighed and said, "Won't that
be nice?")

Does Nina believe in her own unsung excellence? She should.
She's smarter and lovelier than I ever was. Truly, Nina does not
belong here. But it's equally true that she belongs wherever she
wants. Wherever she is.

"They're the ones parading around in public," Nina points
out. "They *want* people to see."

"But isn't Deerling kind of like Vegas?"

Nina looks concerned for me.

"I mean, don't people expect that what happens here, stays here?"

"Why should I care what they expect?"

The internet contains little proof that Deerling exists. Google
it, and you'll find images of derailed trains, farm animals giving
birth, multiple couples posing for engagement photos in front
of the same abandoned barn. The right tweet sent at the right
moment—and possibly, this whole summer qualifies—will put
our hometown on the digital map.

Longtime residents of Deerling know the Harts. They've
admired Nina's grandpa's cherry-stained patio furniture. They've
brought their babies to the library to hear Rosalind read *Peter's
Chair* and *The Night Kitchen*, her voice as clear and comforting
as church bells. Even Carrie, with her single motherhood and
tattooed calves, is revered by a certain kind of Ohio woman—the

kind whose hair is bobbed and dyed red to indicate sass levels, of which Carrie is presumed to have an oversupply.

But the Hart family's status in Deerling won't protect Nina if she picks a fight with a dead white boy. This town loves nothing so much as our dead white boys.

"Nina, no," I say again. "It's not safe for you to share those pictures."

She doesn't need to ask why, nor does she need to remind me that I'm not the boss of her. Nina nods, taking my opinion into consideration. And then she shrugs, flashes me a polite smile, and gets out of the car.

* * *

The last time I hung out with Nina before today, she was three. Carrie was on a date then too, with an older man she met online. Gabe and I were in town, and we offered to babysit, figuring Carrie—who had recently moved from her parents' house into her first apartment—could use a break.

It was the tail end of the time when Carrie and I still considered ourselves friends. We rarely spoke when we were apart, but a trip to Deerling meant seeing her at least once, maybe twice. At twenty-one Carrie had emerged from the fog of early motherhood; she could think and speak on subjects other than her daughter. Having reclaimed some semblance of autonomy, Carrie was less distracted but more guarded. Before leaving to meet her date, she poured three glasses of wine and, while Nina sat at the table and sliced a toy loaf of wooden bread, quizzed us about New York. She asked about my job recording wholesale orders for a plastic jewelry manufacturer in Long Island City, Gabe's classes in American literature, and our roach-infested apartment in the East Village, paid for by Gabe's parents, who were still pretending to believe I was a frequent visitor with an address of my own elsewhere. (When the Feldmans visited, we hid my toothbrush, plus my foil packet of birth control pills, beneath the bathroom sink.)

Carrie was polite. More polite—and so much more distant—than I could bring myself to be. Instead of asking reciprocal questions about her blog and tattoo apprenticeship, I gulped my wine faster than a babysitter should, and I pouted. I let Gabe do the talking, the fawning over Nina's culinary skills. What impressed me about Carrie's maturity was that she had the self-discipline required to perform it in front of me, never resorting to our old rapport. I was supposed to be teasing and blunt; she was supposed to be sincere and unfazed. I still longed for these roles, useless as they'd been.

It was only as Carrie attempted to exit the apartment that her confidence wavered.

"You'll call me if something happens?" She slid her purse strap over her bare shoulder. "I mean, *anything*. Like if she gets hurt, or cries for more than a minute."

"Of course," I said.

"Please don't worry about bothering me. If something's wrong, I'd rather be here than there."

Impulsively, I hugged her. Gabe was distracting Nina, letting her ride him around like a horse. For a second, Carrie relaxed in my arms.

"If your baby so much as stubs a toe, we'll call you." And then, when she did not immediately break the embrace: "You look hot, by the way."

She did, with her chaos of hair and liquid-lined eyes, but

an East Coast irony had seeped into my voice and stained the compliment. Carrie pushed me away, laughed. Sighed.

"I miss you," she said before she left. And I thought it was criticism—an observation that, even though I was standing in her apartment, vowing to keep her daughter safe, I had ceased to be a person in whom she could take any comfort.

Now I wonder if I misunderstood Carrie that night. Maybe the circumstances compelled her to be formal and proud, but she still wanted me to know my leaving mattered. That her life would have been easier, in some respects, if I had stayed. Our friendship was not entirely fucked; one day, she would describe it as "remarkably healthy."

There were so many nights after which things between us were never the same, beginning with the night she told me she was pregnant (Halloween, neither of us in costume) and ending with this one. We didn't know it, but this was the last time I would babysit Nina. The only time I would make myself at home among the furniture repurposed from the Harts' living room, the frosted Goodwill drinking glasses, the pictures of Nina in their dollar store frames. If we were going to let each other go, rip out the seams that had held us together since prepubescence, why didn't we do it earlier, back when I had given Carrie every reason to hate me?

When I remember the years between eighteen and twenty-one, I remember Gabe. The tension between us and our parents, between what was supposed to have happened and what had. I hardly remember Carrie at that age, except in flashes, a skeletal epilogue. It's easy to forget she and I were in each other's lives at all, but we were. We made an attempt to change the terms, to be friends as defined by the dictionary: two who assist each other; bound by mutual affection; of the same nation (not hostile). We gave it a shot and discovered what my mother, the contented divorcée, must have already known: it's harder to love someone *less* than to stop altogether.

Gabe and I took Nina to rent a movie from the two-story Blockbuster on Center Street. Rather than presenting her with a handful of options, we made the mistake of asking her which film she *wanted* to see, as if a three-year-old might maintain a mental wish list. Later we learned the DVD she'd selected, *Happy Feet*, was one she already owned and had seen approximately fifty times.

I carried Nina on my hip. It thrilled me, the way her small body fit perfectly into the curve of mine. She pointed at the tubs of licorice, the packages of microwave popcorn. Cardboard cutouts of Disney characters, suspended from the ceiling and spinning in the air-conditioned breeze, made her laugh hysterically. Gabe spending a dollar seventy-five on gumballs and shoving four into his mouth at once made her laugh hysterically. An older couple in matching shorts and tightly laced hiking boots stared at the three of us, hesitating before they smiled. Before the wife said, "Your daughter is gorgeous."

It thrilled me to hear Nina mistaken for ours.

Carrie had told us not to bother with bedtime. She said Nina wouldn't fall asleep without her mom beside her, and she was right; it was past ten by the time Carrie got home, and Nina was still up, riding a post–*Happy Feet* high. She ran full tilt toward the front door and threw her arms around her mother's bare legs.

It was midsummer, and Carrie was dressed for a bistro in Paris or a wine bar in Tribeca. She and her bearded date must have turned every head at Buster's Backyard Barbecue.

What I remember clearly is the genuine pleasure with which Carrie greeted her daughter that night, after only three hours apart. She dropped to her knees and squeezed Nina tight. "Tell me everything you did while I was gone," she said.

"We went to my movie store," Nina said. Everything was *hers* back then—every store, every park, every yappy little dog tied to a porch railing. "We got my *Happy Feet*."

"Anything else?" Carrie asked, looking up at Gabe and me for confirmation: *No meltdowns? No injuries?*

But there was nothing else. Our night, having gone off without a hitch, was easily summarized by a three-year-old.

* * *

On Sunday morning, Nina corners me in the bathroom, where I'm brushing my teeth while bouncing Jack in my left arm. At first I think she's here to take the baby, and my whole body goes slack with relief. But no. She's showing me something on her phone. The Twitter account of a contributor to *The Atlantic*—Angela Beatty, a twentysomething black woman with seventy thousand followers.

"She writes about the election. All the hate it's stirring up. Should I send her my photos?"

I squint at the screen. In her headshot, the writer looks hip and self-assured. Her lipstick is a deep plum color.

Jack did not sleep last night, which means I did not sleep last night. At one point, I brought his car seat into the guest room and left him to weep within its protective curve while I, upright in bed, pressed the heels of my palms into my eyelids. Eventually I saw stars. That was the closest I came to unconsciousness.

"I mean, look." Nina shows me the best photo of the album.

The casket wrapped in the battle flag is the focal point. The faces of the riders are turned away from the camera—to recognize those men, you'd have to recognize their horses or the suntanned backs of their necks—but the teenage driver of the Chevy must have been watching me from the start. I didn't notice at the time, but now I see his smirk. Scornful, defiant. Internet gold.

"I know she might not use it for an article," Nina says, "but if *she* tweets it, people will pay attention. And she won't have to say I took the photo. I can be her anonymous source."

Technically, I took it, but Nina seems to have forgotten. She savors the phrase *anonymous source*.

If the photo goes viral, the family will claim bereavement, a right to privacy—but the look on this kid's face will render their rights irrelevant. And then what? Tomorrow morning, Nina will join her classmates in a moment of silence for the dead kid?

No one will ask who snitched?

Jack cries. My one-armed grip on him is inadequate. "Can we talk about this later?"

Offended, Nina shrugs. She backs out of the narrow bathroom and disappears down the hall.

I want to dismiss her feelings. Lately I'm capable of dismissing a lot of people's feelings, the way a kid hardens herself against a sibling's vulnerability because there are never enough resources to go around. Who, besides Jack, can claim to need *me* anyway? Who can't appeal to some other woman, whose arms are empty, whose body did not bleed for five weeks straight?

I find I can't dismiss Nina. My affection for her is sudden. I have no control over the avalanche of it, which coincides with the moment she gives up on me.

* * *

In the afternoon Carrie invites me to go hiking at the dump. From her attic she retrieves a spit-up-stained infant carrier last used to transport Nina. It's the kind certain celebrities made popular ten years ago and that people now say may give your baby hip dysplasia. It pleases Jack like nothing else. To me, wearing him feels exactly like being nine months pregnant. My fear of downhill slopes returns. The carrier presses the baby so tightly to my chest I can barely breathe, and still I walk with a protective hand on his head.

On the trail, we don't acknowledge that this is our place. We ignore the bench where we used to sit and get high, on which someone carved, *Be still and know that I am God.* Carrie is walking too fast for me, swinging her arms and humming something beneath her breath. It's annoying.

Jack thrashing his head from side to side is annoying.

The sound of my own labored breathing is annoying.

"Tyler Cox?" I say.

Carrie shifts her gaze from the sky to the ground. "Nina told you?"

"Yup."

"I was going to mention it before I left, but you and Jack were passed out in the guest room."

"You could have woken me up."

"Just to say I was leaving the house?"

"Just to say you had a date with my ex-boyfriend."

Carrie actually laughs. "Tyler is not your ex-boyfriend. You kissed twice."

"Three times."

She side-eyes me. "He says twice."

Why would Tyler omit our third kiss? We were in Maddie Baker's above-ground pool. He had one hand on my back, covering the knot of my swimsuit top. I fantasized about him untying the strings, even as I worried he would actually try it.

Probably he didn't omit our third kiss. He simply forgot.

"That's depressing," I say.

Carrie laughs again. She hasn't slowed down; if anything, she's walking faster, aglow with health and energy.

"Do you remember what he did to me?" I ask, indignant.

"He brought it up on our second date. He feels terrible."

"Your *second* date? How many have you had?"

Steadily, she says, "We've been dating for a year."

I shout, "*What?*" and Jack's eyes fly open. I pat him through the carrier until they close.

On our first day of high school—after the summer of three kisses, the summer of Enrique Iglesias—Tyler cornered me against the back row of the school bus. I was thrilled, terrified. He straddled me and, without technically touching me, began rhythmically thrusting his pelvis at mine. Crowded three to a seat, his friends cheered. They said things I either couldn't hear through my confusion or have since blocked out. The driver, a middle-aged woman who kept the radio tuned to a gospel station and ate sunflower seeds by the bagful, kept driving, not even bothering to threaten the boys through her intercom.

It was Carrie who seized Tyler around the waist and pulled him off me. She called him a *disgusting horndog* and kneed him in the balls so hard his face turned faintly green.

I'm ashamed to admit that until she rescued me, I hadn't known whether to feel violated or flattered.

"He pretended to rape me on the school bus and then never spoke to me again," I say.

"I know."

"I was mortified." It's only a partial lie. Mortification did set in, eventually.

"Teenage boys do shitty things," Carrie says. "It's an old story."

She was always bolder around boys than I was. Quicker to kick them where it hurt but also to kiss them when she felt like it. Her ease with the opposite sex was, in our youth, the first development to challenge the ideas we had of ourselves and of each other. Carrie could be daring; I could be hampered by self-doubt. Who would've thought?

"A year, huh?" The sun is creeping higher in the sky. The baby is covered in SPF 40, plus long sleeves and a floppy hat. My shoulders are bare, my face not even moisturized. Soon I will have a sunburn and Carrie will not. Another old story.

"I really like him," she says.

"Has he lived here the whole time?"

"He was in Columbus, but his dad had a stroke and he moved home to help."

"So, he lives with his parents."

"For now, yes."

"Honorable."

"Amanda."

"Sorry. How did you meet? Or, meet again?"

Carrie's smile is not for me but for Tyler in absentia. "He came into the shop. He wanted a custom piece, a rainbow trout on his biceps. He and his dad used to go fishing in Michigan every fall. It's sweet. The tattoo took three sessions—full color and everything—so we got to talking." She shrugs, still smiling.

"I guess you've tattooed half our high school class by now," I say, trying to steer the conversation elsewhere.

"People come in sometimes. Not as often as you'd think.

Tyler has a lot of ideas about expanding the business. He works at the bank, so he's good with numbers, investments—that kind of thing."

I don't want to talk about Tyler Cox. Imagining them together leaves a bad taste in my mouth, and I refuse to believe that Carrie can't find someone better in Deerling or nearby. She lives here; it's not impossible that someone worthy of her also lives here.

For a while we walk without speaking. I order myself to enjoy the hay-scented air, my heart beating hard, the expanse of prairie rolling toward the horizon. But I'm too busy questioning whether I'm capable of enjoying anything. Aren't I too hot? Too tired? Hasn't my skull been throbbing with my life's worst hangover for the last three months?

Jack wakes with a long, miserable wail. Eyes squeezed shut, he roots against the fabric of my T-shirt.

"Shit," I say, looking over my shoulder as if the car might materialize in the long grass. "He's hungry."

Carrie turns in a slow circle. "We can start walking back. Or if you want, there's some shade up ahead where you could sit and nurse him."

Neither option appeals to me, but Jack is launching into a decibel level that makes my palms sweat and my breasts harden with milk. "Shade," I say, trotting in the direction of the trees. "Now."

Carrie follows with a tight-lipped tolerance. As we enter the grove, the temperature drops and mosquitos whine in my ears. I loosen and unfasten the carrier, shoving the baby into Carrie's arms so I can sit on a rotting tree stump and deal with my bra. The shirt I'm wearing won't stay rolled up or tucked into my armpit. Driven insane by the sound of Jack's cries, I pull the shirt over my head and toss it aside. When he latches on, it's with comical urgency, but I can't laugh.

I'm half naked in the woods

"You really should get a breast pump," Carrie says, arms crossed over her spandex top. "We could have brought a bottle."

"I ordered one, but it has a million little parts and a novella of an instruction manual. I'm never going to have time to sit down and figure it out."

The purchase required making a new Amazon account so Gabe couldn't see where I'd had the package shipped.

Looming over me, Carrie claps a mosquito between her hands before it lands on my hairline. "I can hold your baby while you learn how to use a breast pump."

"You already have to hold him while I pee and while I wash my hair and while I tie my shoes."

Another mosquito hovers too close to Jack, and Carrie murders it. The sound shocks the baby and he ejects a mouthful of milk onto my thigh. "I can also hold him while you use a breast pump."

Her self-possession, her nonstop helpfulness, is grating on me. What's it going to take for Carrie to lose her cool?

"You could have warned me, you know," I say.

"About breast pumps?"

"About all of it."

Carrie looks bored. She excels at looking bored. "I would have, but you didn't ask."

I close my eyes and clench my jaw. Jack is sucking so hard, the pain makes me want to abandon him on this tree stump. Observing my discomfort, Carrie says, "Look, I know this seems like a lot right now. But I swear it's not as bad as you think. Mostly, you need some sleep."

Drenched in sweat and milk and my infant's spit: "I need so much more than that."

We are silent, actively not saying his name.

"Do you remember when we babysat Nina? That night you went out with Roy?" I ask.

"God, I forgot about Roy."

"And she tricked us into renting *Happy Feet*?"

"I remember."

"After that night, we went back to New York and I decided to see how long it would take for you to talk to me if I didn't talk to you first."

Carrie's eyes narrow.

"Six months went by. And then you emailed me a picture of Nina sitting on a pony."

"What? When was this?"

"She was four."

Carrie appears to be racking her brain, straining to remember the parking lot carnival or county fair that produced the pony.

"I wrote back, 'Cute!' and got another six months of silence. By that point, it had been a full year since you had voluntarily spoken to me, and I just . . . gave up."

Gave up is inaccurate. It doesn't imply thinking about her daily, googling her name on my lunch breaks, or taking a perverse satisfaction in the months slipping away, as if I were stronger for every season in which I did not hear Carrie Hart's voice.

Carrie is giving me the same look she used to shoot across classrooms, at scatterbrained teachers or illiterate children forced to read aloud. "Amanda, I had a kid."

I stare back at her.

"Have you ever spent time with a four-year-old? Parenting

a four-year-old is like trying to keep a perpetually drunk person from getting killed. She was always running into traffic or trying to do a somersault in a shopping cart. If I forgot to text you for a while, it wasn't intentional."

"You're saying you *accidentally* didn't speak to me for a year?"

"You didn't speak to me either. On purpose, apparently."

It's aggression dressed up like kindness, this idea that Carrie never stopped wanting to be my friend. To hurt me, all she has to do is pretend she would never bother. She has always known this.

Jack spits out my nipple and rests his cheek on my breast. Having finished his lunch in the muggy, bug-infested woods, he would now like to nap in the muggy, bug-infested woods.

I would like to put a shirt on. I would like to drive back to New York.

Reading my mind, Carrie stoops to retrieve my T-shirt. She shakes off the dirt before handing it to me. When I reach for the carrier, she says, "Let me wear him."

I shrug, and she slides her arms through the straps, adjusting their length and fastening all the right buckles from muscle-based memory. Carrie should have had ten babies.

We walk fast. I feel buoyant, like a dog let off its leash. Like I could go bounding down the path mowed through the wheat if I wanted to. The sky out here is so big and blue and earnest. Maybe Gabe and I should try moving to Ohio. They would hire him at my old high school in a heartbeat. We could buy a house. At Christmastime, we could decorate the house with unironic lights. In the summer, Jack could swing in a tire suspended from a tree.

Why has it never occurred to me, moving back home? In this moment, I can't think of a problem it wouldn't solve.

I consider texting a picture to Gabe and asking if he

remembers this place, but there's no way he would believe my hike was self-motivated or solitary. He knows me. It's tempting to imagine that by the time he flies into Cleveland—less than a week—I'll be a new version of myself. Maternal and disciplined and kind. Because the problem isn't that having Jack changed me; the problem is that it didn't. Not even a little bit.

As the dirt trail merges with the gravel parking lot, Carrie says, "Tyler wants to move back to Columbus, once his dad is doing better. I'm thinking about going with him."

No matter how hard I try, I cannot picture Tyler Cox as anything other than an untamed child.

"How would Nina feel about that?" I ask.

"I think she'd be thrilled."

While we're on the subject of Nina—while we're on the subject of skipping town—I should tell Carrie about the funeral procession for Jared Jenkins. How Nina tricked me into front row seats, Her plans for the incriminating photos on her phone. But something holds me back. It's impossible to say how many secrets Carrie's daughter is allowed, how many decisions are hers to make. Sometimes Nina seems wiser than the adults tasked with raising her; at other times, like a child still liable to sprint headlong into traffic.

When it comes to deciphering Nina, I do have one advantage over Carrie: I still remember what it was like to be a nearly teenage girl; parenting one has not warped my perspective. So I know that if Nina has an exit fantasy, the theme is agency. The theme is independence. Moving to Columbus so your mother can hook up with an adult man named Tyler is about the worst thing that can happen to anyone.

If Carrie and Nina leave Deerling, seeing them will require admitting I want to. Driving eight hours in the ostensible direction of my mom's trailer and veering toward Carrie's house at the last second won't be an option. I'll have to pick a date. Warn her.

Being a coward, I will probably opt to stay home.

It's obvious our friendship will never be what it was. But after the last ten days, the idea of losing her again leaves panic ringing in my ears. Without Carrie, I can be an adult, a partner, a half-decent friend to other women. Maybe even an artist someday. But I can't be a mother.

I try to tell myself that Carrie's potential move to Columbus has nothing to do with me, that it's about her and Tyler and the improbable connection they've formed, left to their own devices out here. But I don't believe it.

How many times did one of us try to replace the other with a boy?

With Gabe, it almost worked.

CHAPTER SEVEN

I don't know exactly what time it is. I don't look at the clock, because I no longer subscribe to the notion of time. Somewhere in the wild there must exist a creature—not a human woman, but some other kind—whose body only sleeps when it's convenient, whose body trusts sleep to come when it comes, in doses brief or lengthy. Something with a lot of predators or a precarious treetop living situation. I'll be her.

I'm her already.

It's not even that Jack is crying; he's simply awake. His eyes are wide and haunted. He's waving his fists, squealing like a cheerful rodent. I tell him, *I love you.* I tell him, *don't grow up and become an asshole.* Forty-three minutes pass, or would pass, if I believed in them. Without looking in a mirror or changing the disposable nursing pads wedged inside my bra, I load Jack into the car.

The Fitbit I gave her for Christmas, my mother warmed to it eventually. Not for counting the steps she's taken or stairs she's climbed, but for tracking her sleep. My mother loves to boast about how little rest she requires. Four or five supine hours, and she's ready to face another day.

Tonight I'll call her bluff.

Jack cries in the car. The radio plays Journey and Sting and Bon Jovi followed by Journey again. The gravel crackles beneath my tires, and my mother's light is on.

Inside, I give her a second to extinguish her cigarette before I hand her the baby. Momentarily I worry her clothes have absorbed the smoke and Jack will press his little nose into her pajama top and inhale. I can imagine the punctuation, the frantic typos with which the concern would be posed to BabyCenter.com.

I let it go, opting to collapse facedown onto my mother's couch.

She tosses me a blanket and tries to sing "Hey Diddle Diddle" to the baby, but she's forgotten what happens after the cow jumps over the moon. She transitions seamlessly into "Edge of Seventeen."

I laugh, already half-asleep.

"You shouldn't have driven," she scolds me.

"To Ohio?"

"To my house."

In my current state—sober, but nonetheless wasted—driving was dumb. I agree. But every once in a while the ever-whooshing windstorm of fear subsides, and I know—I'm certain—I would never hurt Jack. Not by blowing through a stop sign at sixty miles per hour or splashing hot coffee on his velvet cheeks. Tonight I swear I could pilot a plane he was in and keep us aloft.

"Mom," I say.

"Mm-hmm?" She sounds deliriously happy, breathing in the smell of him.

"Did you ever read my diary?"

She scoffs into the baby's scalp. "Her *diary*," Jaclyn murmurs. "Are you hearing this?"

"What about my desk? Did you read the stuff I scribbled all over it?"

"Yes, Amanda, I read what you wrote on the furniture. Most of it was not very good. I liked your drawings more."

"Did you ever worry about me?"

"All the time."

"I don't remember you demanding to know where I was or what I was doing. I never even had a curfew."

"Now you're mad at me for not giving you a curfew?'

"Not mad. But I don't get it. You let me make all the rules."

"No. Children don't make the rules. But they remake the world until the old rules don't apply. I bet you told yourself *your* baby would sleep through the night, didn't you? That all the moms struggling not to nod off in their rocking chairs were spoiling their kids? That you'd put him in his crib at 7:00 P.M. sharp, shut the door, and not open it again until seven in the morning?"

"Mom, that's absurd. I never thought that. Jack doesn't even have his own room."

"Still. You thought the baby would be a participant in *your* life. That his needs would adapt to yours."

The couch cushions smell like smoke and Febreze and a springer spaniel we had twenty years ago. My mother's greatest skill is making things last forever. "Maybe."

"By the time you and your brother were teenagers, we all needed some space. I figured it was your God-given right to take some risks. Just watch, Amanda. Try to keep that boy on a leash, and you'll both lose your minds."

"So, when I was in high school, you just lived in a constant state of panic?"

"I wouldn't say constant."

"Did you trust me?"

She scoffs again. "Not for a second."

The floor creaks as she sways back and forth. My son sighs. In the marshland across the road from Green Acres, bullfrogs bellow like foghorns. At some point, a cat hops onto the couch and settles against the small of my back. It's unexpected; we've never had a cat. Then I remember she does. It's the summer of 2016—my mother is thin, has a cat named Van Morrison, and may or may not vote for Donald Trump.

If I were to lose everything—my apartment, my friends, my health insurance, the Netflix subscription, the car, the bar on Wyckoff Avenue, the love of my life—the universe would deposit me here. With hair unwashed and limbs akimbo and my baby clinging to me. (Even in my most negative fantasies, the baby stays with me.)

I'm almost asleep when she says, "I trusted Carrie more than you. I always thought she had a good head on her shoulders."

If I weren't so tired, I would laugh.

* * *

I nurse Jack twice before daybreak. Otherwise, my mother holds him, and I sleep. Around seven thirty she kicks us out so she can get ready for work, and I drive back to Carrie's house, singing along to the same embarrassing songs that, in the dead of night, made me want to renounce the Midwest.

After parking the Subaru at a jaunty angle in the driveway, I practically float into Carrie's kitchen, my nose buried in the swirl of hair at the back of my baby's head. When you have a newborn, your body is like one of those derelict houses on the side of the interstate, tenants long evicted, roof partially caved in, more leaks and loose screws than you can count. You feel tired in places that aren't supposed to feel: your hip bones, your kneecaps. But four hours of uninterrupted sleep gets you high. Four hours of sleep makes you think about the future, some distant day when, maybe, you'll remember who you are.

Carrie is already up. I expected her to sleep in. Yesterday was the last day of seventh grade, and Nina spent the night at Maxine's house. Today is the start of the first real vacation Carrie's allowed herself since opening shop, and the studio will be closed for two weeks. Although she's booked solid through the rest of the summer, Carrie is still anxious—superstitious, maybe—that the vacation will mark the end of her professional life.

"Did Jaclyn feed you?" Carrie asks. She's perched on a barstool, her knees pulled to her chest. A cup of coffee rests on a Deerling Middle School newsletter. It figures Deerling would be the last district to go digital.

"No," I say.

"Can I make you something? Eggs, maybe? Pancakes? You need to eat."

Her attention is enough to feed some hollow part of me. I soak it up.

"Eggs *and* pancakes," Carrie proposes, clapping her hands together.

There will be a mess. Hardened batter adhering to the countertop and a baby crying before we can finish our food. I imagine wet eggs clumping in the sink, blocking the drain. Preemptive guilt compels me to shake my head. "I'll have some cereal," I say, regret tightening around my throat as I pass Jack to Carrie.

He smiles at her, and I can't ignore the look of love that washes over Carrie's face.

* * *

Around noon, I go with Carrie to pick Nina up from her sleepover. Mostly I go because I want to get a look at this mansion. I want Maxine's parents to invite us inside and insist on giving us the grand tour. Ohio opulence is, to me, a novelty. When we were kids, no one around here had an attached garage, let alone an in-ground pool.

Maxine lives on the same edge of town as my mom, where the roads have no speed limit and cows sometimes stand too close to the shoulder. The farms we pass are Amish; you can tell by the rows of outhouses and the wooden signs advertising JAMS & PIES & ROCKING CHAIRS in eerie, childlike script. I was a teenager before I realized our Walmart's designated parking area for horse-drawn buggies wasn't standard.

A grassy slope shields the mansion from the road. As we approach the driveway guarded by an elaborate wrought-iron gate, a hidden camera or sensor detects our presence. Some person inside approves our entry. Slowly, the gate swings open.

Over the hill, the house appears. It's a disorienting mix of penitentiary stone, New England shutters, and California excess. Palm trees peer over the roof, erect and robust and completely impossible.

"They're fake," I tell Carrie.

All she says is, "Money is money."

The driveway culminates in a roundabout. We park, arbitrarily, halfway around.

Through the panes of glass flanking the front door, we can see a man at least fifteen years our senior hurrying to greet us. White tennis shorts expose his long, sinewy legs. He has a T-shirt wrapped around his head and a sun visor jammed over the T-shirt. When he throws open the door, we're besieged by the smell of Banana Boat and sweat. In studious silence the man regards the tattoos netting Carrie's arms, the wide-eyed infant in mine.

"I didn't realize . . ." he begins, but our blank faces dissuade him. ". . . that Nina had a sibling."

"He's mine," I say, as if there were any doubt.

"Just hers," Carrie adds.

"Aha." The man steps aside and lets us in. He introduces himself as Keith, and I realize Carrie has never actually met this person.

"Pardon my . . ." Keith gives his headgear an affectionate pat. "I've been taking tennis lessons. I'm not bad, but I could be better. Do you play?"

The question is aimed at Carrie. She shakes her head. "No, I never have. Do you know if Nina's ready?"

"The girls are in the pool. We can go get them. Unless you'd like a tour?"

Before Carrie has a chance to decline, I say, "We'd love one. Your home is incredible."

I can sense Carrie's concurrent desires to laugh and to drag me from this man's property.

Keith leads us through the rooms of his own home with the excitement of a child exploring an unfamiliar playground. Someone, at some point, was paid to decorate—we pass free-standing sculptures, exotic potted plants. We walk across Spanish tiles and beneath postmodern chandeliers. Entire walls are painted bright red, slate gray, or papered in black and gold. The refrigerator is stainless steel and cavernous enough to conceal several bodies. A central vacuum system makes dirt disappear. The light fixtures respond to verbal commands.

Twenty million is the amount of money that this man won playing the lottery. I know because Nina knows, because she's heard him and his wife throw the number around in casual conversation, like it's their favorite song or alma mater. According to Nina, the couple's mood darkens only when they recall the chunk of cash the IRS *decided* to take. As if the IRS reviews fortunes on a case-by-case basis.

After making us climb one of two symmetrical staircases, Keith shows us a guest room. The attached bathroom features "both a tub *and* a shower, so you can go either way."

Here, my *ooh*-ing and *ah*-ing yield to a helpless giggle. Carrie's fingers dig into my upper arm. Amused in spite of herself, she sounds midwestern and friendly as she says, "Thanks for showing us around. This has been . . ."

"A real treat," I supply.

Carrie wrinkles her nose. "Right. Exactly. But we should get going. The pool is just . . . ?" She waves, imprecisely, in the direction of the outdoors.

Keith holds up a finger. "One more thing. Kind of saved the best for last."

At the end of the hall, he pushes open a soundproof door and welcomes us to the *bonus room*—named as if the others were obviously essential. The bonus room is a teenager's paradise, complete with a ginormous television, gaming consoles, a foosball table, and several leather sectionals.

"Wow," Carrie says. "This is a lot."

"It's extra," I agree, borrowing a linguistic quirk of Nina's.

Is this what Carrie meant by Maxine's family being a bad influence? As a kid, I would have salivated over a room like this.

Tapping the tip of my baby's nose, Keith says, "What do you think, buddy? You want to live in a big, fancy house someday?"

It's true that Jack is taking in his surroundings with a sort of reverence. I don't have the heart to mention to Keith that it's the same way he looks around a grocery store or a McDonald's restroom.

On our way to the pool, we run into Maxine's sister, Trinity. Dressed in her Deerling Drive-in uniform—a burnt-orange polo shirt with brown-capped sleeves and a black miniskirt—Trinity looks like a bit player who stumbled onto the wrong film set.

"*You* must be Nina's mom," Trinity says, confidently matching Nina's skin tone to Carrie's. "And *you*"—she leans toward Jack, who's bear-cubbing my shoulder—"are still the cutest thing."

"Thank you," I say, and mean it.

Something about Trinity impresses me. She's poised. At her age I wanted to sink through floors or, alternatively, to burn things down. Undignified urges that have recently returned.

Outside, Nina and Maxine are lounging in a pool shaped like a kidney bean, each of their bodies framed by a plastic inner tube. Nina's braids are pinned to the top of her head at a safe distance from the chlorinated water. As we step onto the patio, she sees her mother and blinks, as if emerging from a movie theater into the brightness of midday.

She avoids my gaze entirely.

"Hey, baby," Carrie says. "Ready to hit the road?"

Maxine and Nina slip from their inner tubes into the water and heave themselves gracelessly over the pool's edge. Maxine's suit is a bikini, which seems to be performing a Wonder Bra–esque function, accentuating her newest, most symmetrical body parts. Nina's is a sporty one-piece, presumably chosen to hide what isn't there. It's lime green, slightly pilled. Endearing.

The girls go upstairs to get dressed. Maxine's father offers us cocktails, and I nearly accept, but Carrie steps on my foot to silence me. We wait in the foyer, hovering close to the door. The girls reappear and hug each other goodbye. Their embrace is prolonged, and I wonder if something happened between them—a heart-to-heart or a late-night fight they've already resolved.

My hope is that Carrie, in the seclusion of her car, will release the laughter she suppressed in front of Maxine's father. But she's quiet as we round the driveway, quiet as the gates close behind us. It's the way she used to get after I had persuaded her to cut class but failed to deliver on a promised adventure.

Nina is receding inside a similar gloom.

She's mad at me.

I had forgotten, but I remember now, how easy it is to offend a kid her age. She's so afraid of being belittled or dismissed that she convinces herself it's happening even when it's not. That morning in the bathroom, I was tired. Too tired to shame white supremacists on the internet.

"Nina," I say.

Her grunt is noncommittal.

"Say you win the lottery to the tune of, I don't know, twenty million. What do you buy first?"

With a sigh, Nina plays along. "Um, I'd take a trip somewhere awesome. Australia. No, Tokyo. No, Los Angeles."

Carrie snorts.

"What would you buy?" Nina asks me. "A car stereo?"

"Maybe a brownstone in the East Village."

"And *then* a car stereo?"

"Sure. If there's anything left over."

"Mom?" Nina says. "Your turn."

Carrie says, "I don't know. I'd probably invest half, donate the rest."

"That's not the game," I say.

"How is that not the game? The game is I win the lottery and do what I want."

"No, the game is choosing the *first* thing you're going to buy. Investing takes a minute."

"Oh, but closing on a twenty-million-dollar brownstone is instantaneous?"

Nina groans. "Mom! Just play the game!"

"Fine." Carrie closes her eyes, and she keeps them shut for a second too long. The road is narrow and I'm tempted to grab the wheel—passenger-side steering is a game we used to play—but then her eyes pop open. "An original Basquiat. I'd hang it in the kitchen and every morning, drinking my coffee, I'd *look* at it."

Nina says, "That's so you."

I say, "You're going to hang a Basquiat in your kitchen? In Deerling?"

Carrie shoots me a look. "What's wrong with my kitchen?"

"Nothing. All the citrus-shaped pottery would go great with some neo-expressionist street art."

Carrie's shoulders shake. Finally, laughter rearranges her face, creasing her eyes and lifting her cheeks. Carrie's liable to wake the baby laughing so hard, but I don't even care.

"You're so damn sarcastic," she says. "How have you not grown out of that? Do you ever say something and mean it?"

"She doesn't," Nina laments.

"I do. To other people. Just not to you."

"There it is," Carrie says, knuckling tears from her eyes.

"There's what?" Nina asks.

"The truth."

A minute later, Nina looks up from her phone and announces, "A painting by your Basquiat guy sold for fifty-seven point three million dollars last month."

"Shit," Carrie says. "I'm going to need a bigger Powerball."

The road widens as we get closer to town. Farms yield to schoolyards and junky apartment complexes. Deerling's downtown used to be semiquaint, with a bakery, a hair salon, and an antique store, before Walmart set up shop and ran everyone out of business. Main Street's last standing attraction is a fountain, its granite bottom layered with nickels and dimes, in the center of a small park. Technically, Carrie and I met there, age seven. Softly, gravely, she informed me I had been occupying one of two operative swings for over ten minutes. It was only fair that she have a turn.

I conceded. Though tentative, Carrie radiated a moral authority. She was right. To stay on the swing—the cold of the metal chains seeping through my gloves—would have been wrong.

Carrie and I met for real on the first day of junior high, where kids from each of Deerling's elementary schools merged into one student body. Carrie had gone to the newer elementary school, with the up-to-code playground and the real gymnasium. I had gone to the old one. My brother and I qualified for free lunch—we would find a week's worth of faded blue vouchers in our cubbies every Monday morning—until 1994, when our mom was promoted at the DMV.

Assigned to the same sixth-grade homeroom, Carrie and I recognized each other from the park, but neither of us admitted it. She sat in the desk next to mine. The teacher kept confusing

Carrie with the only other black girl in the class. Carrie was tall, lean, with an abundance of gravity-defying curls. Kim was short, chubby, and wore her straightened hair in a low ponytail. After mixing them up a third time, the teacher laughed. "You two look so much alike," was her apology. "I should make you wear name tags!"

So far under her breath that only I could hear, Carrie said, "Yeah, that wouldn't be racist at all."

She was the one who introduced me to sarcasm, the subtle power of negating the truth. But she never taught me to use it sparingly. Moderation was Carrie's specialty, not mine.

Today the park downtown is cluttered with lawn signs. As we approach, I expect advertisements for the county fair or the local nursing home's karaoke night. But the signs are vibrant, professional. Political, I realize. Someone has driven at least fifty of them into the grass, and they all say, I'M WITH HER.

Carrie's excitement is immediate. "Look!" she says to Nina, tapping a fingernail on the window. "Hillary signs!"

"Yeah," Nina says. "Coolness."

"Oh, come on. You were *just* asking me if we're the only democrats in Deerling! Looks like we're not."

Carrie hangs a right past the park, slowing and admiring the signs as if they're flowers she planted herself. Rarely optimistic and never delusional, Carrie is nonetheless charmed by these signs, as if each represents a citizen of Deerling both old enough and registered to vote. In reality, the entire display must be the work of one or two radicals, tops.

Still, I sympathize with Carrie's compulsion to drive slowly, to linger in the moment. She may be searching for reasons to finally leave Deerling, but isn't she also searching for reasons to stay?

I refrain from saying what I'm thinking, which is that the park is municipal: city employees will tear down the signs within an hour. Instead, I opt for a platitude, sincere and Ohio: "A sight for sore eyes."

Carrie agrees.

* * *

The next day is hot, and Carrie wants Nina and me to go with her to the town pool, but Nina has cramps and a bad attitude and is "sick of swimming, anyway." Personally, I want nothing more than to submerge myself in cold water, but the logistics overwhelm me. Do I have a little hat for Jack? Will he sleep? Will he cry? Will he poop? Will one of Carrie's old suits fit me, and will my lopsidedness—the result of the baby gradually favoring one side—be obvious?

No matter how many boobs are on display, I know some midwestern mom will shoot me the stink eye for nursing in public.

I decline. Aware of my ambivalence, Carrie tries again. "You sure? I'll hold Jack while you swim."

It makes me emotional, turning down an invitation that in my prebaby life I would have accepted without a second thought. It's a raw, completely unreasonable grief. I shake my head, and while Carrie loads up her gym bag with snacks and trashy magazines, I hide myself in the guest room.

A crisis of bodily fluids ensues. Jack's fluids, not mine. I've just slid a clean diaper under his butt, when he releases a torrent of mustard-hued poop. In the three seconds it takes for me to produce a second clean diaper, he pees. Straight into the air so that the urine arcs, splashing against his belly and pooling in his armpits.

The moment he is rediapered and outfitted, he regurgitates sour milk all over his onesie.

The onesie says, TINY BUT MIGHTY.

A half hour has passed since we entered this room. The air is warm and stale. Carrie is at the pool, and Nina has gone back to bed. Is it too late for me to apply to college? Maybe I could learn a trade. Carpentry, or silk-screening.

When I was growing up, we lived across the street from the Dewdneys, a couple whose youngest daughter, Ashley, was six years older than me. Their house was like any other in the neighborhood: cats roosting in windows, shingles littering the lawn after summer storms. Ashley Dewdney was an honor student, which meant her picture hung on corkboards in the supermarket, the library, the bowling alley. When she left for Notre Dame, she had what my brother called Mormon hair, and when she returned home five years later, she was driving an Audi packed with elaborately wrapped Christmas gifts. At their mailboxes, bathrobes cinched tight against the cold, Ashley's mother explained to mine that her daughter had been recruited by a firm of financial analysts during her senior year of college. She had money now and expected her money to proliferate. Her short hair reflected sunlight. She went by "Ash."

I had never heard of a financial analyst. The marriage of the two words was nonsense to my ears. Still, I decided I would become one, for the express purpose of one day popping the trunk and sheepishly asking my family to help me carry the loot inside.

I unsnap the bottom of his onesie, and Jack begins to wail. He is tired of being pinned to the floor, tired of being messed with.

"I don't know what you want," I mutter at him. But it's a lie.

What he wants is to be held tenderly but firmly against my chest while I power walk through a climate-controlled world, waving to women with high-pitched voices and dogs with jingly collars. What he wants is to lie nose-to-nose on the bed while I sing pop songs from my mother's childhood. What he wants is to nurse and nurse and never get gas.

My phone rings. When I see his name on the screen, I think, *He knows.* Of course he knows. Gabe is the one person from whom I've never successfully kept a secret.

With an ache in my throat, I say, "Hi."

"Hello." In that languid, late-night radio voice.

The silence between us, which should be strained, is warm and pleasurable. I can't help it—when Gabe speaks, I feel his fingers on my ribcage. I picture our graves side by side. Love is absurd.

"What are you doing?"

We never ask each other *how* we're doing. Only what and where and why. Implicit in these interviews: *Shouldn't you be here with me?*

"Sitting in my empty classroom." Gabe taught his last day of school yesterday. "Packing up my desk."

"Get anything good this year?"

"You know how, last year, a girl gave me a mug with my own face on it?"

"Your mug shot mug." The mug shot mug travels back and forth between our apartment and the high school. Gabe doesn't believe in thermoses or to-go cups. He likes to walk down the street sipping from an open beverage, as if all of Queens were his living room.

"Well, this year, a student gave me a mug with a picture of myself holding last year's mug on it."

The baby is startled by my laughter.

"And which do you prefer?" I ask Gabe. "Mug shot mug or perpetuity mug shot mug?"

"They're both so good."

We slip into another silence, and this one lasts too long. Desperately, I want to present him with a worthy anecdote, but my best material—Maxine's mansion, Carrie dating Tyler Cox—would reveal what he maybe, probably, already knows. "My mom got a cat," I offer.

"Oh?"

"Van Morrison. He pooped in her neighbor's sandbox."

Gabe hesitates, then says, "The cat's not sleeping in the same room as the baby, is he?"

"No."

"Because I've heard of cats curling up on kids' faces at night." Gabe's voice contains a tremor of parental anxiety. The tremor is genuine; no one has told him I'm not staying with my mom. I could break it to him right now: I'm here with Carrie and Nina. They're beautiful. Neither of them can stand me.

I'm afraid the information would hurt him more than I already have.

"I won't let Van Morrison smother the baby."

"How is he sleeping, by the way?"

A loaded question.

"Some nights are better than others."

"I feel like I haven't seen you guys in forever. I feel like Jack's going to be a completely different baby by the time I get there."

I should apologize. It's in my best interest to apologize, and I want to do it, but I want something else more.

Isn't Gabe the only person in the world who can offer me relief? Not momentary relief while I scarf down a microwaved burrito—or even half a day while I get my hair cut and challenge a parking ticket—but actual, permanent relief.

Instead, when I begged him for it, he said, "You're the one

who wanted this." As if either of us had any idea what we wanted. Does Gabe think that because I'm female—or because I was so close to Carrie when she had Nina—I already understood what a baby was? Does he assume that because I have a body designed for childbirth, I am also designed to be screamed at and sucked dry and spat out?

"Jack smiles now," I say.

Gabe laughs. "No way. Really?"

"At me." *And at Carrie.*

"I want to see him smile at you."

"You will."

"Has Deerling been everything you wanted it to be?"

His question is a Get Out of Jail Free card. Saying yes will be as good as saying *case closed.* We will quietly agree that, like a sickly girl in a Jane Austen novel, all I needed was a dose of my native air, a break from the relentlessness of society.

A fast drive down a country road.

Something I've suspected for a long time is that Gabe is always, however unconsciously, daring me to be less than satisfied with our life. The idea that he rescued me from a certain fate is one I'm guilty of perpetuating. Drunk, and in love with him, I've begun sentences, "If not for you, I'd be . . ."

Married to a car mechanic. Working at the DMV alongside Jaclyn. An alcoholic.

A single mother in Deerling, Ohio.

Maybe that's the truth, and maybe it isn't. Before Gabe, I had a plan, originally inspired by Ash Dewdney but which I had since tailored to reality. I would go to the best university that offered me a scholarship (not Notre Dame, not even Ohio State). Carrie would come too and major in art or else live an ungoverned artist's life in comforting proximity to my ordinary one. By the time we were seniors in high school, art was strictly Carrie's thing. I had forfeited my own sporadic creativity. She had the talent; all I ever had was a reckless streak, a lack of inhibition that occasionally seemed profound.

After college, I would get an MBA, then work in marketing or management for a large corporation. Whatever this entailed was not the point. The point was the salary. At seventeen, I dreamed of owning a dishwasher, taking vacations, buying shoes that weren't from Payless. Specifically, I imagined reporting the balance of my checking account to my mother and watching her light up, impressed and proud and envious. A goal that raised the eyebrows of teenage Gabe.

It baffled me how he could claim not to care about money when his family had so much of it.

I was young.

After we moved to New York, I meant to apply to colleges in and within spitting distance of the city, but I never did. From the outside, it probably looked as if my ambition flatlined when I met Gabe. *Stick with this guy*, I must have thought, *and you'll never end up in a double-wide.* The other possibility—of which, I believe, Gabe and I were both aware—was that I no longer felt like I deserved to go to college.

For a couple of years, Gabe encouraged me to try. His idea was to write my admissions essay about Carrie. "You don't have to spill every detail, but you can describe how it felt to watch your best friend give birth and become a mother. Most people our age have no idea what that's like."

Not for a second did I consider writing that essay.

The answer to Gabe's question is no. Deerling remains less than what I want it to be.

Sometimes, watching the wordless intimacy between Carrie and Nina as they reach over each other to assemble their respective breakfasts or stand side by side to brush their teeth, I think Carrie might inadvertently send me home with some assurance that motherhood is worth the suffering. But then Nina berates Carrie for spreading the last of the butter on her own toast, or she says, "Mom, I hate that tattoo," pointing to the one of her own name wrapped around Carrie's left wrist, and I realize the suffering never ends.

"It's been good," I tell him.

"Will you pick me up from the airport, or should I rent a car?"

A plan forms. It's reckless, and maybe a little bit cruel, but I can't resist it.

"No, don't rent a car," I say, as if the idea offends me. "We'll be there."

* * *

After Gabe's first semester at NYU, we went back to Deerling. He stayed with his family and I stayed with mine, an arrangement that felt like a good deed we were doing. On the morning of Christmas Eve, I drove my brother's seafoam-green Chevy Impala to visit Carrie, who was still living with her parents. Snow covered the streets, and I had to guess at the exact boundaries of the driveway that separated the Harts' property from their neighbors'. The whole town smelled like fresh paint and just-split firewood.

Pushing through Carrie's front door, I was surprised by the warmth and sourness of the house. The oatmeal-colored living room rug was strewn with plastic toys, stuffed animals, bibs, diminutive socks, board books, and piles of hastily folded laundry. I navigated the mess and found Carrie in the kitchen, wrenching the lid from a small jar of puréed peas. Nina was smacking the tray of her high chair. When she saw me, she screeched and grinned maniacally.

"Does she remember me?" I asked. Nina was six months old.

"No." Carrie put the peas in the microwave and set the timer for seventeen seconds. "That's a standard greeting."

"She's beautiful," I said.

She was.

"Thanks." Carrie had adopted a beleaguered way of speaking that seemed designed to excuse the unwashed dishes in the sink, the all-too-personal stains on her sweatpants. I went to hug her. I would have held on to her for a long time if the microwave hadn't started beeping.

From the beginning of the visit, it was clear we wanted to talk about different things. I wanted to talk about how the girls in the coed bathroom looked at Gabe and me when he squirted a glob of toothpaste onto my toothbrush; how Dawn, my boss at the wholesale jewelry company, sent me fervent, unpunctuated emails requesting I stop undermining her authority; and how my friend Paige, who was twenty-two and resembled me in no physical way, had given me her old driver's license to use as a fake ID.

Carrie wanted to talk about her baby.

Compromising should have been easy. The problem was that I believed my life was inherently fascinating, whereas Carrie's routine with the baby was monotonous. A snooze fest. Her mind may have been cluttered with Nina's relentless needs and achieved milestones, but deep down, I believed, she wanted vicarious thrills.

How generous of me, I thought, to drive through the snow to Carrie's house and regale her with stories about being young, in love, and childless.

As I spoke, Carrie spoon-fed Nina the puréed peas. Nina's mouth popped open, birdlike, in anticipation of each bite. Closing her lips around the spoon, she would arrange her features into a deeply critical expression before swallowing and whining for more.

This process had been repeated ten or twenty times, when suddenly, Nina brought her fists to her face and screamed. For a few seconds, I kept talking, as if Nina were a lunatic on the subway whom we ought to ignore. Carrie looked pained. I shut up.

There was green slime everywhere—on the wall behind the high chair, on Carrie's shirt, on Nina's cheeks, forehead, and onesie.

"Do you ever wish you could skip the baby phase?" I asked. "Blink and become the mother of an eight-year-old?"

Nina was still doing her best impression of a tornado warning. Like a mom in a movie, Carrie pinched the bridge of her nose. "You don't have to be here," she said. "You can leave."

"No, no," I reassured her, rummaging around in the fridge for a Diet Coke. "That's not what I meant. I'm having a good time."

I have since considered apologizing to Carrie for what I said that morning. After Jack was born, I experienced the same moment from the other side—a friend covering her ears against Jack's colicky cries or squealing in disgust after he spat up in her hair. The same Paige who gifted me with the fake ID insisted on coming to see Jack a week after the birth. She brought us a jar of olives and a corkscrew, two items that struck me as both extravagant and useless. Watching me breastfeed, she announced in a bored, sullen way, "Those noises he makes are pornographic."

When your friend has a baby, nothing more or less than unwavering admiration is required of you. Being kind to an infant and to that infant's mother? It's the easiest thing in the world.

I have never apologized to Carrie. The time I remember is probably one of countless offenses I committed. To rehash it would be selfish—both a grab for easy absolution and an attempt to show off. *Look at me now. Look how self-aware.*

Still, the shame gnaws at me.

What did I think I had accomplished, exactly? I had fallen for a boy who pronounced my name, first and last, like it was the conclusion of his favorite novel. I had accepted the first minimum-wage job offered to me. I had learned to drink and dress and pontificate like your average college freshman, revealing only as a 2:00 A.M. punchline—a party trick—that I was not a student at all but a stowaway aboard my boyfriend's life.

Carrie, at eighteen years old, had fallen in love with her daughter.

* * *

When Carrie gets back from the pool, she is sun-drunk and too lazy to cook. She pulls three kinds of potato chips from the pantry and cracks open a beer. Nina emerges from her bedroom and slumps way down in a chair to commence chip-eating, her movements mechanical as she reaches again and again for the bag.

I have left Jack sleeping on the bed in the guest room, surrounded by a fortress of pillows in case he spontaneously rolls again. Already I miss the weight of his body in my lap, the curve of his skull against my lips.

"So," I say, "Nina's birthday."

"It's coming up," Carrie agrees.

"I was thinking, to get the celebrations underway, do you guys want to spend a night in Cleveland? My treat? And we can get Gabe from the airport in the morning."

His name is like a foreign object in my mouth.

Nina perks up. "Yes," she says. "Can I get my own room?"

"No," Carrie answers.

Nina tries again. "Can we get a room with a minibar?"

I say, "Yes. You're thirteen now. You can have all the overpriced Skittles you want."

She turns to her mother. "Please, Mom?"

Carrie narrows her eyes at me. "Are you just trying to get away from the fireworks?"

Gabe's flight lands on July fifth. On the fourth, all of Deerling will be ablaze, the hot air saturated with the fumes of Black Cats and Lady Fingers. It's occurred to me that Cleveland's pyrotechnics will be contained, supervised by firefighters, and over by 10:00 P.M.

"That's a perk but not the reason," I say.

Carrie frowns, working her tongue over her teeth. "Are you sure you want us to come? You and Gabe haven't seen each other in a while. Have you ever been apart this long?"

"Sure," I lie.

She's skeptical. "When?"

"Gabe travels. I travel."

"Ah. Didn't realize you two were such jet-setters."

"Please, come to Cleveland with me."

"All right," she says. "If that's really what you want."

Nina pumps a fist in the air. She grabs her phone from the counter and begins furiously texting. I'm still curious to know what happened between her and Maxine two nights ago, causing their goodbye hug to be so solemn and prolonged. Before I can think of a delicate way to ask, I become aware of Carrie studying me. She holds her beer to her lips, obscuring her expression.

"What?" I say.

"Nothing. It's weird to see you without Jack."

"I feel naked," I admit. "Like when you realize you left your purse in the bar."

"Can I ask you something?" Carrie's tone is more deferential than usual.

"Sure."

"Is Gabe good with the baby?"

I remember the night before I left, waiting in vain for Gabe to relieve me of our inconsolable newborn. He was tired, but he was also mean, which was unprecedented. Before the baby, we were so consistently sweet to each other that once, after Gabe called me out for underreporting the price we'd paid for a crate of organic peaches, Paige turned to the woman she was dating and snapped, "See? They fight. They're not perfect."

Certainly not anymore. In the middle of the night, I would have said anything to Gabe if it meant guilt would compel him to take the baby.

Maybe Gabe is not "good with the baby" if the standard is checking the baby's temperature obsessively, always remembering to refill the wipes dispenser, and loving the baby's mother exactly as much as he did before she unraveled.

After Jack was born, the nurses were preparing to move us into a recovery room—where we would stay for forty-eight hours, a curtain separating us from some other newly acquainted mom-baby pair—when one of them mentioned that Gabe would not be allowed in the room between the hours of 10:00 P.M. and 8:00 A.M.

To me, this seemed inhumane, but so did everything else.

Gabe said, "Amanda's supposed to be alone with the baby all night?"

"Wellll," one nurse intoned, "if she's really having trouble, we can take him to the nursery for a bit. But we usually like to keep Mom and babe together."

Gabe looked down at me. I was in a wheelchair. I had tried to walk, but it hadn't worked out.

Over my protests, Gabe asked the nurses about a private room. I was trying to say we couldn't afford it; I had already spent an afternoon on hold with our insurance company to confirm that postpartum privacy was not an expense they would cover. Dubious, the nurses explained that only one private room was currently empty. It was $850 a night. When Gabe stared at them, expressionless, one nurse shrugged and said, "It has a view of Central Park."

Gabe paid. He put $1,700 on a credit card already attached to a balance we may never pay off. In our private room with a view, Gabe was allowed to stay with me all night. Delighted by what they perceived as his selflessness, the nurses brought him a cot to sleep on—but as far as I know, he never used it. If Jack was not asleep in the hospital's lettuce crisper of a bassinet or attacking my nipple, he was in Gabe's arms. Gabe scooped our son up every time he cried. He changed every diaper. He did not let me get out of bed.

In the morning, we failed to pull back the curtains and feast our eyes on the park. The hospital could have been on the side of a highway in Illinois for all we cared. I remember getting up to use the bathroom, denying my body's urge to defecate, even though the nurses had warned me that a successful bowel movement was my only ticket home. Gabe and the baby weren't where I'd left them. I stepped into the hall—no longer paper-gowned, but feeling svelte in my own sweatpants—and found Gabe rocking our son in his arms, singing George Harrison's "My Sweet Lord" beneath his breath. I'd put the song on a playlist for Gabe when I was thirty-eight weeks pregnant, and he'd fallen into the habit of listening to it every day on his way home from work, imagining, he told me, that the lyrics referred not to George Harrison's infatuation with a Hindu god but to our own unborn son.

Finally, they were together. I had united them, and I couldn't look away.

It seems neither appropriate nor feasible to explain the caliber of Gabe's fatherhood to Carrie. All I can think to say is, "He was around Nina as a baby sometimes."

She shrugs. "Barely."

"Well, he's good with Jack. He's great with Jack."

"But?"

I didn't mean to imply any *but*. But, of course, there is one. "Day to day, I am more alone in this than I thought I would be."

For some reason, Carrie looks pleased. She takes a satisfied swig from her beer.

"What—does that make you feel better?" I ask.

She glances at Nina, whose chin is still dipped phoneward and who appears to be tuning us out entirely. "Sort of, yeah," Carrie says.

It's not what I meant, but I can see how it might comfort her—the idea that she hasn't missed out on anything.

CHAPTER EIGHT

I have some idea that we will go to a nice restaurant in Cleveland—a place with a wine list, at least—but Nina has a different vision. She wants to go to Happy Dog, a bar on Detroit Avenue where you pay six dollars for your basic hot dog and then choose from an unholy list of toppings including bacon, SpaghettiOs, mac 'n' cheese, peanut butter, fried eggs, and coleslaw. Nina has never been to Happy Dog, but Maxine told her about it. Because the dinner is ostensibly to celebrate Nina's birthday—and because, as Carrie points out, Jack might cry throughout the meal—I concede.

It's about a ninety-minute drive from Deerling to downtown Cleveland. We take my car. Carrie rides up front, and Nina distracts Jack with a board book titled *I Love My Mommy*, in which a baby elephant and his mother have a good time. The narrative makes me vaguely uncomfortable. I feel inadequate compared to the elephant mom. Jack and I never stand beneath waterfalls or go stomping across the savanna.

Mostly, he cries, and I beg him to stop.

By the time we get into the city, everyone's hungry. We delay checking into our hotel and drive straight to Happy Dog, which resembles an ordinary dive. A neon sign promises GOOD FOOD and chrome stools surround a polished oval bar. As we slide into a booth, Carrie slips her arm around Nina's shoulders. For once, the two of them are getting along. They have been in good spirits since we passed another display of I'M WITH HER signs on our way out of Deerling. The new batch, sprouting from the rock garden outside the library, may actually last a while—if anyone in Deerling County leans left, it's the librarians.

A server appears and asks if we want a high chair.

"Um," I say, holding Jack in my lap, "he's too little for a high chair."

The server is bepimpled and college age, wearing a Levi's shirt with pearl buttons. "Really? Was he, like, just born?"

"Yes," Carrie says. "We rushed straight here from the hospital. Amanda needed her postpartum Happy Dog fix."

He laughs nervously. The creature in my lap produces a new sound, a cross between a cough and a quack. Only when I look down and see the grin stretched across Jack's face—his eyes bright and fixed on our server—do I realize he has giggled.

Carrie, Nina, and I burst into cheers, inspiring yet another giggle. Jack's second ever. The sound leaves me flushed. It's a particular ebullience I haven't felt since I was a child prone to flinging myself down grassy hillsides.

"What can I get you guys?" the kid asks, staring at his notepad and understanding nothing. He has no idea humans aren't born sitting up, eating hot dogs, laughing. I might envy his combination of maleness and youth if I weren't so pleased by my baby's sense of humor.

I order the most expensive beer on the menu for five dollars and fifty cents. I let Nina design my hot dog for me and, too busy cooing at Jack, fail to listen to the toppings she rattles off. The server jogs away. Nina produces her phone, thumbs already twitching across the screen. In general, I've noticed, Ohioans are less captivated by their phones than New Yorkers, but Nina is an exception. It's a relatively recent addition to her life, obtained halfway through seventh grade, but she treats the device like an appendage she acquired in the womb.

"How's Maxine?" I ask.

It's the ensuing silence more than the question that eventually causes Nina to look up. "What?"

"Maxine," I repeat. "What are you guys talking about?"

Nina's phone disappears beneath the table. "I wasn't talking to Maxine."

I don't believe her.

Carrie changes the subject. "Hey, have either of you seen a Hillary sign on private property?"

The answer is no, but I lie and say, "Haven't really been paying attention."

Nina shrugs. "I've seen a couple of bumper stickers."

"Doesn't it seem weird that someone's willing to stick signs all over town, but no one's dared to put one in their own front yard?" Carrie asks.

"Maybe the hopefuls are from out of town," I say.

"Then why canvas in Deerling? I mean, realistically, it's a lost cause."

Nina frowns at her mother. "Maybe you should put up a sign."

"Seriously?" Carrie says.

"I mean, you're voting for her, right?"

"Yes."

"So, put up a sign. Maybe other people will see it and copy you."

Carrie wrinkles her nose. Slogans and logos depress her. "We're not lawn sign people, are we?"

"Maybe *you're* not," Nina says, smoldering.

Carrie lifts her hands. "Hey, if you want to put up a sign, we'll put up a sign. We can erect a Hillary Clinton billboard in our yard if it'll make you happy."

Nina smiles at her mom, but it's the way you smile at someone who has given you a gift meant for a much younger child. Why are mothers consistently several steps behind their daughters? Jaclyn never thought to warn me about anything—menstruation, credit card debt—until long after I was already dealing with it.

Guilt somersaults in my stomach. I should tell Carrie about the photos on Nina's phone. For all I know, Nina has already messaged the *Atlantic* writer, and Deerling has already made headlines. I can't bring myself to check.

My beer arrives, along with Carrie's gin and tonic and Nina's pop. Jack puts a hand on my pint glass, admiring the neon lights reflected in the ale. He's like a seagull that way—drawn to shiny things.

"What about Maxine's parents?" Carrie asks. "Think they'll put up any signs?"

"They say they 'don't want to shove their politics down people's throats.'" Nina makes air quotes.

Carrie seizes the chance to roll her eyes in solidarity. "Cowards."

"Totally," Nina says.

My hot dog appears before me. I know it's a hot dog only because we are at a hot dog restaurant; the wiener itself is not visible beneath the chili sauce, the nacho cheese, the fried egg, or the Froot Loops.

"This is an abomination," I inform Nina.

She beams with pride.

Trying not to squish Jack, I lean across the table for a handful of tater tots, a side dish we ordered to share. Carrie is making faces at Jack, pursing her lips and wiggling her eyebrows. He's in love.

"He looks like you when he laughs," Carrie says.

"I know. I can't wait for Gabe to hear him."

At the mention of Gabe, Carrie straightens. "Do you guys have any plans for the next few days?"

"Not really. I mean, we'll spend some time with Jaclyn."

"But you'll keep staying with us, right?"

"Um . . ." I shift the baby higher on my lap. Carrie assumes I've filled Gabe in, that he's expecting the four of us to welcome him at the airport tomorrow morning. "I guess I was thinking we'd get a room."

"In Deerling? You mean the Super 8?"

"I think so?"

"Don't take your infant to the Super 8. Just stay with us."

"Yeah," Nina chimes in. "Please."

"I'll ask Gabe what he wants to do," I say.

"He'll want to stay with Mom and me," Nina says.

I watch as she submerges a straw in her Coke then covers the top of the straw with her finger and lifts the bottom end to her mouth. Carrie used to drink her pop in the same annoying way. I regret letting Nina order my food. It's almost a thing I could eat, if not for the garnish of sugarcoated cereal. I'm suddenly starving— too starving to do anything except pick off the Froot Loops and endeavor to stomach the rest.

A shadow of disappointment crosses Nina's face. I try to ignore it.

Oblivious to my mood swing, and maybe a little bit buzzed, Carrie says, "You know, when I was pregnant, I always pictured this."

"Dinner at Happy Dog?" It seems possible. Carrie's pregnancy cravings went way beyond pickles and ice cream. I remember her crushing a handful of Cool Ranch Doritos into an open can of baked beans, grabbing a spoon, and going to town.

"You and me, hanging out with our babies."

Nina looks disturbed to be categorized with Jack, who is heavy-lidded, starting to slump against my abdomen. He always falls asleep in the loudest places. It's the silence of a dark room at bedtime that he finds offensive.

When Carrie was pregnant, I was no more inclined to imagine myself with a baby than I was to imagine opening a 401(k) or dying the gray out of my hair.

"I didn't think it would take thirteen years for you to have one," Carrie admits. "Why'd you guys wait so long?"

I look down at Jack as his eyes close. I'm speechless. None of our friends in New York have children. Gabe and I are thirty-one; we started trying to have a baby when I was still twenty-eight. My feeling has always been that I proposed parenthood at the earliest possible moment.

But how much longer has the last decade felt to Carrie? Time does not necessarily slow down after you have a baby, but the conditions of your life change so constantly that each month constitutes an era, each year a lifetime.

I say, "I guess we were waiting to become adults."

Carrie laughs and eats a tater tot. "Not a prerequisite, as it turns out."

She would claim to be talking about herself, but we both know she means me.

* * *

In the fall of our senior year, Carrie was sick.

Gabe, who grew up with three identical golden retrievers—whom he can still tell apart in old photos—once explained the phrase "sick as a dog" to me. Allegedly, certain dogs are prone to vomiting without any kind of warning onto the center of the living room carpet.

Carrie did not vomit onto the carpet, but she did vomit into the toilets at school, on the grass surrounding the track, into an empty Kentucky Fried Chicken bucket, and once, bewilderingly, into the glove compartment of my mother's car. Whenever I encounter a depiction of pregnancy on TV, I'm amazed at the ease with which the writers have downplayed the first trimester. Puke appears only for comic effect—for instance, when the woman is in her boss's office, her performance under review—and always into a conveniently located trash receptacle. We see the woman's eyes dart from side to side as she struggles to remember the date and duration of her last period.

By the next scene, her stomach protrudes adorably beneath a perfectly fitted T-shirt.

Carrie and I learned at an age younger than most that there is nothing adorable about the first trimester. Carrie was so sick that I sometimes insisted she must have eaten a bad clam strip or drunk the warm, murky water produced by the fountain outside the science labs. I wanted to take her to the ER, particularly during her ninth week when she couldn't keep anything down—not toast, not her prenatal vitamins, not watermelon slices, not the antinausea meds her GP had reluctantly prescribed after noting that "some ladies" were "grateful" for their morning sickness, thought to indicate a healthy pregnancy. As Carrie gripped the toilet, struggling to breathe through the bile climbing her throat and blocking her nasal passages, I fretted to her mother, "This can't be normal! This is so fucked up!" and Mrs. Hart shushed me. She pressed a cold washcloth to the back of Carrie's neck and said, "Hart women have rough pregnancies."

Between Halloween and Christmas, Carrie was hospitalized twice for dehydration. She lost ten pounds and missed twenty days of school. Her mother was forced to confess Carrie's secret to the administration so Carrie could complete her assignments from home and graduate on time.

In the same two months, I missed nine days of school. I wouldn't let Carrie go to the hospital alone. Armed with a list I'd printed from the internet of everything that might ease a pregnant person's symptoms, I drove to the drugstore and bought Tums, digestive enzymes, ginger candies, hemorrhoid cream. At Carrie's house we camped out on the couch, watching hours upon hours of reality television and eating pudding from individually sized containers. I tried to amuse her by echoing random lines of dialogue in a grating falsetto. Her laughter was feeble at best.

Eventually, my mother summoned her latent authority and forbade me to cut class. "The two of you are different people," Jaclyn said. "Only one of you is pregnant, and only one of you is going to college next year."

I no longer knew if I was going to college. Leaving Ohio, now that Carrie couldn't, became an imprecise pipe dream. What I never explained to Jaclyn or to anyone else was that Carrie's pregnancy—though devastating—was a kind of consolation. Months before her chosen method of birth control (luck) failed her, when Carrie, with her good grades and raw talent, seemed to have all the options in the world, it had already become clear that hitting the road with her best friend was not her top choice.

The summer before our senior year, something between us had soured. We had been studying each other's faces, making the same jokes, fighting the same fights, and loitering outside the same fast food establishments literally all our lives. My willful opinion was that our boredom with Deerling sometimes masqueraded as boredom with each other. We needed a change of scenery, that was all. The more I begged Carrie to make plans—one school, one apartment, one future to be shared between the two of us—the more she distanced herself. Slowly at first: Summer nights alone with her sketchpad. Sunday morning sermons with her parents. A boyfriend who threatened to eclipse me completely.

And then we were seniors. Pregnant, Carrie needed me. Is it ridiculous to say it felt like I had won?

The only college I applied to was thirty miles away.

After New Year's, when Carrie's nausea had more or less subsided—and we had heard the gallop of the baby's heartbeat, and Carrie had named the baby Nina, Nina Evelyn Hart—our homeroom teacher made us fill out a survey in service of some kid's project on teen pregnancy.

- Did you know that five out of every two hundred girls become pregnant by the age of nineteen?
- Did you know that teen pregnancy rates are even higher in states that practice abstinence only education?
- Did you know that two students at Deerling High School have missed class due to pregnancy complications this year?

No, no, no, I replied to every question. Carrie wasn't even showing yet; claiming absolute ignorance seemed best. Teen pregnancy? Never heard of it.

I glanced over at Carrie's desk, worried I would catch her hyperventilating.

In response to question number three, she had written, *I'M ONE OF THEM.*

CHAPTER NINE

"When are you and Gabe driving back to New York?" Carrie asks me, checking out the view from our room. Fireworks are already exploding over the Cuyahoga, but from our glass-encased suite on the fourteenth floor, we can barely hear them.

Too full of hot dog to pillage the minibar as planned, Nina is lying with Jack across one of two queen beds, tickling the souls of his bare feet. Yesterday I tried to book a separate room for me and the baby, but Carrie insisted I save my money: we could all share, no problem. I regret it now. The prospect of trying to keep Jack quiet while Carrie and Nina sleep causes more than a hundred and twenty-four bucks worth of stress.

"No firm plans," I tell Carrie. "He has the rest of the summer off, so I guess we'll play it by ear."

Nina looks up. "Can we take him to the Dairy Barn?" she asks.

The Dairy Barn is a highway-side institution, a purveyor of cheeses, pepperoni sticks, ice cream, mustards, jams, and assorted kitsch—socks adorned with specific breeds of dogs, picture frames that make it look like Jesus is gazing beatifically at your own kid, and T-shirts that say I CUT THE CHEESE AT THE DAIRY BARN IN DEERLING.

Even for a local it's a lot.

Carrie uses her mom voice. "Do you think he would *enjoy* going to the Dairy Barn?"

"It's, like, our only tourist attraction," Nina says.

"Gabe's from here," Carrie reminds her.

Nina squints, like she has registered this fact only dimly, if ever.

"He's not *from* here," I say. "He lived in Deerling for one year."

"A formative year," Carrie says.

"How about the pool?" Nina asks. "Or the dump?"

"Yes. We can do both." Carrie is perched on the windowsill, her back disconcertingly close to the glass. I follow her gaze to the bed, where Jack's face is in the process of crumbling. He rubs at his eyes, rocks his hips. He wails.

I scoop him up. Though freshly changed, fed, and burped, he is distraught. When shushing and swaying proves ineffective, I announce I'm going to take a walk with him, grateful for an excuse to leave the room. Before I can slip away, Nina jumps to her feet. "Can I take him?" she asks, already reaching.

I hesitate. "You want to walk with him?"

"Yeah. I want to help."

In Jack's entire life, only Gabe and Carrie have ever taken him out of my sight. Charging a thirteen-year-old with his care seems reckless, perhaps illegal, but Carrie is looking at me hopefully. She wants to reward her daughter's interest. Nina has spent plenty of hours fawning over Jack when he's happy, but this is the first time she's offered to step in when he's sad.

Carrie and Nina have been getting along all night. I'm supposed to say yes.

Forever in my friend's debt, I hand over my screaming infant. "Stay on this floor," I tell Nina. "And come back as soon as he calms down."

"I will," she promises, and her gravity cannot conceal her delight. She's like a teenager turning the key in the ignition for the first time. If my baby weren't the family sedan in this scenario, I would be impressed.

"They'll be fine," Carrie says. The heavy door clicks shut. "They're right outside."

My hands are on my face. My palms are cold and sweaty. "Look," I say, trying to outrace my mounting anxiety, trying to disguise it as something else. "I don't know if Gabe will have time for all that stuff."

"What stuff?" Carrie asks.

"The dump, the pool, the fucking Dairy Barn."

"What do you mean? I thought you had *no firm plans*."

"I mean, I'd like his help with the baby. And we *should* spend some time with my mom, not to mention some time as a family. Just the three of us. It's been forever."

She slides her thumbnail between her front teeth. "It's Nina's birthday tomorrow."

"I know."

"Nina's birthday is the whole reason for your trip. And it's not like we're planning to abandon you with the baby. Everyone's going to help. Even Nina is starting to bond with him. Can't you be happy about that? I mean, they are siblings."

Carrie looks down at the retro hotel carpet. She studies its threat-level-orange honeycomb pattern. Then she changes her mind and looks me in the eye.

I wish it didn't break my heart, Jack having a sister. I have fantasized about alternative versions of my life in which it doesn't bother me at all—Gabe and I meeting in our midtwenties, New York City. On our third or fourth date he confesses to me that he has a daughter, the result of a brief and otherwise unremarkable relationship in high school. He loves her to pieces; he visits twice a year; he and the girl's mother are on friendly terms.

In the fantasy, I take a deep breath and say, "Okay."

Once Gabe asked me, "Is it because you didn't help make her?" We were drunk on a futon in Nashville. It was New Year's, and we had driven down to Tennessee after spending Christmas in Deerling. The conversation was the kind you can only have hundreds of miles from home, as if words unheard by the artifacts of your everyday life are somehow off the record.

"No," I said, my face half-buried in a pillow. Everything in the Airbnb we had rented—the towels, the futon mattress, the insides of the water glasses—smelled like pulled pork from the restaurant downstairs. "It's because it feels like I did."

To Carrie, I say, "I miss him."

"You're the one who came here without him."

"It was a bad idea."

"Really?" Carrie leans back against the window. I wish she would move toward the center of the room. "I think it's been pretty great."

"Um, you didn't even want me here. When I knocked on your door, you looked at me like I was your landlord."

"What landlord? I own the house."

I roll my eyes at her pride. Houses in Deerling cost less than a year of Gabe's salary. "I know that. I'm saying you looked at me like I was going to make you move all your furniture into the kitchen so I could paint your living room an ugly color and justify raising your rent."

It's Carrie's turn to roll her eyes. "I was just surprised, that's all."

"You didn't look surprised. You looked like you'd been dreading my arrival for years."

"Yeah, well." She throws up her hands. "Maybe both things are true."

I am moving gradually toward the door, straining to hear Jack's cries. All I can hear is the whine of the elevator. "Seeing you has been great," I say. "Spending time with Nina has been great. But I'm finally starting to feel like myself again, like maybe I'm going to wake up from this postpartum nightmare soon, and I want to get home. I want my life back. You have to remember how that feels."

"Not really." She has slipped into that strategic boredom, her expression opaque. I could shake her.

"What do you want from me right now?"

She gnaws on her thumbnail. "I want you to stay in Deerling another two weeks."

"Why do you want that?"

"Nina's excited to see her dad."

"We can come back another time."

"No."

"Carrie, he's my husband."

While technically untrue, it's something I say in New York all the time. No one there knows the difference. Now, claiming Gabe as a member of my own small family while excluding him from Carrie's is the equivalent of shaking her. As she rises from the windowsill, her lips curl into a smile—one part disbelief, two parts scorn—and I know I'm doomed.

"You know, you've never even thanked me? I could have said no."

I swallow. Swallowing hurts. "No to what?"

"When you told me Gabe kissed you. That you wanted to go to New York with him. I could have said no."

"I wasn't asking your permission."

"Well, Gabe did."

Not knowing where my baby is makes my heart pound twice as hard.

"When?"

"Before he kissed you, he asked if I wanted him to stay. He had already talked to NYU, and they were going to let him defer for a year. We would've moved out there after Nina's first birthday, and then gotten married after Gabe finished school. He had a whole plan."

I can feel my lips twitching into a defensive smile. "You're telling me Gabe proposed to you."

"He said if we were 'reasonably happy' we could get married."

My laughter is stunned and hollow. "How were you guys going to determine if you were 'reasonably happy'?"

Carrie sighs. "I don't know, Amanda. We didn't get that far."

My breasts choose this moment to fill with milk. The sensation is like turning into stone. I grip my shoulder and hope Carrie can't tell I'm applying pressure to my nipples, countering the pain. Through the window behind her I can see the city's final burst of fireworks. It's an antagonizing eruption of color and sound and God-bless-America. I try not to cry.

The colors blur.

"He never told me any of that," I say.

It's almost imperceptible, but Carrie softens. She was correct to guess that he never told me, but it was only a guess. "Yeah, well, Gabe always tries to do the right thing."

"Which would've been . . . marrying you?"

"You know that's not what I meant."

"I need to go get my baby." Refusing eye contact, I turn and rush out of the room, letting the door slam behind me. It was insane to let Nina take him away. He's heavy and squirmy and Nina's arms appear as thin and weak as raw spaghetti. What if she decided to joyride the elevator? What if she carried him outside to roam the streets of Cleveland?

What if I can't find them anywhere?

It will be Gabe's fault, my panic decides. Gabe's fault for not being here already. Gabe's fault for offering my life to Carrie before he offered it to me.

I find them about twenty feet down the hall, swaying beside a vending machine. Jack is sleeping peacefully, his cheek flattened against Nina's shoulder.

"He likes the sound," she says, meaning the electric hum of the machine.

"He's a connoisseur of white noise. Supposedly, it reminds him of the womb."

Nina arches an eyebrow. "Your womb sounds like a vending machine?"

"With a thunderous heartbeat, I imagine."

She appraises me, her concern sweeping my body. In the course of the evening, Nina seems to have aged a decade or two. "You look weird," she says.

"Weird how?"

"Like, nervous weird."

"I didn't know where you'd gone."

Nina strokes the top of my baby's perfect head. "Literally nowhere," she says.

CHAPTER TEN

"I read on the internet that she, or he, is the size of a blueberry," Carrie told me. "I know I should be freaking out, but I actually feel so calm."

It was Halloween. We were sitting on the porch of my childhood home, swaddled in sweaters and scarves, depositing handfuls of candy into the pillowcases of neighborhood Spidermans, Harry Potters, and Tinker Bells.

"You're having it?" I asked as one group of trick-or-treaters receded and another approached. What I meant was, *You're not getting an abortion?* Abortion was a word, maybe the only word, I couldn't bring myself to say aloud. In 2002, in rural Ohio, teenage girls made their choices quietly, without slapping pro-choice stickers on their notebooks. Someone would have complained, the librarian with the crucifix around her neck or maybe Mr. Wallace, the chemistry teacher, who relished September and June, when nearly every day granted him the opportunity to summon a girl to the chalkboard, ask the class to identify her violation of the dress code, and send her to the office. There, she would be made to don an oversize DEERLING HIGH SCHOOL sweatshirt of shame.

Carrie nodded.

"Just because you go to church?"

Snow White asked how many peanut butter cups she could take, while a pirate plundered the bowl. When they were gone, Carrie said, "Look, the test turned positive, and I expected to fall apart. To sob or something." She looked at me. "If I felt like sobbing, I would terminate. I really would."

What if I *feel like sobbing?* I wanted to ask but didn't. Carrie was making a body with her body. Privately I wished she wouldn't, but intuitively I understood the project demanded absolute deference.

"What I felt instead was . . ." Carrie pressed her hands into her midsection. With a sincerity that made me uncomfortable, she said, "pure joy."

My lips formed a word which began as *Carrie* but. against my will, veered into "Congratulations." And as soon as I'd said it, I meant it. When you love a person, there is no way to avoid loving that person's child. Trust me, I've tried.

Carrie rested her head on my shoulder.

"We should tell Gabe," I said, my heart breaking on the smooth stone of his name. They had been a couple for approximately six weeks. (Fewer than two menstrual cycles, I've since noted.)

She hesitated. "We?"

"Yeah?"

She took a breath. "I don't want to tell him until after my first trimester. There's some chance I'll miscarry before then, in which case, he might as well not know."

I knew what a miscarriage was—Jaclyn would sometimes refer to the discovery or nausea of a pregnancy between me and my brother, one that hadn't lasted—but I believed it was a tragedy particular to my mother's relentlessly difficult life. If I had understood it was common, maybe I would have rooted for Carrie's pregnancy to fail.

Luckily, I was naive enough to dismiss Carrie's concern as paranoia. From the beginning, I took her baby for granted.

* * *

The Feldmans showed up the summer before our senior year. Mr. Feldman—as I'll always think of him, though I've tried calling him "my father-in-law" or "Jack's grandpa" or "Hank"—was temporarily transferred to Deerling after his employer, an East Coast consumer goods corporation, acquired a handful of midwestern factories. The day Carrie and I first laid eyes on Gabe, we were fighting. Or else not fighting but bickering, pausing to get high, and laughing at ourselves for having achieved old-married-couple status—until our buzz faded and we resumed bickering.

It was August, and we had passed most of the summer this way. I kept pestering Carrie to review and contribute to the list of colleges I'd assembled. Schools that boasted both art and business programs. All were out of state, none Ohio-adjacent. Carrie shared my restlessness, my impatience with the full year of high school looming ahead of us. But while the list gave me hope and purpose, it seemed to fill Carrie with dread.

We were walking through the woods when she confessed, "I'm not sure I even want to go to art school anymore. I feel like art maybe can't be taught."

"Fine," I said, annoyed with her apathy, which was supposed to be my affect. "Then pick a part of the country, any part. I'll go to school there, and you can do whatever you want."

"That's stupid. You're the one with actual goals. You should have the final say."

"So, you'd rather I pick?"

"I'd rather talk about something else."

"What else is there?"

It was the last question I would ask as the version of myself who did not know Gabe Feldman. Since then, most things I've said have had something to do with him.

He was sitting cross-legged on a footbridge, hunched over a paperback copy of *Self-Portrait in a Convex Mirror*, a title that sounded to me like heady nonsense. Carrie and I froze on the path approaching the creek. She threw out an arm to prevent me from walking ahead, something she'd done in this spot before. In the spring we'd spotted a coyote, surprisingly slim and projecting a feline calm. In July we nearly tripped on the corpse of a turkey vulture, its clenched talons and wrinkled red head the stuff of nightmares. But this was different. Our shock merged with thrill. Here sat an uncharted boy. He was reading an actual *book*.

At some point in the last twenty-four hours Carrie had straightened her hair, which meant she'd gone somewhere without telling me. Maybe to a church member's wedding or funeral. Maybe to a classmate's party. Now the humidity was restoring the curls near her temples and behind her ears.

"Yo," Carrie said, comically confrontational. Flirtatious. "We've never seen you here before."

Gabe studied her, then me. Her again. "I've never *been* here before."

"Ah," Carrie said, "Mystery solved."

* * *

When school started a few weeks later, Gabe and I were in the same English class. The teacher relied heavily on the alphabet to govern her classroom; not only were Feldman and Flood seated in neighboring desks, but we were assigned to work together on our inaugural assignment: a portrait of Deerling. A joint expression, either poetry or prose, of what our town meant to us.

On the first Saturday of the school year, I drove the Toyota—the truck technically belonged to Carrie, but we shared it as casually as we shared sweaters, hair elastics, and tubes of cherry-flavored Chapstick—to the development where the Feldmans had leased one of a dozen identical homes. Two dormer windows were positioned like eyes above a garage door paneled with gritted teeth. I pulled into the driveway as the sun was breaking through storm clouds, restoring the premature dusk to broad daylight. Gabe answered the door, his trio of purebred dogs squeezing between his legs and the doorframe. He led me into the kitchen, where his mother was unloading the dishwasher.

Mrs. Feldman did not work but was dressed the way my mother might have for a job interview. She looked down at my mismatched socks and said, "Oh, you didn't have to take off your shoes."

My cheeks burned.

She offered me *soda* instead of *pop* and a sleeve of seedy crackers. Or she could slice up an apple, if I preferred. Overwhelmed, I declined everything, though I wanted all of it. I expected Diane to leave the room, but she resumed segregating forks from spoons while Gabe and I sat down to work.

"I guess I'm kind of drawing a blank," Gabe said, "on what Deerling means to me."

Diane snorted. Behind Gabe, stuck to the fridge, was a certificate declaring him the winner of the Gladwyne Middle School

1998 Ravenous Reader award. The certificate perplexed me. I couldn't fathom how it had come to be displayed so prominently in a house the Feldmans had occupied fewer than thirty days. Had it been on their refrigerator back in Philadelphia? Had his mother packed it up carefully, among the plates and wooden salad bowls? Did it belong to a rotating set of awards and blue ribbons exhibited throughout the house?

Already, I understood that Gabe's parents took him more seriously than anyone had ever taken me.

Since discovering him at the dump, Carrie and I had been including Gabe in our daily non-adventures. He rode in the narrow back seat of Carrie's truck and followed us through the aisles of Walmart willingly if not eagerly, amused if not enchanted. Carrie stopped seeking excuses to spend hours away from me, which was a welcome return to normal. Slightly unbearable was the way she always sat on Gabe's side of the booth at Denny's, plus the way the two of them sprang apart, like corn kernels in hot oil, whenever I returned from the bathroom.

In the Feldmans' kitchen I said, "Our teacher's super Christian. We could probably get an A if we wrote about how Deerling has more churches per capita than any other town in Ohio."

Diane looked up, aghast. "Is that true?"

My palms were sweating. I couldn't tell if I was sitting too close or, awkwardly, revealingly far from her son. "I have no idea," I said.

It was Gabe who finally proposed we get out of the house, buy a disposable camera from the drugstore, and make a photo essay. He was boyishly confident the teacher would love us for redefining her assignment, and I didn't care about our grade; I wanted to be alone with him. We drove west, racing the sunset. Gabe rode shotgun and through the window snapped a picture of an apple orchard—the fruit still green and unreachable—and another of a man in a tank top tussling with a punching bag suspended from his front porch. Above a barn in the distance loomed a plume of bluish smoke. Gabe was alarmed.

"Something's on fire," he said.

"Probably just brush. Or garbage," I said.

"People set fire to garbage?"

We passed a man and a woman standing in grass to their knees, their arms around each other as they watched a couch and two mattresses burn to nothing.

"Amazing," Gabe said.

"You can say it. I won't be offended."

"Say what?'

"That you hate it here."

"What if I don't?"

"You do. It's small and depressing." *Small* didn't feel accurate—in fact, we had been driving in one direction for nearly twenty minutes without reaching another town—but it was something I'd grown up believing anyway.

"It's real," Gabe said. He brought the camera close to my face. The shutter clicked. "You're real."

We turned back toward residential streets. Deliberately, I drove Gabe through Carrie's neighborhood, where houses looked plausibly suburban, lawns mowed and driveways paved. I stopped the truck when I spotted a soft-bellied dad and his two sons hanging a Cleveland Indians flag above their garage door. The three of them wore red T-shirts and matching baseball caps. Taking the camera from Gabe, I rolled down my window, trusting the family was too preoccupied to notice us, and hardly caring if they did. It was almost dark. We could speed away; they'd never catch us.

This was the photo that Gabe and I would submit to our English teacher. What did Deerling mean to the new kid and me? *Family*, we claimed. *Baseball*, we bullshitted. *Lingering in the warm glow of a porch light after the September sun went down.*

We got an A.

* * *

When I returned Carrie's truck to her driveway that night, I told her Gabe had called me *real*. "What do you think it means?" I asked.

My best friend shrugged. She was furtively smoking a cigarette. Only her dad was home, and if he emerged from the house Carrie would thrust the Marlboro into my hand, a trick that never failed to soothe her parents, who weren't fools but maintained a foolish faith in Carrie's goodness. "That he's a snob?"

"He's not a snob."

"That he's trying to Velveteen Rabbit you?"

I could have told her Gabe's attention meant something to me. That I liked him, actually, and had since the day we met him. My gut feeling is that if I had asked her to, Carrie would have left Gabe alone. Perhaps, in her aloofness, she was daring me to ask. To admit aloud that I expected her to yield.

But instead of admitting anything, I mimicked Carrie's shrug of indifference, tacitly giving her permission to finish what she'd started.

Several years into my friendship with Paige, when she was twenty-six and I was twenty-two, I finally revealed to her the real reason behind Gabe's seasonal trips to Ohio. In boozy desperation—Gabe was in Deerling for Nina's fourth birthday; I missed him; I missed her—I laid bare the devastating sequence of events and asked Paige what I'd never had the guts to ask Carrie.

"She was my best friend. Why would she hook up with Gabe when she knew I liked him?"

When I'd first met Paige, working in Long Island City, I assumed we had certain things in common. Her teeth were slightly crooked, and she was always asking to borrow two dollars for a Coke from the vending machine in the warehouse. She turned out to be from Scarsdale, a kid who hadn't liked wearing her retainer. She found my background fascinating, and while I was prone to exaggerating Jaclyn's shortcomings and my occasional run-ins with the Deerling police force, the premise at which Paige most often marveled was a hard fact: from the time I turned twelve, no certified adult thought to keep track of where I was. Now Paige was savoring the moment, reacting as if I'd kept Gabe's daughter a secret for the sole purpose of spilling it tonight—a salacious gift on an otherwise ordinary Tuesday. Throwing up her elegant, semimasculine hands, Paige said, "Why does anyone do anything when they're seventeen?"

We were sweating in an un-air-conditioned bar in Bushwick, as far from Deerling as I'd ever been. At twenty-two, I owed my overall happiness to the state of Pennsylvania, which I imagined as a barricade between my childhood and me. Only when I saw the state on a map, crowded between Ohio and New York at the base of the country's thumb, did I doubt it was up to the task.

There's something to the idea that Carrie, Gabe, and I acted impulsively—we were kids, and kids burn things down; they drive cars into rivers and behave like animals toward the people who love them—but I don't have the luxury of believing it's so simple. If I don't take seriously the things we did and felt at seventeen, then my entire adult life becomes a joke.

"What makes you so sure she knew how you felt?" Paige asked. "Gabe's a hard guy to resist. The dignified, brooding type. Maybe she genuinely wanted him for herself."

Carrie did want him for herself—casually, experimentally. I have never doubted the pleasure Gabe and Carrie took in each other's company (or, to my grief, in each other's bodies). But this was a girl who could correctly predict the onset of my period by the way my stomach protruded, barely, over the waistband of my jeans. Watching a movie together, she would say, "Don't cry," in the second before my shuddery inhale. When I told her about Gabe and me turning a homework assignment into a joyride, making it last as long as possible, she knew how I felt. She always did.

"Before Gabe showed up, I'd been talking about going to college together, moving in together. Maybe she was telling me no. Maybe she was trying to say she'd had enough of me."

Paige was skeptical. "But you still had a year of high school left. *Maybe* your friend was just trying to get through it. *Maybe* you're overestimating the extent to which her life revolved around yours. She needed a pick-me-up. And it doesn't sound like your hometown was crawling with interesting men."

Gabe wasn't merely interesting. Gabe was a time traveler, an ambassador from the future.

He was proof of life outside of Deerling County.

* * *

A few days after Halloween, Carrie threw up. We were leaning against the counter in my kitchen, sipping Diet Cokes, watching my brother search the fridge for his after-school snack. Lifting the lid from a Tupperware container, my brother sniffed and theorized, "Old turkey burgers?" The moment the smell reached us, Carrie blanched. She turned and vomited into the sink.

"Sorry," Carrie croaked, running the water over the bile-splattered dishes. "Hangover."

My brother, bewildered, said, "It's Tuesday."

"She's been hungover since Sunday," I said.

"Yeah," Carrie agreed. "Interminable hangovers run in my family."

Still clutching his Tupperware of spoiled poultry, my brother said, "That's quite a curse."

Miserably, Carrie nodded.

* * *

The next two months were a blur, during which Gabe, in his ignorance, slipped farther down Carrie's list of concerns. When I think back to our mornings on the bathroom floor or our numbing afternoons in class—the room's aroma of boiled hot dogs and pencil shavings—my stomach churns, as if mine were the body in revolt that fall. The number of humans I've gestated is one. I know that. Still, a dozen years after Carrie's pregnancy, when an ultrasound tech squirted a cold curl of gel onto my belly and asked, "First baby?" I struggled to produce the correct answer.

There was a night in November when I drove Carrie to the hospital to receive intravenous fluids. Squished together on the narrow bed—Carrie's hand resting on her still-flat abdomen, mine on the remote control—we watched the episode of *Dawson's Creek* in which Joey Potter loses her virginity. The premise: during an improbably lavish school trip to a ski lodge in Vermont, Joey and

Pacey share a room. She wears a pink camisole with no bra and he brushes her hair, slowly, without encountering a single knot.

From there, the camera is mostly concerned with the undoing of buttons.

"Was it like that?" I asked.

Fluid dripped into Carrie's veins. "Sure."

But could it have been so romantic, or reverent, even in their imaginations? Gabe and Carrie were not in love—he would assure me of that later, whenever I questioned what we'd done. In essential, unyielding ways, Gabe and Carrie were too similar. Each was judgmental and quick to become self-righteous when his or her judgements were questioned. Whimsical observations escalated into fights. Often their fights concerned Ohio. Gabe, echoing his parents, maintained that our town had no culture. Carrie challenged him to define *culture*: Overpriced restaurants? Rush hour traffic? She relented when Gabe described visiting MoMA on vacation in New York City with his parents or listed the indie bands he had seen live. Carrie and I hadn't been to a concert since we were fourteen, when my mother dragged us to hear a Lynyrd Skynyrd cover band perform at the golf course.

Though Gabe, like Carrie, was proud to a fault, he had a domestic silly streak that was all his own. In the privacy of a bedroom or a car, he spoofed on radio hits. He broke awkward silences by smiling to reveal an orange peel wedged between his lips. His comedic timing left me doubled over, gasping for air, while Carrie looked from him to me like she was considering dropping us both off at the pound.

I kept prodding. "Was there a fireplace, casting flattering shadows across your faces?"

"No," she said. "No fireplace."

"How many times?"

"Once."

I put some space between our shoulders. "Just once? Are you kidding me?"

She sighed. "No, not kidding you."

And there was no joy in her response, this time.

There were things I didn't need her to say. I understood that, whatever her motivation for sleeping with Gabe, she hadn't meant to permanently tie her life to his. If Carrie's goal had ever been to bruise me, it hadn't been to bludgeon me. She'd broken up with him a couple of weeks before learning she was pregnant, in no small part because my infatuation with her boyfriend had become intolerable to us both. The unspoken plan was to give Gabe a second to catch his breath before I claimed my pass to make out with him. Due to the cells accumulating personhood in Carrie's uterus, the pass was now null and void. I got it. I didn't expect her to accommodate my feelings for the father of her child.

But I did, however unfairly, wish she would say she was sorry.

She never did. Either she believed the blue paper gown and tubes taped to her wrist absolved her or else she already suspected what was coming.

* * *

Gabe was the third person we told, after Carrie's mother and after mine. Driving to the highway exit Denny's where we'd asked him to meet us, I was more nervous than Carrie seemed, my hands slipping against the steering wheel.

"Why breakfast?" I asked. "Why not dinner? Isn't that when you're supposed to have serious conversations?"

Carrie stared out the window. "I've never heard that rule."

"Sure you have. Dinner is official. People, like, join hands and pray before dinner."

"You want to pray before we eat our pancakes?"

"Maybe we should." I was concerned she did not feel the weight of our mission. Carrie talked to me less and less as the pregnancy progressed. I felt jealous of the fetus, who was presumably keeping her company.

"Look," she said, "you can't go around dropping bombshells at dinner. It's too close to bedtime. How would Gabe ever get to sleep after that?"

I turned into the Denny's parking lot. Mounds of shoveled snow buried the medians. "No, you're right. Better to tell him at 9:00 A.M. In another twelve hours, he'll be over it."

In the months since their breakup, Gabe Feldman had become a subject of fascination among our peers. No one in Deerling had ever heard the term *emo* and so couldn't apply it to Gabe's swooped bangs, slim-fit corduroys, Elliott Smith T-shirt, or scratched leather messenger bag. If pressed for a description of the new kid, most locals would have sooner produced the word *homo*—but that wouldn't have fazed Gabe, and so no one bothered. Gabe slammed his locker and moved through the halls like a businessman impatient to cross an airport terminal. None of us was used to thinking about our town as a pit stop; to us, Deerling was home, and home was a concept as unyielding as the broken-down cars in our backyards and the generations of junk cluttering our grandmas' attics. Gabe had moved here from Philadelphia. Before that, he had lived in Boston and New York. He didn't care whether he was liked by the teenagers of a small midwestern town—therefore, he was beloved.

Later he told me he had started his senior year pretending to be a spy, dispatched to observe the habits and rituals of
Middle Americans. He said yes to everything: yes to parties, yes
to football games, yes to driving an ATV through the center of
town, yes to the county fair, yes to using empty Budweiser cans
as target practice in Bruce Stout's backyard. It wasn't until Carrie
and I walked into Denny's hand in hand—both Carrie's nerves
and nausea had surged in the parking lot—that Gabe realized his
life in Deerling was more than a game.

My job was to answer the practical questions—thirteen weeks
along, due at the beginning of July, feeling sick but excited—
while Carrie engaged Gabe on the delicate subject of his paternity.

"I don't want us to get back together, and I'm not asking you
for anything," she said. "I know this is primarily my fault."

I flinched. My assumption, until now, was that their chosen
method of birth control had failed them. My understanding of
fertility was vague, rooted in our health teacher's assertion that
you could be struck pregnant at absolutely any time—no matter
the day of the month, no matter the brand of pill or condom.
Even if you didn't fully have sex, but just kind of gestured toward
intercourse. Sperm were sneaky.

If, in fact, Carrie and Gabe had declined to take precautions in
the heat of the moment? It wasn't a moment I wanted to imagine.

"Not your fault," Gabe said quickly.

His hair fell in his eyes as he dipped his chin toward his coffee.
A moat of empty sugar packets surrounded the mug. His fingers
shook as he tore open another.

"Still, you don't have to, like, be a dad. I can leave that line
blank on the birth certificate."

Gabe frowned. "Don't do that."

EMILY ADRIAN

"You want to be a dad?"

"I mean, no. Not really. But if I *am* a dad, I don't want to pretend I'm not one."

"Okay," Carrie said. "That's honest. Thank you."

Gabe laughed. "This is surreal. Don't you guys think this is surreal?"

Carrie and I exchanged a look. This morning was no more surreal than our past one hundred mornings. Still, I ached for him. I wanted to cradle Gabe's head in my lap while he cried.

"We don't have to figure everything out right now," Carrie said. "You can think about how involved you want to be and then get back to me."

Outside the restaurant, Gabe used his remote key to unlock his Volkswagen Beetle, a car that looked like a rotund space invader among the pickups and Wranglers of Deerling. He watched Carrie and me climb into her truck and called out, "Hey, Care?"

The nickname revived all the affection of their brief romance. She looked up.

"Do you know if it's a boy or a girl?"

"Not yet. It's too soon."

"Are you going to find out?"

The wind whipped his hair away from his face. His forehead, unblemished, was creased with concern.

"Do you think I should?"

"Yeah," he said. "It would be cool to know."

The two of them shared such tentative smiles, I had to turn away.

It's funny, now, to remember the assumptions we made—primarily, that the adults in our orbit would leave it to three teenagers to dole out custody and care for an unborn child. Carrie and

168

I were still waiting for Gabe to call and define the parameters of his fatherhood when Mr. and Mrs. Feldman drove up to the Hart house one Friday night, mid-January. I was at home, chatting with Carrie on the bulky Dell desktop my mom had begrudgingly set up in one corner of our kitchen. Back then, Jaclyn was bewildered by the hours my brother and I spent on the internet, bewildered by the internet itself—the atonal beeps and screeches of the dial-up connection—and unable to imagine a future in which all of us stroked our handheld screens for comfort. Carrie typed, *Um. The Feldmans are here.*

> **Me:** all of them??
> **Carrie:** just Gabe + parentals + some random dude??
> **Me:** what do they want??!
> **Carrie:** brb

I stared at the computer, my heart pounding. At the top of my buddy list, Carrie's screen name turned gray to indicate inactivity. After fifteen minutes I typed, *everyone still there??* and received an automated message in response: a couplet of Nick Drake lyrics, one of the morose musicians to whom Gabe had introduced us.

More than an hour later, the away message came down and Carrie typed, *finally they're gone.* She gave me the verdict: Gabe had been accepted early decision to NYU and would be attending college in the fall. As long as things remained amicable between him and Carrie, he would not file for custody. Mr. and Mrs. Feldman would make child payments until Gabe graduated and began earning a minimum salary of $40,000 per year, at which point he would assume responsibility for the payments himself.

Gabe would see the baby whenever he was in town—Christmas, spring break—and at least once per summer.

The random dude turned out to be a family mediator.

My fingers were still hammering away at my keyboard when Carrie told me she was logging off, going to bed. By the time I saw her the next day, the meeting was already in the past. To rehash the details, she told me, would stress her out, and stress was among the things—caffeine, hot baths, deli meats—that Carrie avoided on the fear-mongering advice of that prenatal bible, *What to Expect When You're Expecting*.

My first vicarious glimpse into that night wouldn't come until Gabe and I were twenty-five, on vacation in Rome. Again, a conversation made possible by foreign surroundings and two bottles of Chianti at lunch. We began by talking about how neither of us had ever been to Europe until now.

"When I was a kid, I always thought I would go the summer before college. I thought I'd schlep a backpack around and sleep on trains," Gabe said.

"Oh, yeah? And then what happened?" Talking to Gabe about Carrie always made my cheeks hot. The topic was equal parts terrifying and exhilarating, like taking a sledgehammer to your own house.

Gabe played along. "Got a girl pregnant. Spent the summer waiting for her to go into labor."

"What a drag."

We sank into silence. The wrought iron table wobbled against the sidewalk. On Gabe's plate, a few remaining bites of gnocchi drowned in red sauce.

I took a breath. "When Carrie and I asked to meet you at Denny's, what did you think was going on?"

"Honestly? I thought you two were going to inform me of some arrangement you'd cooked up, wherein you and I got to date. Maybe with some conditions, as predetermined by Carrie."

"Wouldn't that have been a little dramatic?"

"You two *were* a little dramatic."

That fall, following the positive pregnancy test, Carrie and I had mostly avoided Gabe. I'd talked to him a couple of times only because we still shared an English class. Once I told him I liked his T-shirt. Against a black background, a reddish circle was labeled MARS. "Is Mars your favorite planet?" I asked. Gabe had looked down at his skinny chest and replied, "It's my favorite planet shirt."

"We were dramatic because she was pregnant," I said.

"So I learned."

"Would you have dated me?"

Gabe smiled. "I'm not sure. At the time, I thought of you as Carrie's sarcastic friend who maybe had a crush on me. I didn't fall for you until a few months later. You guys invited me over to bake cookies, which sounded so unbelievably wholesome, I figured it was code for, like, *do meth*, until I remembered Carrie was going to be a mom. And moms do things like bake cookies. Do you remember this?"

At twenty-five, I still remembered everything, but I lied and said no.

"The cookies Carrie wanted to make were crazy complicated. The dough wasn't doing what it was supposed to do. She had a bowl full of liquid mess, and she started crying. Hysterically."

"Hormones."

"Your solution was to take the whole failed experiment and toss it into the river behind Carrie's house. You must remember this."

"Vaguely."

"So, we walk down to the river, and it's March, and it's freezing.

And we determine Carrie's too pregnant to walk across the rocks, and so you volunteer. You were wearing a pair of flip-flops, if memory serves."

"Sounds plausible."

"And Carrie kept saying, 'Don't throw the bowl! Don't throw the bowl!'"

I assured her I would not throw the bowl, only its contents. Then, with the water rushing beneath my unprotected feet, I chucked the bowl against the rocks. The river swept the ceramic shards downstream. Gabe turned up his palms in disbelief, but Carrie was instantly cheered. "I told you to be careful! I knew that would happen!"

"You were right," was all I said.

In Rome, Gabe finished this story and summarized, "You knew if you screwed something up, it would be like Carrie's own mistake had never happened. It was manipulative, but in a sweet way."

"You fell in love with me because I broke a mixing bowl?"

He smiled. "Yeah. A little bit."

Because I didn't know if we'd ever again be drunk and abroad, I resisted the temptation to change the subject. There were so many moments from which I'd been excluded that year. Moments that felt crucial to understanding my own history and my own future.

"What happened when you told your parents Carrie was pregnant?"

"I told them on a Friday morning. They were stone-faced. Like, just completely ashen. I was sobbing and begging them to say something, but my dad kept repeating, 'You're going to be late for school,' until I finally gave up and left. I guess that's when they sprang into action. By the time I got home, they'd hired a mediator and arranged the meeting with Carrie's parents."

"I always thought you guys ambushed the Harts."

Gabe shook his head. "All the adults were in cahoots. My dad tracked down Rosalind at the library. I think she was relieved, honestly, to realize he was this business guy with plenty of money and, you know, shame."

"Were you upset?"

Gabe put his hands behind his head, leaned back in his chair. "I was embarrassed. Carrie's preference was to act like we had everything handled, and to me, that seemed noble and mature. I wanted to be like her. I didn't want her to think I'd gone running and crying to my parents."

"But you had."

"Oh, totally." We made deliberate eye contact. "But you know, their involvement was a relief. It took me a week to tell them, and the whole time I was thinking it was a situation they couldn't rescue me from. But then, in the end, they rescued me anyway."

"Not really," I said. "Carrie stayed pregnant. You still became a dad at eighteen."

"Yeah, but what did I have to give up? Nothing. I got everything I wanted—college, New York. I even got *you*." His expression was strained, as if our togetherness was an indulgence Gabe hadn't deserved.

His implication—though never voiced, not even in Rome—was that Carrie had given up everything to become Nina's mother. Maybe it's convenient, my reluctance to agree. But Carrie, who hadn't previously known what she wanted from her life, couldn't have been calmer or more focused during the nine months of her pregnancy. The test turning positive filled her with the sense of purpose that kids like Gabe acquired after touring the green lawns or city campuses of their dream schools.

And *isn't* it more ambitious to raise a child than to get a bachelor's degree?

At least, to try to raise a child without fucking her up?

"I guess, if I'm being totally honest," Gabe went on, "I'm not sure I would've become a high school English teacher in another life. When Nina was around two, it started to really bother me that my parents were still making those payments. I might have gone for a PhD if I'd felt like I had the time to spare. You know?"

The wine plus Gabe's tone, newly laced with self-pity, made me blunt. "Yeah, but it doesn't count as a sacrifice if you only think of it afterward."

He blinked at me. I stared back, as cool and formidable, I hoped, as Carrie Hart herself.

"You're right," he said finally.

* * *

From the night I tossed the mixing bowl into the river, a memory we've never once discussed: Carrie went to the bathroom for the hundredth time. Gabe and I were alone in the kitchen, among the open bags of sugar and salt. There was something he wanted to say to me that I preferred not to hear. As a distraction, I grabbed a yellow legal pad and sketched— without looking at the page and hardly breaking eye contact—a portrait of him. It turned out good. I had captured the light in his eyes, the span of his extravagant smile. With a flourish, I spun the pad in his direction, as if presenting a test score or a puzzle I had solved.

From the bathroom, we heard the toilet flush. Gabe gave the drawing a once-over before looking up at me through the swoop of his hair.

"And you claim Carrie's the artist," he said.

* * *

Because Carrie was long, lean, and fond of wearing an oversized track-and-field hoodie, the swell of her stomach went unnoticed until April. Even once her pregnancy was public, it was decidedly less of a circus than Tatum Barnett's. Though she shared a due date with Carrie, Tatum had been showing—and outfitting herself exclusively in formfitting maternity clothes—since January. Hazy ultrasounds adorned the inside of her locker, and she would recite her daughter's full name, *Madison Grace Barnett-Delaney*, in one breath to anyone who would listen. (Tatum's baby turned out to be a boy, whom she named Pete, a twist I would eventually discover on Facebook.) Maybe it was Tatum's gestational enthusiasm that allowed our peers to go easy on Carrie—or maybe it was simply that people were already accustomed to leaving Carrie Hart alone.

For whatever reason, reactions to her pregnancy were mostly limited to rumors about who the father might be. Gabe's parents had asked her to keep Gabe's role a secret, arguing that the information could cost him his spot at NYU. Gabe, to his credit, insisted it was within Carrie's rights to tell whomever she pleased, but Carrie had honored the Feldmans' request.

And so, suspects included Hunter Locke, who pronounced his name *Hunner* and who had once dared Carrie to hurdle a shopping cart; the youngish track-and-field coach with the goatee, who had always favored Carrie over the other gazelle-legged girls; the possibility that Carrie was so promiscuous she had no idea; and my brother. No one suspected Gabe. Kids in Deerling were largely bad at math, and the weeks during which Carrie and I had comprised the new kid's inner circle seemed, to most, like a lifetime ago.

Then, on a particularly hot day in May, Hunter Locke happened to wander by the drinking fountain in the south hallway as Carrie was struggling to lean over her eight-month bump and reach her lips to the water. Maybe Hunter was going through a rough time. Maybe his truck needed a new transmission or his dog had died. Maybe he resented being in the running for possible father of Carrie Hart's baby or else it may have irked him that Carrie had gone and gotten pregnant by someone else. The two of them had dated erratically—smoking pot in the garage behind Carrie's house, making out in the elevator the school reserved for students with disabilities—prior to Gabe's arrival.

"Hey, Hart!" Hunter's greeting was aggressive, and Carrie spun around, water still dripping down her chin. I stood beside her holding her backpack. I was always holding her backpack. "Think you'll ever own up to being a slut and tell everyone I'm not your baby daddy?"

Hunter's question, shouted across the hall, ignited *Jerry Springer*-esque commotion. Everyone was stir-crazy, counting down the days until the last day of school, desperate for stimulation. The twist of Carrie's mouth made me think she was going to either puke or cry. For Carrie's sake, I hoped for nausea, knowing tears would embarrass her more.

It's one thing to be called a slut when you are the sole occupant of your body. By the time Carrie and I entered our teen years, we were accustomed to degradation. Hearing random men holler *nice ass* through the rolled-down windows of passing cars was the price we paid for having bodies at all.

It's different when your ribcage is stretching painfully to accommodate your organs, which are retreating from your uterus, which is growing as fast as the human it houses. It's different when your body is busy with a colossal task beyond your jurisdiction.

You become protective not only of your baby but of yourself. Of women everywhere.

It's mortifying, then, to have your pregnant body objectified.

Gabe pushed through the crowd. He handed Carrie a bottle of water. The two of them locked eyes as she drank. A rosy glow returned to her cheeks as Gabe placed a hand on her belly and kissed a drop from the corner of her mouth. The kiss was neither dramatic nor prolonged. It was perfunctory, as if they always kissed between third and fourth periods, indifferent to their captivated audience and to Hunter's disbelieving scowl.

Watching Gabe come to Carrie's rescue, I had never loved him more.

It must have been around the same time he proposed.

* * *

There were exactly two moments that year when my resignation veered toward hope. At midnight, a couple of weeks before Carrie's due date, Gabe IM'd me out of the blue. While the three of us sometimes chatted as a group, Gabe and I never conversed in a private window of our own. It was unprecedented.

Gabe: What are you doing up so late?

Waiting for something like this to happen, I thought.

Me: Can't sleep. Worried about C.
Gabe: I guess it could be any day now?
Me: Could be. Most people go past
their due dates though.

Gabe: Then why worried?

Me: It was movie night in birth class.

Me: I've seen some things.

Gabe: lol

Gabe: C's tough. She'll be ok.

Me: Easy for you to say.

Gabe: Hey, I'm gonna be there too.

Me: In the room?

Me: She said yes?

Gabe: Yeah, but if she ends up needing a C-section I guess she can only have one person in the OR with her?

My fingers froze. I had never heard this rule.

Gabe: So if that happens, I'm out.

I relaxed.

Me: Ok, good.

Gabe: Why good?

Me: Oh, you know. Abdominal surgery. Kind of a "girls only" thing.

Gabe: Right. Like pedicures.

Me: Exactly. We don't like boys to see our toenails ... or our intestines.

Gabe: Got it.

Gabe: You're a good friend.

Gabe: I know I'm like the last person she would've chosen to have a baby with.

Gabe: I mean, we didn't really date
that long.

Gabe: I'm pretty random.

Gabe: And totally unprepared for this.

Gabe: But knowing she has you ...
makes me think she'll be ok.

Me: She will definitely be ok.

Gabe: You know when I first met you
guys, I could tell Carrie liked me
but I thought you hated me on sight.

Me: Why?

Gabe: You kept squinting at me. Like
I was a bug in the corner and you
were trying to decide if you needed
a dictionary or just a really thick
novel to smash me with.

Me: Oh, that's just my face.

Me: I'm really sensitive to light.

Gabe: lol

Gabe: No, you have a cute face.

Gabe: This was your cute face twisted
into a hostile expression.

Gabe: But then I realized that's just
how you look at people who aren't Carrie.

Me: Sorry, I should've been nicer to you.

Me: Didn't realize you were going to
sire my best friend's firstborn!!

Gabe: lol

Gabe: Stop making me laugh.

Gabe: I'm going to wake up my parents.

Me: Sorry, Mr. and Mrs. Feldman.
Gabe: Please, call them Diane and Hank.
Gabe: I mean, I do.
Me: Ok, now *I'm* laughing.
Gabe: Do you ever think ...
Gabe: I mean, humor me for a sec. What would have happened if you and I had hooked up instead of me and Carrie?
Me: Nothing would have happened. I have intimacy issues.
Gabe: lol what?
Me: Seriously. I haven't even kissed anyone since the seventh grade.
Gabe: So you're saying there wouldn't be a baby?
Me: Ours would have been a sexless affair.
Gabe: What about hand-holding? Would you have held my hand?
Me: I guess ... if you sanitized it first.
Gabe: lol, ok
Gabe: This is getting weird.
Gabe: We should sleep.

As if we would turn off our monitors at the same moment, slide between the same set of sheets.

Gabe: But first.
Gabe: I know this isn't fair.

Gabe: But I was hoping you could tell
me I'm doing the right thing.
Gabe: By going to college.
Gabe: Leaving Carrie alone here.
Gabe: Or not alone.
Gabe: But you know what I mean.

My hands hovered above the keyboard. Given the chance, would Carrie have asked Gabe to stay? Would the three of them be happiest behaving like a family—because they would be one? I wanted to do the right thing too. At the very least, I wanted to know what the right thing was.

Me: Here's what I think:

(I had no idea what I thought.)

Me: You should go to New York.

(Sabotage.)

Me: Because you're 18. And you're
smart. And you have your whole life
ahead of you. Plus I'll be here with
Carrie.
Me: But you should remember that
Carrie might change her mind and ask
you to come back.
Me: And if she does, you should do
what she says.

Me: Because she's the mother of your
daughter.
Me: Got it?
Gabe: Got it.
Gabe: Thank you, Amanda.
Me: Goodnight?
Gabe: Night.

Two weeks later, Carrie went into labor. A nurse entered Carrie's delivery room and said, "There's a kid out there claiming he's the father."

"That's Gabe," Carrie said. She was between contractions and still in possession of herself. Still reaching up, occasionally, to retie her hair.

"Your boyfriend?" the nurse asked.

"No," I said.

"Can you just let him in?" Carrie requested.

"If he comes in, she has to go." The nurse nodded at me.

Carrie said, "Amanda's not going anywhere."

"Well, unless you want to kick your mama out . . ."

Mrs. Hart crossed her arms. "Mama's not going anywhere."

Carrie looked up at me helplessly.

"I'll go tell him," I said.

The waiting room for the maternity ward was small. No more than fifteen chairs surrounded a low table covered in battered magazines and gnawed-on picture books. Gabe was alone, staring up at a television mounted high on one wall. The television was showing an episode of *Friends*, which was still a year away from airing its series finale. On the screen, Ross Gellar was shouting, "My *best friend* and my *sister*?" Squeaky panic undercut his rage.

Chandler and Monica cowered, contrite, while the other friends looked on.

I've hated that show—any show with a laugh track—ever since.

"They won't let her have more than two people in the room," I told Gabe.

He whipped around. He processed what I'd said, and then his shoulders went slack. Tension drained from his face.

"Is she doing okay?"

"She's doing great so far. She's only at five centimeters, if that means anything to you."

A lesser boy might have winced, or smirked, but Gabe nodded. "I read the books."

"*What to Expect When You're Expecting?*"

"No, the companion text: *What to Expect When a Girl Who Broke Up with You in a Garage Is Expecting.*"

I was the one who smirked. Carrie was always breaking up with boys in the garage.

"I should get back in there," I said, "but if you're going to wait, I'll come out and give you updates when I can, okay?"

It was a well-intentioned promise that I would fail to keep. Over the next few hours, Carrie's labor would progress rapidly, and Gabe would be the last thing on my mind. But for now, he had my full attention as he reached for my arm and whispered, "Wait." Gabe pulled me into a hug—a substantial, ribcage-crushing hug. He clung to my shoulder blades and buried his face in my neck. Heat swarmed my body.

For years I maintained that if I could relive a single moment of my life, this is the moment I would choose.

The maternity ward was slow that night. Carrie's bellows were audible from the waiting room as she pushed Nina, bit by bit, eyebrow by eyelid by eyelash, into the world. Gabe was not allowed inside the delivery room until after the baby had been wiped clean, weighed, measured, vaccinated, and swaddled. Nina's eyes were wide and roaming as Carrie—already standing, a feat I wouldn't manage for a full twelve postpartum hours—placed her in Gabe's trembling arms. I have an improbably vivid memory of the first look Gabe gave his daughter. Maybe I'm actually remembering the first look he gave Jack, or maybe it was the same look each time. I ought to be able to distinguish between the two memories as easily as I can tell a photo of Gabe at eighteen from one of him at thirty—but the truth is, I'm not sure I can do that so easily either.

Gabe, in my eyes, never ages.

It was a look of awe and absolute terror. A crumpling of his brow, a loosening of his lips. Gabe's children undid him.

* * *

Carrie and I spent the first half of July sitting on opposite ends of her couch, passing a curled, slumbering Nina back and forth. The baby was a satisfying eight pounds, as warm and yeasty as fresh bread. Weird urges came over Carrie whenever she sniffed her daughter's hair. She would burst into tears or else declare her desire to have ten more children. She reminded me not of her drunk self, exactly— Carrie became more introspective the more she imbibed—but of a drunk stranger, teetering between despair and bliss.

After those first couple of weeks, as Nina slept less and fussed more, Carrie tried to push me away. Her temporary shamelessness, necessitated by the birth and its aftermath, faded. Her modesty returned, and she no longer wanted me helping her on and off the couch, on and off the toilet, in and out of the shower. She grew tired of my gaze on her breasts, so swollen with milk they were *Playboy*ishly huge, but with chapped nipples that sometimes bled.

A pattern formed. Carrie would snap at me—for a pathetic swaddle job or for occupying more than one and a half of the spit-up encrusted couch cushions—and send me home. Within twenty-four hours, she would call me back. Because her parents worked during the day, there was no one to hold Nina while Carrie peed or showered or scarfed down some toast. In the evenings, Mr. and Mrs. Hart did what they could. Carrie's mom bathed Nina in the kitchen sink while her dad made dinner and stole furtive, rueful glances at the baby. By midnight, both of Carrie's parents were in bed, and she alone was responsible for bouncing and shushing the baby to sleep.

I did not consider that I had a choice. The notion that Carrie had wronged me by dating a boy in whom I was immediately and irreversibly interested had expired. The scorecards we maintained as children were wiped clean in the delivery room. My lingering feelings for Nina's dad—whenever Gabe was on his way over, I frantically reknotted my hair and brushed my gums raw—amounted to more of a betrayal than Carrie's decision to claim him for herself. A year had passed since then. Also, a lifetime.

I came when she called.

Carrie would mumble an apology, thrust the baby into my arms, and disappear into her bedroom for an hour or more. Now I wonder, Did *she* ever consider that I had a choice? Did she recall, with a shudder, how close she had come to pushing me away for good?

When Carrie was still pregnant, she had enlisted my help in cleaning out her closet. Some clothes, she reasoned, would never fit again. Other items were not mom-friendly or would remind her of the type of life that was no longer hers. One T-shirt had bunched offensively in some school photo, and so went directly into the Goodwill pile. But the material was a heathery pink, which I remembered looking good against Carrie's skin, and I convinced her to try it on, just in case. As luck would have it, the shirt flattered her round belly and newly ample breasts, and she wore it almost daily for the duration of her pregnancy.

We had things in common, me and that shirt.

We had both turned out to be useful.

And then it was August, and the heat was blistering. Mrs. Hart installed a window AC unit in the office turned nursery. I remember standing in front of the unit's gust, clutching a scream-ing newborn Nina beneath her armpits until the cold air calmed her down. I sang "Round Here" by Counting Crows because it was the only song I knew by heart, and it happened to include a line about staying up very late. My silent tears were divorced from any feeling but fatigue. When I had the presence of mind, I panicked. Alone in the Harts' bathroom, I would lean over the sink, make eye contact with my reflection, and review the facts that Jaclyn kept trying to impress upon me.

Fact: no matter how much I loved her, or him, I was not a prisoner of the moment when Carrie and Gabe failed to locate a condom.

Fact: I was eighteen years old.

Fact: I was no one's mother.

And yet, Carrie and I signed the lease on a two-bedroom house near the local third-rate Christian college whose dean had informed me of my acceptance over the phone. I took out student loans to cover both the deposit on the house and my tuition. Carrie would get a part-time job; we would coordinate our schedules so that someone was always home with Nina. The child payments from Mr. and Mrs. Feldman were generous—at least by Deerling's standards, where a gallon of milk still cost less than a dollar.

Although I cannot point to any obvious flaw in this plan, I struggle now to understand how we ever believed it would work.

On August fifteenth, I left the airless, milky squalor of Carrie's house to put gas in the truck. It was a beautiful night. I cranked the windows and from the glove compartment unearthed *The Miseducation of Lauryn Hill*. Ignoring my compulsion to return to Carrie and the baby as fast as possible, I burned the truck's last gallon driving the carriage-scuffed roads of Amish country. A small, bonneted child flashed me a suspicious look as she darted through the dusk to a dilapidated outhouse.

My head shook back and forth, denying something both crucial and obscure to me.

When I pulled into the Motomart, he was hanging up the pump at station seven. Registering Carrie's truck, Gabe lifted an apprehensive hand. He'd been at the house earlier that day. After initiating a diaper change, he called out for assistance.

"It's a one-person job," Carrie snapped. "Either you're competent or you're not."

"I don't mind changing her. There's just . . . a lot of poop? And it's quite yellow?"

"It's supposed to be *quite yellow*."

"Is it supposed to be . . . everywhere?"

With a colossal sigh, Carrie had risen from the couch and shooed Gabe from the changing table. "Go home, Gabe. I need help, not a fucking audience."

I hopped down from the driver's seat of the Toyota, and Gabe grinned. "It's you."

"Were you hoping to see the mother of your child?"

"Not even a little bit. Christ, is she always so grumpy?"

I tried to remember the last time Carrie had expressed joy or pleasure or even irony. Had it been days? Weeks? Sometimes her private smog of exhaustion almost lifted. Touring the rental near the college, I had gestured to some old cables hanging out of the wall and said, "We'll have to do something about those once Nina starts crawling." Carrie's lips twitched, as if she'd forgotten that Nina would eventually learn to crawl, would not always need to be held firmly against someone's body. But she suppressed the smile and regloomed her features.

I had been meaning to ask Carrie why she so often seemed to be punishing herself—why she denied herself even fleeting moments of happiness—but I hadn't found the right words or the time.

"It's harder than she thought it would be," I said.

"No shit," Gabe said. "For me, too."

"Helping with the baby?"

We always called what Gabe did *helping*. Despite his best intentions, no one expected Gabe to be a parent.

"No," he said. "Leaving."

"When do you go?"

"Friday."

It was Monday. Ignoring my heart, which had gone and skipped a beat, I waited out the silence.

"Do you want to get some food?" Gabe asked.

I was surprised. "With you?"

"Yes, with me."

I considered the alternative: driving back to Carrie's house. She would be waiting just inside the door, ready to pass me Nina so she could attend to some basic bodily need of her own. Beneath the gas station lights, Gabe's skin looked tan and silky, like the moist underside of a cake. If only I had thought to shout *yo* at a floppy-haired boy reading poetry on a footbridge. If only I had pulled Carrie aside that day or that week and made my case: *Let me have him, and I'll let you go.*

But how was she supposed to know that Gabe was the one person I would love more than I loved her? How was I?

"Under one condition," I said to Gabe. "We don't talk about her."

It wasn't entirely clear whether I meant Carrie or the baby or to refer to them as the same female unit, but he quickly agreed. I parked the truck behind the station's minimart and climbed into his Beetle. We went to Denny's—the same Denny's where Carrie and I had told Gabe he was going to be a dad, because there was nowhere else to eat in that town—and we talked until 3:00 A.M. It was the summer of 2003, and I had no cell phone, no pocket vibrations alerting me to Carrie's impatience turned concern, turned rage, turned fear.

I remember explaining the concept of Denny's secret menu to Gabe and Gabe not believing me. I triumphed by ordering a French toast grilled cheese sandwich from a waiter who didn't bat an eye.

I remember Gabe asking me what I wanted to study at college. On a whim I lied and said philosophy, which impressed him.

We finished our food and slid lower and lower on opposite sides of the booth, until our knees were pressed together beneath the table.

We confessed our middle names: mine Candice, after my grandmother; his Theodore, for no reason.

I said, "Tell me the truth. How bad is Deerling compared to the rest of America?"

Gabe replied, "It's not the best, but I like all the grass."

We crammed a year's worth of awkward adolescent courtship into a single night.

Our discussion of Deerling versus the rest of America landed us back where we'd started: Gabe's departure date. "Don't go," I said, with comic urgency. "Don't leave me with those people."

I meant Carrie and Nina, of whom we were not supposed to be speaking.

For a long, inflated moment, Gabe and I studied each other. His eyes were shadowed and bloodshot, like someone who had lost more than a few nights of sleep that summer. Without warning, he gripped the edge of the table, leaned over our grease-slicked plates and empty Coke glasses and kissed me on the mouth.

"I think you should come with me," he said, sinking back into place.

"I think I shouldn't," I said.

CHAPTER ELEVEN

Jack falls asleep around one in the morning, but I don't. I lie awake thinking of things I've misplaced or thrown out or permanently lost.

Letters from Carrie, folded into paper footballs.

A picture of Gabe and me taken with a timer before our first "date" in Manhattan, he in his blazer with ironic elbow patches, me with one sharp hipbone protruding between my skirt and ribbed tank top.

Every school yearbook.

A poodle-shaped mug from which I drank lukewarm coffee each morning for years, until I dropped it on the bathroom floor, and it broke into four clean pieces. Gabe wanted to glue the mug back together. Holding back tears, I called him a crazy person.

All my baby teeth.

Brochures from the colleges I did not attend.

A vintage locket, whose chain snapped and disappeared somewhere between West Fifty-Eighth Street, where I worked, and Ridgewood, Queens, where we live.

That AOL Instant Messenger conversation between Gabe and me—two weeks before Carrie's due date, three weeks before Nina was actually born—which I printed out, intending to save.

A pair of cowboy boots from a flea market in Pennsylvania.

Countless pairs of formerly trendy, now ridiculous glasses.

A flyer for a studio apartment in Brooklyn—*Perfect for the young, single professional*—which I tore from a bulletin board the winter I was twenty-three and kept in my coat pocket until April.

Concert ticket stubs.

My high school diploma.

It irritates me to lie awake while the baby sleeps, and the irritation makes my chances of sleep increasingly remote. I ask myself, *Why would you need those things when you know you're going to die someday?*

I don't need them, but Jack might.

Jack, who is going to live forever.

* * *

Around eight, the baby and I wake up for the last time. I roll onto my side, expecting to see Carrie and Nina sprawled across the second bed before remembering I switched rooms. Maxing out my Visa, I paid for what the girl at the front desk promised was the hotel's last available suite—two king size beds on the nineteenth floor. The excuse I gave to Nina was that I didn't want to keep everyone up all night. Carrie required no excuse. As a rule, she and I don't explain or apologize. There's no precedent for it; we would feel like we were playacting.

When I tell Jack he's going to be reunited with his dad today, he kicks his legs and hoots at the ceiling. His pajamas, patterned with paw prints, are getting to be too small. The idea of folding them up for the Goodwill pile makes me want to cry.

I can't help how much I'm looking forward to seeing Gabe. I don't know that I've ever, in our entire history, been disappointed to see him. It's the defining cause-and-effect relationship of my life—Gabe walks into a room; I smile.

Lifting Jack to my breast, I lean back against the throne of hotel pillows. From this angle, I can see the sky above Cleveland, an expanse of blue broken by a single helicopter. Will I tell Gabe what Carrie told me? About his proposal, his concession—however he thought of it at the time. Should I confess that I know we were nearly nothing, all our years together contingent on Carrie's stubborn (generous) refusal of his help?

I may not have asked her permission to leave town with Gabe, but I was the one who broke the news to Carrie. Before I told Jaclyn and before I even confirmed my decision with the boy himself. My plan was to inform Carrie I was *in love* with Gabe. In the books and television shows of our youth, the word *love* wielded so much power—love was a plot point; love was a deal-breaker; love was brand-new information. I expected the revelation to be, in Carrie's eyes, all this and more. Love was the only excuse for what I knew would be otherwise unforgivable.

Carrie was on the couch, using her own teeth to trim Nina's hazardous fingernails. The summer's final exhale of heat radiated from the cushions, the carpets, the curtains, the windowpanes. In one breath, I told Carrie my plan: forget college, follow Gabe to New York, disappear from Deerling. Then I threw in my secret weapon: "I'm in love with him."

Carrie looked at me like I was a fool. Since giving birth, she had returned to the hospital three times—once after a clogged milk duct became infected, driving her temperature to 102 degrees, and twice to have her stitches restitched. At her most recent appointment she had cried, and the same doctor who'd delivered Nina looked up from his perpetual post between Carrie's splayed legs and asked, "What's the matter?" Carrie hadn't slept in over a month, and I was talking about love? Was I out of my mind?

"You don't love Gabe," she said. "You just want out of Ohio. You just want out of *this*." She gestured to her environs: the package of Pampers on the mantel, the baskets of unfolded laundry. In the kitchen the breeze from an oscillating fan disrupted the refrigerator's display of sketches, photos, and expired coupons.

Mutely, I nodded. If she needed to control the narrative, that was fine with me. In this moment I was prepared to lose her, but as the seconds ticked by and Carrie said nothing, I entertained other possibilities. Would she give me her blessing? Would my absence bring her some semblance of relief?

"Whatever," she said, nearly choking on the word. "It's nothing I didn't already know."

Looking back, I understand Carrie did know more than me. She knew Gabe's lame jokes put an unrestrained smile on my face, like that of a person clutching a winning lottery ticket. She knew I would be willing to abandon my best friend with a newborn—even after I'd signed my name next to hers on a lease. And she knew that, while I may have been Gabe's first choice, it was Carrie to whom he'd made the first offer. A literal marriage proposal.

Why did Carrie wait so long to deliver that particular blow?

Because she wasn't interested in delivering blows. Only in our worst moments did we mistake our friendship for a rivalry. Before I left her house that night, she threw her arms around my neck.

I smelled conditioner, spit-up, diaper cream, rosewater. She said, "You better fucking call."

* * *

When Carrie and I were thirteen, I bet her she would be the first to get married.

"No way," Carrie said. "I'm not getting married until I'm at least thirty."

"Okay," I allowed, "but I bet someone will ask you. I bet you'll get proposed to way, way before anyone proposes to me."

Was I trying to imply she was more conventional than I was—more inherently *wife material*? Or was the wager supposed to be self-deprecating: Carrie was lovable; I was not?

I remember Carrie sinking into a thoughtful silence before asking, "How much?"

"Twenty bucks," I said.

Twenty bucks was a sum we cited often. As in, *If we only had twenty bucks, we could see a movie*, or, *For twenty bucks we could order a shitload of Chinese food.*

Carrie agreed, and we shook on it. Five years passed. She didn't bother telling me I'd won the bet.

So, maybe it wasn't a proposal. Maybe it was only a bad idea.

Jack murmurs as he nurses, a sound I should record and keep.

* * *

Eager to spot her dad, Nina scans each group of rumpled passengers descending the escalators toward baggage claim. I am just as eager but also racked with anxiety. My tongue has forgotten how to interact with my teeth. I scrape it against my bottom incisors over and over until I taste blood. Before we had a baby, I maintained a constant awareness of Gabe's mood and how to calibrate it if necessary, whether we were together or temporarily apart. Today his mood is an escaped pet, a dog for whom I have no leash. Gabe might feel anything toward me now.

"Here." I shove Jack in Carrie's direction. A smock of drool darkens his onesie. "I have to go to the bathroom."

"Um, can you wait?" She has only a noncommittal grip on the baby. "These guys look like New Yorkers." She nods at a trio of middle-aged businessmen in baggy suits, each staring at a phone in his palm. I don't know how she knows. Carrie has never been to New York.

"Can't wait," I say. "My pelvic floor muscles aren't what they used to be."

Carrie wrinkles her nose at the overshare. Nina bounces on the balls of her feet. "He's here. He's here."

Gabe steps off the escalator, hands in the pockets of his travel sweatpants, which have often doubled as my hangover sweatpants. Trapped in a pair of my prepregnancy jeans, those pants look like heaven to me. Something about Gabe is different. He's more angular than I remember, less self-conscious.

He looks, I realize, like somebody's dad.

Gabe does not immediately locate his own family among the strangers swarming the baggage carousels. His eyes land on Carrie first. I've often wondered if he searches crowds for her, if hers is the face mysteriously replicated on trains and across busy intersections. The leap of his eyebrows seems to confirm my theory, but then he looks automatically to the side of her, to me, as if Carrie's presence simply indicates mine. As if it's always been that way.

"Dad!" Nina skips toward him. Gabe throws open his arms, unmistakably pleased and not at all surprised.

He already knew she'd be here. The person Nina has been texting from back seats and beneath tables is not Maxine but her dad. When Gabe fretted about Van Morrison smothering our child, he was testing me, curious to see how faithful I would remain to my lie. I should have realized. Historically, none of us have had much luck keeping things to ourselves.

If Nina resents Gabe for his long-distance parenting, his fair-weather fatherhood, I've never seen the evidence. My suspicion is that she reveres Gabe the way some kids revere uncles or older siblings. What the two of them have more closely resembles friendship than the fraught, shameful codependence of parents and their children. Someday, I guess, Jack will have a long list of complaints about his dad, none of which will ring a bell to his sister.

"Do you hate the Dairy Barn?" Nina is asking Gabe as they approach.

"Yes." The baby kicks his legs at the sight of Gabe. He knows him. No one could convince me otherwise. "I hate the Dairy Barn, but I *love* going there."

"Oh my god, same," Nina says.

"It's a paradox. Hey, Care. Wow, how huge is this guy?" Gabe reaches for Jack. Carrie smiles as she hands him over. It's obvious that mine is the only heart racing.

"Mom doesn't get it. She just hates it," Nina says.

"That's because your mother is fundamentally sincere. She doesn't share our taste for irony."

The ease with which Gabe kisses Jack's head, it's like they've never spent an hour apart. Maybe I'm wrong, maybe Gabe will have a perfectly uncomplicated bond with each of his children.

My dad's great, I picture Jack saying on some dorm room floor, a bottle of beer clenched between his knees. *But my mother . . .*

"Hi," Gabe says to me.

Was our relationship always prone to these subtle shifts of power? Has Gabe ever looked at me like he's looking at me now?

Like he knows he has won.

"Hi," I say.

Carrie watches, careful to give us our space. It's been years since we were all together, and it's never been clear to me how much Nina herself understands about what happened and when.

I'm starting to wonder if the answer isn't *everything*.

Gabe kisses me. For about three seconds, the rest of these people are secondary to the texture and temperature of the kiss, which conjures our yellow couch with the broken springs, the cast-iron pan that always smells faintly of the last meal we cooked, entire days we passed without saying their names.

"Tell Amanda you're not staying at the Super 8," Nina prompts him.

"We're not staying at the Super 8," Gabe tells me.

She makes a proprietary grab for his hand. "And we're stopping at the Dairy Barn on the way home."

"Nina," Carrie warns.

"And we're stopping at the Dairy Barn on the way home." Gabe's smile is broad. Nina cocks her head at me as if to say, *So there*.

Chastened, and conscious of my gritted teeth, I loosen my jaw and look over at Carrie. She's ready with a commiserative roll of her eyes. "Tourists, both of them," she says. "We can wait in the car while they cut the cheese. Gabe, did you check a bag?"

"Nope."

"Great. Let's get out of here, shall we?"

Carrie walks ahead. Nina automatically falls into step with her mother, allowing Gabe and me a few moments of privacy. When he snakes his arm around my back, my relief is curtailed by my wish that he'd use both hands to hold the baby.

"I'm sorry," I say.

"You did what you had to do."

It's a planned response, one he rehearsed in his head on the plane.

"I shouldn't have needed to do it."

"In a perfect world, no."

"But this isn't a perfect world."

"Correct," Gabe says. "This is Ohio."

Nina is beckoning for us to hurry up. Gabe moves ahead, urgently closing the distance between him and his daughter.

* * *

He and I ride in the back seat with the baby between us. Watching Gabe make fart noises against Jack's bare feet, coaxing his first froggy giggles into bona fide laughter, a kind of vacancy washes over me. I press my forehead against the window and slip into a deep sleep, dreamless and impervious to Nina's chatter, Jack's noises, Gabe and Carrie's small talk. When I wake up, Carrie and I are alone together in the parking lot of the Dairy Barn, amid the life-size, galvanized cow statues, whose bellies are embedded with speakers.

The cows blast country hits of the nineteen-nineties. "Achy Breaky Heart." "She Thinks My Tractor's Sexy." Carrie is watching me in the rearview mirror.

"Gabe took the baby inside," she says.

"I figured."

"They'll be back in a second. Nina wants buckeyes, and Gabe wants some kind of mustard?"

"Yeah. The spicy mustard."

Carrie twists in the driver's seat and examines me the way you examine a knot in your shoelace or a Scrabble board—something you need to solve.

"You guys can stay at the Super 8, if that's your preference."

I shake my head. "We'll stay with you. It's only another two weeks, right?"

As if staying with her has been some kind of hardship.

Carrie takes a breath. "If this is too difficult for you, we don't have to keep trying."

"If what's too difficult?"

"All of us, together."

This topic feels ambitious, like something I shouldn't attempt to navigate for another month or two—however long it takes Jack to sleep more, nurse less. Until I can no longer feel the seam of my jeans rubbing against my scar tissue.

"Carrie, you've done nothing but make things easier for me."

The comment catches both of us off guard. Carrie smiles, and I avert my eyes. "Okay. I'm glad. Still, I get that it's awkward. All of us being together is completely optional. We can have Gabe keep us separate, if that's what you want."

Our original plan was to drive to Ohio for Nina's thirteenth birthday. Jack and I were going to stay with my mom, but Gabe wanted to spend at least a few nights at Carrie's. He was looking forward to introducing Nina to her baby brother, but he'd made no reference to my exact whereabouts during this meeting. In my head, I was drinking a glass of wine at my mom's kitchen table, my jealousy a fair price to pay for my freedom.

The night I left New York, this plan was irrelevant to me. All I wanted was Carrie. Specifically, Carrie's hands on my baby.

Now she and I are alone together—truly alone together, no infants on our laps or children hanging off our sleeves—for the first time in years. And already, Gabe and Nina are emerging from the Dairy Barn, plastic shopping bags hanging from their wrists.

"Do *you* want Gabe to keep us separate?" I ask.

"No," Carrie answers quickly. "I'm over it."

"You are?"

"Look, it was rough at the time. But I never loved him. You know that, right?"

Simultaneously, Gabe and Nina pull open doors on either side of the car. The smell of fudge clings to their clothes. It's a sticky, headachey smell—but I can remember how appealing it used to be.

A piece of strawberry licorice dangles from Nina's mouth.

"Have a good time hate-shopping?" Carrie asks brightly.

Gabe leans into the car and drops the baby into his bucket seat. "Sorry, buddy. Kind of a rough landing."

Jack whimpers.

"Dad spent sixty bucks," Nina says.

As Carrie starts the car, the baby starts to cry. I am chasing an errant thought, one I want to trap and isolate before it can slip away. *If she never loved him—if she never loved—if she never—*

"Amanda?" Gabe says, like he's already said it once before.

"Yeah?"

"Do you think he's hungry?"

"He's always hungry."

* * *

Something is up with Carrie's front lawn. The grass is askew. Flattened, maybe, but only in parts. As we approach, we realize someone has mowed a phrase into the grass. Mowed messages are a Deerling tradition—a celebration of high school football victories, or a fun way to wish your neighbors a spooky Halloween.

Carrie's jaw drops. "Does that say . . . ?"

In capital letters, the grass says, TRUMP THAT BITCH.

We continue idling in the street, all of us needing a second to decipher the phrase—to turn the first noun into a verb, the second into a particular person.

Gabe takes out his phone and snaps a picture.

"What the actual fuck?" Carrie says.

"Um," Nina squeaks.

I point wordlessly at the driveway, which is littered with campaign signs. The same pro-Hillary slogan that invaded the park and the garden outside the library, now battered, slashed, and strewn across the gravel.

Nina starts to cry. Parking along the curb, unwilling to drive over the I'M WITH HER wreckage, Carrie puts a hand on her daughter's leg. "It's okay, baby. I mean, it's disgusting, but we'll fix it." Nina's tears have granted Carrie the eerie calm that moms get when someone's head thuds against a bookshelf.

Nina says, "This is my fault."

All at once, the rest of us go, "*What?*" and the commotion frightens Jack. He looks at me, dumbstruck. I give him my index finger to hold.

"It was Maxine and me. We put the signs in the park, and in front of the library, and, um . . ."

Carrie narrows her eyes. "And where else?"

"The golf course . . ."

"And?"

Nina sniffles. "High school football field. But nowhere else, I swear."

Carrie looks nauseated. "Why would you do that?"

"Um, I guess to see if we were the only Democrats in Deerling?"

"Well, Neen, I think you got your answer!"

"Hey," Gabe says, "there's nothing wrong with being politically engaged. I'm proud of you, honey."

In the front seat, Nina twists to give her dad a tight smile. His opinion, though sweet, carries no weight. It was foolish to think Carrie needed me to bridge any gaps between her and her daughter. The two of them could not be more ensnared in each other.

Carrie says, "There's political engagement, and then there's sheer stupidity. It's not actually legal to stick signs all over city property. And this?" Carrie gestures to her lawn. "How did this happen? Who did you tell?"

"We didn't tell anyone!"

"Then someone saw you. Someone who knows where you live."

"No one saw us! We did it in the middle of the night!"

"Jesus Christ, Nina."

"You liked the signs. You got all excited when we drove past them."

Carrie lets her head fall into her hands. I'm staring at the driveway, at the volume of the debris. "Where did you guys get so many signs?" I ask. "You must have had hundreds."

"We ordered them off the Internet," Nina says.

"How," Carrie demands.

"Maxine has a credit card."

"Of course."

"It's for emergencies."

"The threat of a Trump presidency *is* an emergency," Gabe says, his tone still proud, delighted. "That must have been a massive delivery. Where did you stash them all?"

"We had them delivered to the drive-in while Trinity was working. She stored them in one of their garages for a while. Then she borrowed her boyfriend's truck and helped us set them up." Nina dries her eyes with the back of her hand. Pride has seeped into her tone too. Across the street, a neighbor pulls back her curtains. Her gaze darts between us and the grass. Does she know it's vandalism? Does she think Carrie did this to her own property?

"This is what you've been doing when you spend the night at Maxine's house," Carrie says.

"Only the last few times."

"I thought you guys were swimming. Playing foosball. Making fudge."

"No one makes fudge, Mom."

"When I was a kid, we made fudge."

"No." I interject on the grounds of historical accuracy. "We didn't."

Nina whips around. "*Of course* you didn't."

"Okay." Gabe unbuckles his seatbelt. "I'm going in first. I'll take a quick look. Make sure nothing's, uh, amiss. You guys wait here." He hops out of the Subaru before anyone can argue. He cuts across the lawn, his feet landing in the middle of the *B*. On the front porch, he examines his keyring—crowded with keys to the high school, our building in Ridgewood—and slides one into Carrie's front door.

"He has a key to your house?" I ask.

She doesn't answer.

Jack whines.

A minute later, Gabe reappears and beckons us inside. No one has smashed the windows; no one is lurking behind the shower curtain or crouched in the basement. Pulling the baby out of the car, I offer to mow the rest of Carrie's lawn. "I just need to nurse Jack first."

She shakes her head. "No, I'll do it. Or Gabe can do it."

"You think Gabe knows how to start a lawnmower?"

She smiles, but barely.

I follow Carrie inside, where her keys hit the kitchen table with an exasperated clatter and she pinches the bridge of her nose. She's mad and unnerved and embarrassed—all things that residents of Deerling County have made Carrie and her family feel a thousand times before. In order to make her next move, Carrie needs privacy, and Gabe and I qualify as the opposite of privacy. We are the audience she most resents. I understand, but because Gabe is looking at her with his arms folded, his expression stern, I'm forced to stay in the room. I'm responsible for him, for dispelling whatever parental authority he thinks he can claim.

The other person for whom I'm responsible begins to weep, fed up with this day, which has been far from tailored to his needs. I take a seat and pull out my boob, glowering at the rest of them. However much Carrie and Gabe and Nina would like to escape this moment, at least they get to endure it with their clothes on.

Nina is leaning back against the counter, gripping the ledge of the sink. Her posture leaves her so exposed, the stance almost appears defensive, like someone bluffing, *Go ahead, hit me*. "I'm sorry," she says, no longer tearful.

"For what?" Carrie asks.

"I don't know. You choose."

"That's not how apologies work."

"Give her a break," Gabe cuts in. "She didn't do anything wrong. She was peacefully protesting the political climate."

Carrie says, "Really, Gabe? You can't think of any reason I might be mad?"

Gabe frowns, stumped by the pop quiz.

Carrie turns to me. "What about you?"

I point to the baby's face buried in my breast. "I'm kind of in the middle—" The look Carrie gives me transports me back to girlhood. How often did one of us corroborate the other's story in front of a suspicious parent or ensure, with spontaneous transgressions, that a teacher punished us both equally? "Okay. It seems like you're mad that Nina did all of this behind your back. That she lied about her plans and snuck around town in the middle of the night. Also, personally, I'm concerned that Trinity's boyfriend was even marginally involved. I mean, we're talking about an unknown male entity with a driver's license. That's a red flag for me."

"Thank you," Carrie says.

"Oh, come on," Gabe says. "It's not like they were drinking, or tipping cows . . ."

Nina turns a palm toward the ceiling, a gesture I've seen her dad perform in countless moments of incredulity.

". . . They were trying to make a difference!"

"This is Deerling," Carrie says. "Nothing Nina does is going to make a difference. Best-case scenario, no one lays a finger on her, and she and her friends get to feel like they tried. The worst-case scenario—believe me, Feldman—is so much worse than this." She gestures in the direction of the defaced lawn. Then she turns to her daughter. "Nina, it *has* occurred to me that if raising you in this town makes you want to change the world, that's probably the best result I could have hoped for. But could you please wait a second before you go full activist? Could you be a kid a little while longer? You're twelve, for Christ's sake."

"I'm thirteen!" Nina bellows, causing Jack to spit out my nipple and release his own earsplitting cry. "And if it's too dangerous for me to express an *opinion* in this town, then maybe—maybe!—*we should move!*"

With all the righteous, hopeless fury of a tenured teenager, Nina storms out of the kitchen and slams her bedroom door so hard the walls around us shudder. I am trying to snap the panel of my nursing bra into place, but Jack is crying and I'm flustered, fumbling. It's Carrie who takes the baby from me. Jack falls silent the same moment an engine growls to life in the front yard.

I rearrange my shirt and go to the window. The woman from across the street is outside in her pink tank top and matching Keds, erasing the pro-Trump obscenity, mowing in straight, determined lines. She has schoolteacher hair and khaki shorts down to her fleshy knees. Without pausing her efforts, she gives me a dutiful wave: *Nothing to see here.*

I'm overcome with affection for the stranger, who is roughly my own age. Her body looks solid but yielding, perfect for bear hugs or crash landings. Her uterus, when occupied, must be spacious, accommodating cartwheels and backflips well into the third trimester. I imagine she has three children, that she drives the oldest two to school each morning before rushing home to get the baby down for a nap. Every day, she showers and fixes dinner and keeps her shit together.

"We should do something to show our thanks," I say. "Maybe she likes fudge."

I turn, hoping for obligatory smiles if not laughter, but Carrie's nose is buried in Jack's hair and Gabe is staring at the space Nina vacated, wishing he had the nerve, or the right, to follow her. Whenever he visits Deerling—twice a year since he was eighteen,

EMILY ADRIAN

even after his parents moved back to the East Coast—Gabe falls prey to the same pattern of emotions. He lands in Cleveland giddy with excitement to see his daughter, is immediately rewarded with a glimpse of Nina's best self—her maturity, her effortless cool— but later blindsided by some moment of conflict between Nina and Carrie that exposes his own irrelevance. His uselessness.

"I have no idea what it means to be a dad," he tells me, often over the phone, because I often stay in New York.

The problem, I suspect, has shifted. For the first time in thirteen years, Gabe knows exactly what it means to be a dad.

* * *

I have never asked Gabe

- if he wishes he had been in the delivery room when Nina was born,
- whether the pictures Carrie used to send to his Yahoo! account—files so large they would crash his computer— made him want to book the next flight to Ohio,
- how much it shocked him the first time Nina said "Hi" into the phone,
- why he never fought Carrie for partial custody,
- if he has forgiven his parents for exonerating him from fatherhood,
- if he has forgiven himself for leaving Deerling, or
- if he has forgiven me for not making him stay.

CHAPTER TWELVE

In an attempt to salvage Nina's birthday, Carrie orders pizza and wings from the place near the train tracks, an establishment I almost went the rest of my life without patronizing. Gabe goes to pick it up. The four of us plus Jack sit around the kitchen table, grease staining the corners of our lips fluorescent orange. We're not talking about the lawn, cropped close to the earth like a boy's head buzzed for summer. Nor are we talking about Nina's proposed solution, screamed with such hysteria that she could easily take it back.

I doubt she will.

Gabe finally makes an attempt at conversation. "Thirteen years old," he marvels, eyeballing the last slice of pepperoni. "Carrie, I can't believe you were in labor thirteen years ago."

"I wasn't, technically," she says. "I went into labor on the fourth. Nina was born on the morning of the fifth."

Gabe says, "Hear that, Nina? Your mom was in labor with you for multiple days."

There's so much Gabe doesn't know about those days. How Carrie felt her first contraction in the deep end of the town pool. How we walked home along Center Street, Carrie stopping periodically to bury her face in my shoulder. Cars slowed as they passed, the drivers' concern yielding to something else when they saw the spectacle of Carrie's pregnant body in a bathing suit. No one stopped. At home, lurching between the shower and her parents' California king–size bed, Carrie labored for another ten hours. On our way to the hospital, we saw fireworks from the highway.

It has never felt like the right time to tell Gabe the story of his own daughter's birth.

Nina squeezes her shoulders, unimpressed. "That's rough."

"*Rough?*" Gabe pretends to be aghast. "It's the ultimate sacrifice!"

"All right," Nina says, "but it's not like I asked to be born."

I smile and try to meet Carrie's eyes, but she's distracted by the doorbell. She jumps up, clearly expecting someone. Gabe and Nina and I sit in silence, ears pricked for clues. A minute later, it's Tyler Cox who steps into the kitchen.

My first thought is, *Damn, Carrie. Good for you.*

Tyler is so handsome—with a sharp jawline and a cinematic symmetry to his face—that just looking at him feels like openly acknowledging his beauty. Time seems to fold in on itself. Instantly I am nervous and hopeful and embarrassed. Had I been warned, I would have expected him to look vaguely juvenile, unappealing in his familiarity.

Turns out, no.

"Whoa!" Tyler says, looking at my lap. "A baby!"

He reacts only mildly to my laughter, lifting his eyebrows

in Carrie's direction as he scoops Jack from my lap and hoists him into the air. Tyler is a pro at baby talk, Jack an enthusiastic audience. The baby's gummy smile stretches beyond anything I have ever elicited. Enraptured, he bleats like a goat.

"What a guy," Tyler summarizes, returning the baby to my lap and kissing Carrie on the cheek. The sleeve of his T-shirt rides up to expose the tattoo on his arm. The trout's scales are pink and yellow like a sunset or a bruise, glistening as if wet. With the bent brim of his baseball cap and chest like a billboard, Tyler is not my type, but I get it. I haven't been gone from the Midwest so long that I can't appreciate a man with nothing to prove.

Gabe is looking at me, horrified. At first I think it's because I blushed when Tyler walked into the kitchen, but now I realize it's about Jack. I wasn't supposed to let Tyler toss our son around like pizza dough.

"Tyler," I say brightly, "this is my partner, Gabe."

Tyler is already reaching a tanned forearm across the table. "Feldman. It's good to see you, man."

It's nearly imperceptible, but I catch Gabe's confusion as it flickers across his face. He would recognize the story of Tyler mounting me on the school bus but not the kid's name and not the man himself. Gabe may have been a novelty in Deerling that year, but Deerling was, to him, the indistinct background of the year his life veered off course.

"You too," Gabe says. And then taking a guess, "What are you doing back in town?"

"My dad had a stroke," Tyler says.

"I'm sorry to hear that."

"We're also dating," Carrie blurts out.

"Smooth, Mom," Nina says. Tyler's arrival has darkened her mood.

"Oh." Gabe relaxes. "Sit down, have some wings."

There are exactly three wings left, their sauce cold and congealed. The definition of a good sport, Tyler reaches for one. Our conversation bumbles toward the details of his father's recovery. Mr. Cox can write short responses on a handheld white board more easily than he can speak. Tyler's latest battle with his family's health insurer is over coverage for the wheelchair his father desperately needs. Everyone but Nina has something disparaging to say about health insurance companies.

Everyone, including Nina, is growing bored.

Tyler remembers he has a present for the birthday girl in his Jeep. He goes outside and returns with a pair of hot pink wireless headphones still in the box. It's a gift that astonishes and cheers Nina, one she clearly wasn't expecting to receive from her mother's boyfriend. Carrie watches with critical detachment as Nina digs her thumbnail between the flaps of the box. "Thankyouthankyouthankyou," Nina chants.

Morosely peeling the label from his beer bottle, Gabe appears defeated. His own gift for Nina, which he selected without my input, is inadequate. I can tell.

I hope it's not stickers.

Rising from the table, I'm surprised by the heaviness of my bladder plus a rush of dizziness. "You okay?" Gabe asks, half standing.

"Yeah," I say. "Just gotta—" Out of habit, I pass Jack to Carrie then shuffle out of the room without finishing my sentence.

I get to the toilet at what feels like the last possible moment. Elbows digging into my thighs, I cradle my face in my hands.

I want to be alone. I need to be alone. It blows my mind to remember I'm here by choice. Sitting across a table from Tyler Cox is not a requirement. I'm not obligated to witness all the jealousy and self-loathing play out on Gabe's face. This experience is strictly optional. Another idea would have been to stay in New York. Couldn't I have persuaded Gabe to cancel the trip? Couldn't we have spent these days sinking into our couch and watching Jack get bigger?

Reluctant to go back, I linger in front of the mirror.

The first time I peeked at my postpartum body, I was still in the hospital. I had left a blood-tinged urine sample in a tray beside the sink, as per the nurse's instructions. As the gown fell from my shoulders and into a heap on the floor, I kept my eyes squeezed shut. It wasn't vanity so much as the fear on which so many movies capitalized in the nineties—the terror of waking up to discover you've aged twenty years, turned into Santa Claus or your mother.

But then I looked. And it wasn't so bad. My boobs hung slack, no longer resting on the high shelf of my bump and not yet bursting with milk. My stomach, though squishy, had defaulted to the shape of early pregnancy—month four or five. But I recognized my own bright eyes, thick thighs, and bony feet. I felt like cheering.

After turning myself inside out, I had not disappeared completely.

I no longer want to cheer. Endeavoring to judge myself through Tyler's eyes, I finally admit that the extra weight on my face has formed a second chin. Once, when we were fourteen, he told me I had "massive, spooky eyes—like a deer." They're dull now. And edged with creases. Neither the old tank top I borrowed from Carrie nor the nursing bra beneath it are doing me any favors.

I splash some water on my face and think, *Fuck it.* That girl thought she knew herself, thought she knew what her body was for. She didn't know the half of it.

In the hallway, Tyler is waiting to use the bathroom. Just standing there, as if we're in a restaurant or on a plane.

"Oh, sorry," I say, conscious of the extra minutes I loitered over the sink, ignorant of Tyler's needs.

"No, I want to talk to you. I think I owe you an apology." His brow is furrowed, and he is trying too hard to sound sincere.

"Oh, no," I say.

"Yes. I mean, maybe you don't remember, but that time on the bus . . . ?"

Forcing me to acknowledge the incident is its own kind of violation. "I remember."

"I'm so sorry about that. Obviously, it was forever ago, but I guess it was a big deal to you guys. Carrie almost didn't go out with me the first time I asked."

"Oh, no," I say again.

"I want you to know it was just a joke. I had no intention of . . . you know."

"Um."

"Still, it was inappropriate. I was way out of line."

In the kitchen, Jack starts to fuss. My patience dries up instantaneously. "Sexual assault usually is."

He cocks his head, thrusts his tongue against the inside of his cheek. "I mean, I wouldn't go that far. We were fourteen."

"Nina's thirteen."

"Okay . . ."

"So, if some kid did that to her, you wouldn't call it assault?"

Tyler holds up his hands. "Look, I don't want to get into a political debate. I just wanted to say I'm sorry."

Jack produces a sound like a siren. I hear Carrie say he sounds hungry. Gabe wonders aloud where I am.

My teeth grind. Why can't he take the baby?

"Okay," I say to Tyler, "I forgive you."

I will pardon his every sin if he will end this conversation.

He exhales. "Great. That's great. There's actually something else I want to ask you."

If he hears the baby crying, he doesn't appear cognizant of my obligation to the baby. Tyler Cox, it occurs to me, is stupid. Did I always know that? Does Carrie?

"I want to ask Carrie to marry me, but I thought it would be nice to get your, uh, blessing."

In the kitchen, the screen door creaks open and slams shut, and Jack's cries fade. An ambulance retreating.

"My blessing?"

"I thought it would be a nice gesture. Since you guys are so close."

Close is both an exaggeration and an understatement.

The bet was not that Carrie would be the first to get married, or even engaged, but that she would be the first to find herself on the receiving end of a proposal. Struggling, suddenly, not to laugh, I clasp Tyler's limp hand between both of mine and say, "Yes, you should do that. As soon as possible."

He beams. "I was already planning to do it tonight."

"Tonight is perfect."

"Yeah?"

"Yeah."

"Yeah, okay." His head bobs up and down. "Cool."

"I have to feed my kid, but do me a favor? Don't propose to Carrie until I get back?"

Tyler winks at me. It's a charming, fraternal wink. "You got it."

* * *

In the yard, Gabe is standing in a patch of shade between the picnic table and the ash tree, holding a tear-streaked, hiccuping Jack. I take the baby and sit atop the table to nurse him for something like the tenth time today. Jack's small hand searches the air until it lands on my chin.

My milk is inexhaustible. It's the only part of me that is.

I offer Gabe a smile. I want him to ask how I am or demand every detail of my private conversation with Tyler Cox. Beneath this rational desire for Gabe's attention is the less reasonable wish that he would take care of me. All the time. Forever. Is this what everyone wants, secretly? For another person to accept both the blame and responsibility for all our bad feelings? Maybe the adolescent struggle for independence is misguided. We grow up and fire our mothers, insisting their work here is done, before realizing we cannot hire a replacement.

It should not come as a shock to me that I am no one's baby.

The sun is in Gabe's eyes. He is disheveled and irritated, and I don't have the energy to cajole him from his gloom. So this won't be a moment of connection or respite. It will only be another moment to get through.

I'm staring at the blur of shadows the leaves cast on the lawn, unable to separate the cicadas' drone from my own internal murmur, when Gabe says, "You look beautiful."

I laugh, no less startled than if a stranger on the street had said it—though of course, Gabe has said it more than all the strangers combined. "Pretty sure I look terrible."

"No. Different, maybe. Younger. You look like you did when I first met you."

Pleasure cuts through the static.

Gabe takes a breath. "I've been thinking about what Nina said. About moving. I think we should try to help Carrie find an apartment in Queens. I know we've been down this road before, and she always says no, but things are different now that Nina is older. Do you agree?"

"I agree that things are different."

"Whatever she needs upfront, we could give that to her. The deposit and everything."

"We don't have any money."

"My parents—"

"Carrie's not going to take any more of your parents' money."

He's quiet, indulging or else mourning the fantasy: Carrie and Nina living a few subway stops or even a few blocks from us. Carrie could rent studio space in Brooklyn; twenty-two-year-olds, eager to commemorate their autonomy with tattoos of birds fleeing their cages and old-fashioned skeleton keys, would add their names to her waiting list. She could travel to conventions and festivals, hold guest spots at the famous shops in Chicago and LA, while Nina stayed with us. In New York, our family would be almost conventional: a boyfriend, a girlfriend, an ex. A pink-cheeked infant and a biracial teenager. No one would need to know that our family's origin was Carrie and me, a fortress of a childhood friendship built with ease but not easily escaped. Does Gabe imagine Carrie and I could live in the same city and pretend that he, the father of our children, was all we had in common? Because I have a fantasy too.

In mine, Carrie falls in love with a stranger. A New York stranger who has everything to prove. They have a baby. This time, it's Carrie's mother and her partner in the delivery room— or better yet, this baby is born at home, the furniture pushed aside to accommodate the inflatable birthing pool, that nightmare of landlords everywhere. The birth is quick. Not precipitous but efficient, twelve hours from the first contraction to the final push. While Carrie lies naked and elated, both ravenous and more satiated than anyone has ever been, I sneak into the building armed with champagne and toilet paper and bagels and pad thai and laundry detergent and Epsom salts. I deposit these offerings outside the apartment door, knock, and vanish.

Sometimes love means making yourself scarce. I know that now.

Gabe doesn't dwell on what it would mean for me if Carrie moved to New York. And it's not that he's self-absorbed, or even that he believes his connection to Carrie eclipses mine. To him, Carrie's proximity would be almost beside the point.

He wants his daughter. He wants Nina to need him as much as he needs her.

* * *

Back inside, the party has moved to the living room. Nina is curled into one corner of the couch, scrolling through Twitter on her phone, and Carrie is telling Tyler about a work problem. A prospective client wants his old gang tattoos covered up with the kind of curling ivy for which Carrie is famous, but his existing tattoos are dark, muddy, and spaced far apart. Carrie doesn't specialize in cover-ups. She should refer him to someone who does, but he's so invested in the idea of getting a Carrie Hart original—he's followed her on Instagram for years, memorized the FAQ section of her website—that she wonders if she shouldn't give it her best shot.

Tyler sits in a floral armchair with his legs splayed, one hand on each knee. As Gabe and I squeeze onto the sectional between Nina and Carrie, Tyler swallows three times in rapid succession.

Only now, at the last moment, do I acknowledge the possibility that Carrie will say yes. That she's actually in love with this guy. But there's no time to fret over what might happen next; Tyler rises from the floral chair and it's already happening. Lacking a utensil, he taps his car key against his beer bottle, interrupting Carrie midsentence. The noise intrigues Jack. In my lap, his bobble head lolls backward for a better view of the noise-producer.

"Carrie, I—"

She looks at him the way you look at a person about to ask you for a stick of gum.

"I know crazy romantic gestures aren't your thing, so I thought I'd do this at home. Where you're comfortable."

Carrie squints at him, and I know I've guessed correctly. Tyler Cox will never be her husband.

Tyler's hand goes to his pocket, and Gabe unthinkingly narrates, "Oh! He has a ring!" like an alarmed play-by-play announcer.

With a chuckle, Tyler says, "Carrie, will you marry me?"

Carrie frowns. For a long time, she frowns and says nothing and frowns. Then she clears her throat. "Um, Ty?"

"Yeah?"

"Why would you propose to me on my daughter's birthday?"

At the word *propose*, I extend a flattened palm in Carrie's direction. Without looking at me, she pushes my hand away.

Tyler clears his throat. "Well, I-I didn't want to leave Nina out . . ."

"*Please* leave me out of this," Nina says.

Tyler returns his hopeful gaze to Carrie. When she continues wordlessly gawking at him, he says, "Do you need time to, like, think it over?"

That she's tempted to take the out is obvious in the sudden parting of her lips, her eager intake of breath. The fingers of her right hand release their grip on the armrest. And who could blame her? If I were Carrie, I would excuse this boy from my house as soon as possible and reject him later, over email.

But Carrie's not me.

"No, I don't," she says gently.

Tyler is still standing in the middle of the room, looming over the rest of us. "You don't need time?"

"I don't need time."

Nina releases a long sigh. The look she and her father exchange is the equivalent of a high-five.

When Nina first told me her mother was on a picnic with Tyler Cox, I assumed the wholesome, midday date had been staged to show me how little Carrie thought of our shared past. Even the people who had populated our lives were no longer defined by what they had done and said to us back then but by more recent pleasantries exchanged in the supermarket or over drinks or in bed. Then Carrie revealed she'd been dating Tyler for a year, since before I'd turned up on her doorstep, before Gabe and I had made a baby. I understood her feelings for Tyler were genuine. At the very least, her feelings had nothing to do with me.

Still, could we have dreamed up a better revenge on the boy who mimed penetrating me in front of all his friends? A memory, as vivid as it is fake: Carrie and I ambling down Center Street, sucking chemical-blue ice through straw-spoon hybrids, Carrie spelling out the plan. "I'll grow up, make him fall in love with me, and turn down his proposal."

"Wow," Tyler says. "Okay." He snaps the ring box shut. It's not clear to him—to any of us—how he will get from this unbearable moment to the solitude of his Jeep. It's the most painful distinction between movies and real life: real-life scenes don't fade to black; people don't exit rooms a beat after delivering their punchiest lines.

Not that Tyler has any punchy lines in store for us.

What happens, finally, is that Carrie rises from the couch and takes Tyler's hand—gingerly, as if it's sticky—and leads him into the backyard to talk. The rest of us disperse. Gabe takes Nina to Dairy Queen, and I settle into the guest room for the nursing session that will put Jack to sleep until nine or nine thirty. Ten, if I'm lucky.

He's still pressed against my chest—intermittently dozing and mouthing my nipple—when I hear Tyler's Jeep rev and reverse out of the driveway. A minute later, Carrie creaks open the door to the guest room. She climbs onto the bed beside me.

There's no judgement or curiosity in her stare. She watches Jack as impassively as she would watch her own baby at her own breast.

Why, after everything, is it our comfort with each other's bodies that sticks?

Carrie unfurls her fist to reveal a crumpled twenty, which she places on my thigh.

The baby's eyes are closed. I keep my laughter lodged in my

throat. Carrie whispers, "You win," and I am happier than I've been in weeks.

"Let's move to Cleveland," I say.

"And all live in the same house? Like cult members?"

"Different houses. Same city."

"You think Nina was serious about leaving?"

"I think she's your daughter. I think she says what she means."

With her chin resting on my shoulder, Carrie watches Jack, the most beautiful baby ever born. I believe in his beauty the way I believe that winter lasts longer than summer, that spaghetti tastes better the second day.

"I'm in," she says.

CHAPTER THIRTEEN

Gabe and Nina are gone for a couple of hours, driving aimlessly or maybe waiting for stars to appear over one of the county's unlit parks. Gabe joins me in the guest room just as Jack is waking up. He starts to pull his T-shirt over his head. His arm is behind his neck when I say, "We should move to Ohio."

Gabe freezes. "To *Deerling*?"

"No. To Cleveland. Carrie and I discussed it, and we both agree."

Slowly, his arm falls to his side. His shirt stays hitched up in the back. "You would do that?"

"Gabe, I'm the one who's from here. I love Ohio."

He's stunned. I think he would be less stunned if I revealed I could dunk a basketball or that one of my eyes is made of glass. "I had no idea," he says.

"You want to be near Nina. I want to never again lug a stroller up the steps to the M train. Let's just move."

Slowly, Gabe crosses the room. Leaning over the bed and the baby, he places his hands on the sides of my face and kisses me. I whisper the details of the plan. We'll take a year. Carrie will sell her house, and Gabe will find a new job. Nina will finish junior high in Deerling and be ready to start anew, a freshman in the city.

Gabe kisses me deeper. Something in me tenses, some biological insistence that now is no time for touching. Too much touching is what got us here. But I love him, and he is letting me off the hook, and I need a second. I give the baby to Gabe for a burp and a change. I go to brush my teeth. Spitting into the sink, I remember being pregnant. My body was taut and warm and coursing with extra blood. I felt like a mammal but in the best way. We had sex all the time.

In our room, I find Gabe swaddling a heavy-lidded Jack in a receiving blanket. It feels like it's been forever since I saw Jack wrapped up like a burrito, his arms pinned to his sides. I had practically forgotten he used to sleep like that, snug and immobilized every night.

"That doesn't work anymore," I tell Gabe.

He takes his hands off the baby, who promptly punches through the folds of the blanket. "Since when?"

"Since the first night we spent here. I kept wrapping and rewrapping him, and he kept busting free. He doesn't like it anymore."

Gabe blinks. "The swaddle always calmed him down instantly."

"Well, now it fills him with rage."

Gabe marvels at his infant son. "How could he change so fast?"

I marvel too. And I don't know. I have almost forgotten the way he used to kick against the walls of my uterus—not exactly like a prisoner but like someone trying to get comfortable on a plane. I can barely remember the shocking thrill of his first detectable movements, the ever-heavier weight of him. How I used to walk around Ridgewood with my hands on my belly, never alone. Never alone again. What will I forget next? How he napped straight through the afternoons, curled like a comma on my chest? How he shook his head from side to side before locating the bullseye of my nipple?

The pitch of his cry in my ear?

Gabe sighs. "I guess this is why people have more than one kid."

Jack is drowsy. He's struggling to keep his eyes open. *Why fight it?* I want to ask him. *What do you think you're going to miss?*

We're not done yet; I already know that. My injuries will heal, and our baby will learn to sleep at night, and we'll have another. With a swirl of dread in my stomach, I acknowledge the future versions of ourselves who won't be able to resist doing this all over again.

I show Gabe our new routine—how I sit on the bed with my legs bent, Jack propped against my thighs, and rock him from side to side. The rocking must continue for a full five minutes after Jack shuts his eyes. Rock for fewer than five minutes and you can't be certain he's asleep. He may simply be resting.

Once I've placed him in the center of the mattress and arranged the pillows, I take Gabe's hand and pull him to the floor, to the braided wool rug that's always been in Carrie's house. When we were eleven, the year we met, it was in the kitchen, strictly Mr. Hart's domain. We used to annoy him by walking around the outermost seafoam-green braid as if it were a tightrope, careful to avoid letting our feet spill onto the rug's multicolored inner loops. I don't remember why. Probably it was just something to do as we sucked on popsicles or waited for dinner to be done.

"This might not work," I whisper to Gabe, kissing his throat.

It didn't work the first time we tried. Jack was seven weeks old. A few days earlier, at my one and only postpartum checkup, the OB who had delivered him almost declined to examine me. She finally agreed to take a look after I mentioned that things did not feel "entirely normal." What I meant was that occasionally I would bend my leg a certain way or choose to sit on an unforgiving stool and a flash of pain—the sharp kind associated with lacerations, or having foreign objects yanked from your flesh— would take my breath away. The OB declared that everything looked "perfect" aside from one tiny spot near the base of my vagina where a stitch "must have fallen out." With her fingertip she applied some kind of solution, which stung.

"I'm clearing you for intercourse," the OB announced.

Jack was squirming in a nurse's arms. Both women seemed annoyed I'd come to the appointment alone, but Gabe had used up all his sick days after the baby was born.

"Wait a few hours for that stuff to do its magic, then, you know . . . have a glass of wine, try to relax. And don't put it off too long—we don't want you developing a complex."

The apartment had sunk into squalor. Every surface was covered in dishes smeared with condiments or heaped with dirty laundry: fetid burp cloths and milk-soaked rags. Jack hadn't slept for more than three consecutive hours since birth. I was still dressing myself exclusively in sweatpants. The lanolin cream I used on my nipples had left greasy, asymmetrical stains on each of Gabe's T-shirts, but he didn't dare ask me to stop wearing them. Most of the time, when he got home from work, I wouldn't look at him. If he was even a few minutes late I imagined him lingering over stale coffee in the teachers' lounge or strolling home alongside his female colleague with the shampoo-commercial hair, and I doubled the time I spent cold-shouldering him.

Sex, I thought, would restore me to myself, us to each other. My hopes were not high or orgasmic. I aimed only for the mechanics to succeed—for nothing to rip open or cave in. If I could get through a few minutes of intercourse, wouldn't the rest of my life fall into place?

We waited until Jack was napping in his bassinet. Gabe wanted to shower together, soaping each other up and down like we used to, but I was unwilling to take off my bra. I'd had enough of my boobs; they were not invited to this party.

There was no wine, no laughter. Only urgency and the accidental fistful of lube that the bottle had belched forth.

It was as if Gabe had tried to penetrate an open wound, and I cried out.

Jack woke instantly, desperately needing to nurse. Threatening to fling himself from our fifth-story window if I didn't commence nursing him immediately. There was no time for what I needed, which was to lie flat on my back letting tears pool in my ears while Gabe assured me sex didn't matter. We could try again in another month, or a year, or when Jack graduated from high school.

"We don't have to try," he says now.

And so, like God-fearing teenagers, we do everything but.

Grimaces freeze on our faces each time a door hinge creaks or a neighborhood dog woofs and Jack stirs in response. After his first feeding of the night, there's no telling when he'll wake up; all bets are off. But miraculously, the baby sleeps on. Gabe and I take turns finishing each other with our hands. For me, at least, the end is mild—not a volcanic eruption but a warm bloom. Still, coming at all is an indication—the first I've had—that my body will recover. All of this, from my overgrown hair to my unclipped toenails, will be mine again.

Someday.

"I'm glad you're okay." Gabe rests his hand on my stomach.

"I didn't know how long the pain would last. No one warned me."

"The birth wasn't exactly routine," he says.

What I want to tell him, but don't, is that I'm afraid it was.

Gabe goes on, "When I think about those nights in the hospital, it's scary to remember how little I knew what I was doing. I look back on it and think, *I never should have let that guy touch my baby.*"

"I'm sorry," I say. Guilt overwhelms me whenever I remember the hospital.

Halfway through his second night outside my body, Jack became hungry. He alternated between sucking my nipples raw and screaming himself hoarse. Those screams were mad, beseeching. I was not yet producing milk, only colostrum, which resembled Vaseline in color and texture and would, according to the La Leche League breastfeeding manual, satisfy the baby. But the baby was far from satisfied, and I couldn't tolerate his suffering.

"We need formula," I told Gabe at 3:00 A.M.

Though he too had read the book's warning that a single drop of formula could render our son birdbrained and unemployable, Gabe agreed. Our night nurse, with whom we were a little bit in love, cheerfully showed Gabe how to feed Jack through a tube taped to his index finger. The baby latched onto Gabe's decoy nipple. His frown yielded to drowsy contentment as the formula began to flow.

In the morning, after the 7:00 A.M. shift change, our daytime nurse—whose tight ponytail lifted her eyebrows into a look of permanent skepticism—watched Jack guzzling his breakfast of premade poison and remarked, "I guess you've already given up."

Had I been able to get out of bed, I would have throttled her.

Everyone says labor is difficult but, at the end, you get a baby.

Another possibility: the difference between labor and a near-fatal accident is that at the end of labor, everyone expects you to take care of a baby.

"You're not allowed to apologize anymore," Gabe says.

I watch the ceiling fan spin above us. I wonder if we could surprise Jack by having a ceiling fan installed in our bedroom in Queens. I don't know when infants are capable of being surprised. I don't know when they get teeth or sit up or say *Mama*. I keep meaning to download an app that will tell me when to look out for this stuff.

Sometimes I doubt the birth was any easier on Gabe. Could I have watched the love of my life endure thirty-six hours of ceaseless pain without breaking down myself? Could I have paced the corridors of the hospital, haunted by the late-night howls of women laboring behind closed doors, soothing a rumpled newborn I'd barely met? Who could have been anyone's baby?

Across the hall, a toilet flushes. Nina informs Carrie they're out of toothpaste.

"Okay," I say to Gabe. "I won't be sorry."

"Will you marry me?" he asks.

* * *

You know how everyone thinks that when you have sex you, like, lose your innocence?

In the woods that day, I resented Carrie for invoking her own innocence.

Of course, I loved Nina. And I was too enchanted with the baby's pursed lips and violet eyelids to wish her existence away, but I hated thinking of her as the result of Carrie and Gabe having sex. That Carrie had brought it up during the one afternoon I might, conceivably, have thought about anything else; that she had done so casually, as if commenting on the humidity; that she was still pretending not to know I was in love with Gabe—all of it prevented me from hearing what she was trying to say.

I think I might have lost mine when I gave birth.

In the delivery room, Carrie felt pain for the first time. Not the dishrag twist of menstrual cramps or the jabs of food poisoning. Not the throb of nose fractures, sore shins, or however many twisted ankles she sustained during three years of high school track. Real pain, for which she had no metaphor or simile. From which she could not distract herself. At first, she didn't know if she would live, and then she did not know if she wanted to.

Because with the realization that she might die came the certainty that she *would* die, someday. And so would I, the childhood friend holding onto her knee, and so would Mrs. Hart, stroking the sweaty hair at Carrie's temples. Worst of all, the baby who hadn't yet taken her first breath would also take a final breath, maybe in an identical hospital room, with monitors tracking her heartbeat and anesthesiologists wandering uselessly in, out, and onward to the cafeteria.

What is innocence if not living your life without this preview? Without subjecting a child to as much pain and possibly more—all of which will be your fault, because you decided it was a good idea to build her in your body?

It took me thirteen years, but I get it now.

* * *

Gabe offers to run out and buy formula so I can sleep tonight. And it's tempting, the prospect of closing my eyes and not opening them until morning, but chances are that after four, maybe five hours, I'll wake up with my breasts rock hard and aching. Plus, I don't want to give the baby formula. My body keeping him alive is the *fuck you* I failed to issue to the nurse who accused me of giving up. Once we were home with Jack, my milk arrived overnight. My breasts were pale and heavy with it. He latched on lazily, but when his first few experimental pulls paid off, Jack went slack with relief. He nursed and has since nursed like he's never known another way.

So I feed Jack every two or three hours, but it's Gabe who paces and bounces him back to sleep. In the morning I feel, if not well rested, then functional. Like I could pass a basic multiplication test or recall, on demand, the maiden names of both my grandmothers.

In the afternoon, we drive to Green Acres to see my mom. We've been engaged for a full day, but Gabe and I are the only two who know. It would have felt cruel announcing it to Carrie over breakfast, the morning after her uncoupling with Tyler Cox. Besides, I can't decide if our engagement is even a big deal. If I want the hugs, the tearful congratulations.

Last night, Gabe said, "Will you marry me?"

ME: (*after a stunned silence*) I thought we decided we didn't care about that.

GABE: We did.

ME: Is this because I walked out on you? You want to make it illegal for me to leave?

GABE: It's 2016. Even married women are allowed to take vacations, I'm pretty sure.

Here my excitement began to simmer. I imagined myself in a flattering nonbridal dress from a boutique in Brooklyn. Everyone we know drinking whiskey cocktails from mason jars in a bar strung with fairy lights. Jack, a few months older than he is now, wearing a button-down onesie but changing into pajamas right after the ceremony.

ME: Would you want, like, a wedding?

GABE: If you do. But that wouldn't be the point.

ME: What would be the point?

GABE: The point would be to celebrate a choice we made a long time ago.

I turned to face him, my cheek resting against the braided rug. We didn't have much time before Jack's next wake-up. Between us hovered all the reasons we hadn't gotten married, like everyone else, when we were twenty-eight or twenty-nine.

ME: I should be the one proposing.

GABE: That's probably true

ME: Who should we invite?

GABE: Jack.

ME: Good call. Anyone else?

GABE: Nina.

ME: I'll add her to the list. Carrie, too.

GABE: What about your mom?

ME: If she'll fly to New York.

GABE: You don't want to get married in Ohio?

No, I decided. We will do this one last thing in New York before we give the city up for good.

As we approach Green Acres, the sun baking us through the windshield, I'm self-conscious of our timing. People will suspect we had a baby to fix what was broken between us, and, when that didn't work, got married to fix what was broken by the baby. At best, they will think our decade out of wedlock was a failed experiment. *Who needs a piece of paper from City Hall?* our younger selves scoffed.

We do, we admit, chastened at thirty-one.

My throat is dry as we approach my mother's trailer. The stone statue of Van Morrison props open the screen door.

We're not going to tell her, so why am I so nervous?

Because, I think, *she'll look at me and know.*

Jaclyn appears before we can knock or ring the bell. Some sixth sense has alerted her to the baby's presence. Her hair is wet from the shower. She's wearing a man's flannel with the sleeves rolled to her elbows. It's possible the shirt belonged to my father twenty years ago. Mom doesn't update her wardrobe until it's absolutely necessary, and even then, only one item at a time: A single pair of thick hiking socks. A black sweater from Walmart, which will pill and collect cat hair before its first wash.

She makes grabby hands at her grandson. Jaclyn has never been comfortable around Gabe, has never known how to greet or exchange pleasantries with him, but now the baby is a buffer between them. "Here's your grandma," Gabe sings, hoisting Jack into her arms.

My mom croons in the baby's face. It annoys me, the way she avoids looking Gabe in the eye.

I don't know what it's like to have a child old enough to have a child of her own. When I consider that my willingness to live five hundred miles from my mother—that I don't even miss her, most days—is not the result of some unique coldness in my heart but an American norm that will inspire Jack to one day make the same clean break, my throat tightens with panic. It's not fair how much we are required to love our children and how little they have to love us in return. It's fucked up that I can't observe the imperfections of my mother's aging body—her weathered toenails, the slack skin pooling at her elbows—without feeling ashamed. Her body evokes the beginning of me: all the swollen diapers, all the years I spent making poop jokes and asking what sorts of organs strangers were hiding beneath their clothes. It's embarrassing having a mother.

It's embarrassing being one.

"Mama, we're getting married."

I hold my breath as she looks up at me. I experience a jolt of that childhood fear: *Can I get in trouble for this?*

The last time I saw my father I was sixteen and had recently obtained my driver's license. As always, Dad called me on my birthday, but instead of hanging up at the earliest moment, he asked me to have dinner with him. He and his new girlfriend, Heidi, were passing through Deerling on their way to Akron to visit Heidi's parents. That he wanted to "introduce me to Heidi" rather than to see me, his only daughter, should have been my cue to decline. (The same invitation was extended to and wisely refused by my brother.) But one week later, I climbed willingly into my dad's Dodge Caravan, which he proudly told me he'd won in an auction of items repossessed from Indiana state prisoners. At Buffalo Wild Wings—called *B-Dubs* by my father and Heidi—with a tray of heavily sauced chicken wings between us, Heidi apologized to me for being "only twenty-nine."

"That's okay," I said, confused. Twenty-nine didn't strike me as young; it was older than I had ever planned on being. "You can't help it."

It was 2001, but Heidi's bangs were curled like it was 1990. She had big teeth, big boobs, big dreams. She worked for a cruise line's inexplicably South Bend–based marketing division, a company that offered its employees one week of ordinary vacation time or two weeks if they opted to vacation aboard a ship.

"I choose the ship every year," Heidi told me. "Who wouldn't?"

"Some people might prefer a week on land to two at sea," I said.

"Not me!" Heidi said, unfazed. "Me and my last boyfriend cruised to Jamaica *and* to the Bahamas. Next I'm hoping to take your dad to Cancun."

She winked at me.

Did my father ask me a single question? Did he touch me or breathe his ex-wife's name or use the word *love* in a sentence? My memory says no. As a parent, every part of me resists the memory, longing to dismiss it as impossible.

They dropped me off at home, and by the time they drove away, leaving tire tracks in the fresh snow, I was crying. My rattled sobs bewildered me. I didn't think I had expected, or needed, anything from my father. I had agreed to dinner at B-Dubs out of sheer curiosity and because I was interested in becoming a person who had seen her father recently, rather than a person who had last seen him when her age was a single digit. On the porch, in the cold, I waited for the emotion to pass. To clear up like bad weather. But my mother had flicked back the living room curtain in time to see an Indiana license plate departing. She emerged from the house, yanked a knit hat over my ponytail, and ushered me into the cab of her truck. Without asking, she knew I'd seen my father, and she also seemed to know everything that had transpired: his girlfriend calling me "Doll," the way Dad sat back in his chair, half watching a Cavs game and half watching me, waiting for me to be impressed. With him, I suppose, but for what? For having rustled up a woman who did not yet resent him?

Jaclyn and I drove with no destination. I stopped crying long enough to ask her for a cigarette; she mumbled, "Fat chance," our old routine. Out in the country, among the numbered roads on which she had so recently taught me to drive, we approached an intersection that had become a source of contention between us. There was a stop sign, but as you descended into the valley— cornfields, a frozen riverbed, a barn begging to be torn down or else vandalized—you had complete visibility. No blind corners, no place for a cop to hide. When I had been the one behind the wheel, my learner's permit ratting in a cup holder, I'd threatened not to stop. "It's pointless," I argued. "People who stop here are too scared to think for themselves."

"You stop because you don't want to wind up dead," Jaclyn had always told me, but this time I watched, in hushed disbelief, as she accelerated through the intersection. I felt elated and betrayed.

"Why'd you *do* that?" I asked, thinking she was trying to make a point. Something about rules, how some of them were fine to break.

For example, the rule of loving your father solely because he made you with his sperm.

Jaclyn gave me a blank look. Then, with a smile containing traces of guilt, she said, "Oh, I never stop there."

In 2001 she was still plump. She still barked her laughter as if punctuating a sitcom. For most people my mother was sweet and accommodating, but for me a fierceness smoldered in her eyes. In my favorite photo, Jaclyn is cross-legged on the center of her unmade bed. My brother, a toddler, rests a meaty hand on her knee. I am in a *Winnie the Pooh* nightgown and scaling her shoulder, my mouth wide open as if I'm about to nip her ear. The unflinching stare she gives the camera both distances herself from my brother and me and challenges the photographer, the whole world: *Just try and touch them.*

My beautiful mother. Who could leave her? I swore I would never get married, and I meant it. There's a version of my life—so plausible I can taste it, can hear the luxurious silence of it—in which I never fall in love, never reproduce, never answer to anyone but myself.

One year after Jaclyn ran the stop sign, Gabe Feldman moved to town.

My mother's instructions were clear: *Love him less.* But I've been trying to love him less since the day I met him, and I've never had any luck.

"Married?" Still standing in the doorframe of her trailer, she squeezes the baby close to her chest, as if Jack's the one who has delivered good news. "Oh, Amanda. Oh, Gabe."

We beam at her, proud of ourselves.

"You're going to be so much happier than I ever was."

She says this firmly, conclusively—as if it's been her goal all along.

* * *

After Jack was born, we weren't discharged until I'd answered a series of questions pertaining to my mental health. I nearly blew it when the doctor opened with "Are you doing okay?" and I replied evenly, "No, of course not," believing only a truly unstable individual would describe herself as "okay" forty-eight hours after giving birth.

At my bedside, Gabe widened his eyes until I realized what I'd said. I corrected myself: I was doing fine.

To the hospital, to give birth, I had worn ankle boots with two-inch wooden heels. By the end of my pregnancy, they were the only shoes into which I could still slide my swollen feet without having to bend over. They weren't comfortable, but they worked. As we were leaving—our baby strapped tight into his car seat, engulfed in pale-blue pajamas—I heard my boots clomping against the floor of the maternity ward, and the sound made me cry. It was the sound I'd heard everywhere in the final weeks before the birth, that era in which, it now seemed, I had been blissfully innocent. Naive enough to hope for a quick labor and an epidural that worked and, in the minutes after delivery, skin-to-skin cuddles—anything approximating relief.

Carefully, Gabe set down the car seat and gripped my shoulders. "Amanda, when we get home, you can cry for a year. But right now, I need you to put a big smile on your face and walk confidently past the nurses' station. Got it?"

Gabe was losing his patience with the hospital staff, who had already detained us an extra six hours. "It's a Sunday." Our nurse had shrugged. "There's a lot of paperwork."

In the hallway, gravity straining the floor of my pelvis, I laughed through my tears. "I still love you more than the baby," I told Gabe.

Granted, this was before I'd ever spent an entire afternoon with Jack's cheek resting on my shoulder, before I noticed his chin dimple, identical to mine. Weeks before his first coo, first cold. Before the needles in his thighs. But it was true then.

Is it wrong to hope it's true forever?

* * *

As we're leaving Green Acres, my mom says, "Whatever kind of wedding you have, even if it's just at city hall, I'd like to be there."

"Of course," I say.

Ostensibly to Jack, she says, "Your mama has a tendency to leave me out of important events."

I don't know what she means until I do. It honestly never occurred to me to ask my mother to be present at my son's birth. Even if she had suggested it herself—which she didn't—I'd have been overwhelmed by logistics. Was I supposed to call her the moment I felt my first contraction? What was the going rate for last-minute airfare between Cleveland and New York? Who would drive my mom to the airport? Would she succeed in navigating the mess of taxis outside the terminal at JFK, or would she fall prey to one of those guys who pulls you into his BMW, calls you *sweetheart*, and charges you $200 for a ride downtown?

It would have struck me as impossible, calling up my mother and asking her to meet me at Mount Sinai at her earliest convenience.

Of course, if I'd asked, that's exactly what she would have done.

Waiting for Gabe to unlock the car, there's a flash of movement in my peripheral. I turn to see a man exiting the trailer two doors down, stepping onto his plywood porch to light a cigarette. It's Brian, I think. The one who has it out for Van Morrison. His yard is festooned with a new MAKE AMERICA GREAT AGAIN sign—this one with a weather-resistant sheen— along with a family of those plastic flamingos people stick in the ground for no reason.

Brian is younger than me, but I can't tell by how much. There's a spark in his eye as he shuffles his feet and surveys his surroundings, like he's looking for a kid to tease or something he can set on fire.

A girl steps outside and huddles beside him. The girl is Trinity, Maxine's sixteen-year-old sister. She stands on her tiptoes to kiss Brian's scruffy cheek.

When Nina referred to Trinity's boyfriend, I imagined a teenager, a boy who proudly slid his driver's license inside the transparent sleeve of his wallet mere months ago. I did not imagine a man closer to my own age than to Trinity's. A man with mud caking his work boots and a week's worth of stubble crawling down his neck.

Brian's truck is parked in the grass. Its bumper bears a single, faded sticker: IF JESUS HAD A GUN, HE'D BE ALIVE TODAY.

"Gabe," I hiss over the roof of our Subaru.

"What?" he whispers back dramatically.

I jerk my head in the direction of Trinity and Brian—though Gabe has never seen either of them before in his life. He doesn't know Trinity is Maxine's sister, cannot suddenly imagine, with perfect clarity, how she sweet-talked her boyfriend into letting her borrow the truck once or twice. She would have been coy, secretive about the project until he coaxed it out of her. The whole thing—young women canvassing for a detested female candidate—rubbed him the wrong way. Unwilling to retaliate against

Trinity's own family, he set out to punish the girl who didn't matter to him.

Or maybe, simply, to correct her.

"That's Trinity," I say.

Gabe frowns. "Nina's friend?"

"Nina's friend's sister."

"That man is forty."

"Twenty-five, tops."

"Still gross."

"He vandalized Carrie's lawn."

"No. Come on."

"Trust me."

I consider slashing Brian's tires. My mother would have a suitable knife. The task would probably thrill her.

I note the truck's license plate and imagine trying to explain to the police: it's not only that he trespassed; it's not only that he messed with the grass; it's that he crushed the pure-hearted activism of two little girls. In my mind, Maxine and Nina are as innocent as children offering daisy chains to fairies, cookies to Santa. They asked the universe, *Are we alone out here?*

Brian replied, *Hell yes, you are.*

"We should do something, right? On behalf of Nina?"

"*Do* something?"

"Now's our chance. Let's exact our revenge."

Gabe grins at me, pleased by my loyalty to his kid. Assuming I'm kidding, he says, "Amanda, you're holding an infant. Let's maybe avoid exacting revenge on a guy so passionate about gun ownership he wishes he could go back in time and give one to Jesus."

I place a hand on Jack's head to calm myself down. Gabe's

right. My only option is to get in the car. But Brian chooses this moment to squeeze Trinity's ass through the pocket of her embroidered jeans.

"Hold the baby."

Marching up Brian's porch steps, I feel weightless. Uncivilized and unrestrained. He's already sputtering some confused obscenity even before I smack him across the face.

My right arm is strong, which shouldn't surprise me: I spend approximately twenty hours a day holding a fifteen-pound infant.

Gesturing in Gabe's direction, I tell Trinity to get in the car.

"Who the fuck're you?" Brian wants to know. His fingertips are pressed into his cheek. I hope it throbs.

"Nina's stepmom," I say.

"Who the fuck's Nina?"

Trinity, dazed but composed, says, "My sister's friend," as I answer, "The little girl whose house you vandalized two nights ago."

Trinity shouts, "*What?*"

He tells her, "Sweetie, we were wrecked. I mean, just obliterated."

"Obliterated is what you're going to be if you go anywhere near these girls again," I say. "Got it?"

Trinity's eyes go comically, theatrically wide. "What did you do?" She screams the question. It's the scream of someone who knows what Brian's capable of.

Two doors down, my mother emerges from her trailer. "Amanda?" she calls. Her voice crackles with excitement. I should be mortified, but this is exhilarating.

"Get in the car," I tell Trinity.

"Don't get in this psycho's car," Brian says.

"Get in the car," I repeat.

"We'll talk later," Brian says.

"No, you won't."

For whatever reason, Trinity trusts me. She turns her back on her boyfriend and walks calmly across the grass to the Subaru, where Gabe and the baby stand marveling. Astonished, they look identical. When Gabriel Theodore Feldman was born in 1985 in Hartford, Connecticut, his parents—had they been the gambling type—would have bet against their son ever stepping foot in a mobile home park, let alone witnessing any trailer-side altercations, let alone marrying a girl who instigates them. Lucky for me, Hank and Diane only got to guess at, not choose, Gabe's future. And now he's looking at me the way he did in Carrie's truck that hazy September nearly fourteen years ago. The click of the disposable camera was satisfying. Something mechanical, magical, that could also be thrown away. *You're real*, he said.

Before me, it was all fake.

Brian's last retort, delivered with a sneer is, "Who are you— my mom?"

Over my shoulder, I say, "I'm someone's mom, Brian."

* * *

In the car, I show Trinity the pictures Gabe snapped of Carrie's front lawn. Trinity weeps as she flips through the collection. Gabe was fastidious, photographing Brian's landscaping efforts from every angle. Did he imagine us presenting our evidence in court?

"I don't even care about politics," Trinity says. "I was just trying to be a good sister."

"I'm sure you're a great sister," Gabe says, navigating the twists and valleys of the rural road.

I say, "Look, Trinity, it's not your fault. You can't choose how Brian spends his leisure time. But maybe consider dumping an asshole who vandalizes the homes of thirteen-year-olds and has legitimately threatened to shoot my mother's cat."

Trinity grimaces, clearly no stranger to the cat saga. "Do *you* think I should break up with him?" she asks Gabe. At some point in the last ten minutes, she has shifted her blind faith from me to him. Probably because I'm coming across as a little unhinged, and Gabe, as a good-looking man of a certain age, is Trinity's exact type.

"Um, how old is he exactly?" Gabe asks.

Trinity sniffles. "Twenty-four."

Gabe and I exchange a look. "Dump him," he says. "Posthaste."

We drop her off at home, rounding the circular driveway and making our getaway before her parents can rush out and question us—though as Gabe points out, "They seem pretty hands-off." By the time we get back to Carrie's house, our baby is sound asleep. His head lolls as Gabe lifts the car seat, but he doesn't wake up. It's possible we have overstimulated him.

In the yard, Carrie is sitting on top of the picnic table, her bare feet resting on the bench. Shielding her eyes against the setting sun, she waves at us.

"Go hang out," Gabe tells me. "I'll come get you when Jack wakes up."

"You don't have to," I say. "I've been pumping. There's breast-milk in the freezer. You can feed him."

Gabe hesitates. His resistance is subtle and brief, but I catch it. *You have a baby*, I think. *So feed him.*

"To thaw the milk, I just . . ."

"Run the bag under lukewarm water. Bottles are in the cupboard above the fridge."

"Right. Okay." Gabe smiles at me and, having summoned the courage, marches his son into the house. I go to Carrie.

From my back pocket I withdraw the crumpled twenty she gave me last night. I hold it in the air in front of her nose until she, comprehending, takes it between two fingers.

"You still lost, technically," I tell her. "But only by a couple of hours."

I'm not prepared for Carrie's reaction. Her features collapse in a display of unveiled emotion. Tears spring from her eyes. "No shit! Are you serious?"

"I think Gabe might've proposed ten years ago, if I'd let him."

"Of course he would have. You know, people don't normally love other people as much as Gabe loves you. It's kind of weird. Congratulations, Amanda."

I stare at her, willing myself to speak. This is my chance. We are alone. No one is hungry or sobbing or otherwise needing us.

Someday, when my son understands language, I will tell him I'm sorry. Probably I will tell him multiple times a day: Sorry for yelling at you in the grocery store. Sorry for roughly yanking your arm through your coat sleeve. Sorry for plopping you on the floor and immediately distancing myself, as if every second you're not climbing up my leg is precious. Sorry for screaming into a pillow. Sorry for behaving as if you're the problem or your dad is the problem or the collection of unpaid parking tickets is the problem when I am and have always been the only problem.

Though I fantasize about communicating with Jack in English, I also doubt our relationship will ever be truly shaped or altered by words. Who has ever said of their own mother, "She screamed into pillows, but she always apologized after"? We remember what our parents did and how they made us feel. Jack won't consider what unspeakable actions my screaming into a pillow replaced. The sin was needing to scream at all.

When I was thirteen, I went to retrieve my lip gloss from the cup holder in my mother's truck, and I left an interior light on, draining the battery overnight and preventing Jaclyn from getting to work on time. I was still half-asleep when she pulled me out of bed and slapped me. What shocked me was not her capacity for violence—of which I was already aware: the way she choked the air in front of my brother's face or hammered her own fist against her thigh, tenderizing the strongest part of her—but that she had hit me over something so trivial. Thirteen was an age at which I often told my mother, *You have ruined my life.* Not that she was in the process of ruining it, or that she behaved as if she *wanted* to ruin it, but that she already had. My life, finished. Once she ordered me to wash a saucepan in which I'd allowed the remains of Kraft Macaroni & Cheese to cluster and calcify. Already mad at her for some forgotten reason, I filled the pot and tossed its contents, murky with soap and cheese and waterlogged noodles, at Jaclyn's chest. The bile splashed against her chin and soaked through the cotton of her white sweater.

She didn't hit me then. Why did she hit me over an honest mistake? When I compared notes with Carrie, she confirmed that Rosalind Hart was similar in her unpredictability. Our mothers' moods were frighteningly, almost offensively, unlinked to our deeds, good or bad.

Jaclyn never apologized for the morning of the dead car battery. Though I'm sure she felt remorse, apologizing would have been futile. Even now, when she talks to me over the phone, I barely hear her. All that she says and has never said merges into a fixed and immutable impression of my mom. I love her and I dread her. I forgive her and I never will. How can I expect Jack to feel differently about me?

I've always thought of my relationship to Carrie as familial, nearly as intuitive, vital, and maddening as that between me and my mom. As kids, we ended handwritten notes, passed between desks in our sixth-grade classroom, with *LYLAS*. Our own children, blood-related to each other, have further ensnared us in this idea of ourselves as grown siblings, guaranteed to reappear at holiday parties and funerals, drunkenly impervious to the proof of each other's adulthood. But what if I chose *not* to love Carrie like a sister? What if we redefined the terms?

"I'm sorry," I say.

She looks surprised, and then the opposite. "Are you really?"

"For some things."

"Which?"

"For showing up at your house without calling first. For not calling at all, ever. For becoming a stranger to Nina. For ditching you with a newborn when you were eighteen."

Carrie frowns. "You don't have to call before you come over."

"I'm not sorry about Gabe."

"I wouldn't expect you to be."

"I mean, it was an objectively terrible thing to do. Skipping town with the father of my best friend's child."

"But it was worth it." A statement, not a question.

"Yes."

Carrie is silent. I still want what I wanted when we were squeezed into the same hospital bed, watching people on television lose their virginities without consequence. What I did to Carrie was

EMILY ADRIAN

worse than what she did to me. Only in hindsight do her actions seem especially cruel, whereas my betrayal was never more acute than the moment I announced I was following Gabe to New York. Still, I'm mad. Not on behalf of my thirty-one-year-old self, who's going to be fine. I'm mad on behalf of the girl I was. The girl with whom Gabe would make impish eye contact as his hand remained buried in Carrie's hair. Who was expected to bear the news of her friend's pregnancy with stoic resignation then tender resolve.

I liked him first.

Carrie reads my mind, the way she used to. Her hands grip the raw edge of the picnic table. "Gabe and me . . . I mean, insofar as we were ever anything . . ."

My cheeks are hot. I want to know everything and also nothing about the brief period of time in which Gabe and Carrie's relationship took precedence over what I had with either of them. Given a film reel of those six weeks, I would pause and then return to the footage again and again.

"Sleeping with him . . ." Carrie is speaking circuitously, the topic awaiting clearance to land.

I nod.

She exhales. "I would love to say it had nothing to do with you. That I was seventeen and I went after the new kid because he appealed to me. Which he did. Obviously he did, especially in the moment. But if I'm being honest, I knew it would hurt you. And hurting you both did and did not appeal to me."

"Why would you want to hurt me?"

The question is a reflex. I once took pleasure in deleting Carrie's number from my cell (as if I didn't have it memorized). And I was twenty-three or twenty-four the time I let Paige answer Gabe's phone, unattended and vibrating on the kitchen counter, caller ID flashing Carrie's name. I could hear Carrie's confusion through the speaker, and yet I did nothing to disguise my drunken laughter. Gabe returned from the bathroom and wrenched the phone from Paige's hand, shooting venomous looks at both of us as Carrie told him Nina was in the ER with a fever of 103.

"I don't know," Carrie says. "When we were kids it seemed to me like you always got what you wanted. And I was crazy about you—so when it was me or my attention you wanted, you got it. But then we were older, and the stakes felt higher, and I couldn't tell where you ended and I began. I know that's a cliché of codependency, but . . ."

We're having trouble sustaining eye contact. We ought to have had this conversation in a bar in our twenties, in the neon glow of a beer sign, pint glasses sweating in our hands. But we waited too long. Now we're old; we're sober; mosquitos keep landing in the creases of our elbows and on the napes of our necks.

She says, "You were ready to Moon River it all over America. And I just needed something else. At least, I needed to need something else. So maybe sleeping with Gabe was an experiment in you not getting what you wanted. In me taking something from you. For once."

I slap at another bug. "You were schooling me in loss?"

"Maybe. To see if you could handle losing me. Or me winning. But God, I didn't know the effects would be so irreversible. Before it happened, I'd have sworn that if I ever got knocked up, I'd be the first girl in line at the Mansfield Planned Parenthood in the morning. And I had no idea the *ridiculous* tension between you and Gabe was, like, the foundation of a lasting relationship. I mean, it's a fucking miracle you two are still together. What are the chances?"

In between Nina's birth and Jack's, there were entire years in which Gabe seemed as guaranteed as a brother or a comfortable piece of furniture. I forgot he wasn't my husband. I forgot he was never *mine* to begin with. On long subway rides or treks to the hardware store, I would fantasize, innocently, about leaving him. Pressing my body against a stranger's in a bar. Fucking a man who didn't know my middle name. It was only after Gabe impregnated me that I saw him as a hologram, shifting between the most familiar person in my life and the boy I once desired so fiercely it made me physically ill not to have him. I used to look at him across the booth at Denny's, knowing his hands were interfacing with Carrie's beneath the table, and realize we would either end up together or we wouldn't.

Both outcomes felt equally impossible.

Carrie takes a breath. She says, "When I found out I was pregnant, I loved my daughter. Immediately. I couldn't change the way it had happened. I couldn't give Gabe back to you."

Finally, I sit beside Carrie on the picnic table, my left knee colliding with her right. As children we rarely fought, and when we did—after I borrowed Carrie's favorite jeans and washed them with an uncapped Sharpie in the pocket, or after Jennifer Rollins passed Carrie a note that read, *Plz rate Amanda's hotness on a scale of 1–10*, and Carrie rated me a 6.5, and Jennifer promptly dropped the note on my desk—the experience was traumatic for both of us. We sobbed until our noses ran. We went home and called each other, hung up on each other, got busy signals as we tried to call each other back. And when it was over, when we'd made up and Carrie had slung her skinny arm around my neck, our friendship felt brand new. As fresh as daybreak, and as full of potential.

It's a feeling I had assumed was lost forever.

"Well," I say, aiming for relief, for levity, "I took him back."

She heaves a sigh and plays along. "Typical."

"And now we're staying in your guest room."

"I love having you in my guest room."

"We had sex on the floor last night."

Carrie wrinkles her nose. "Rude."

"On the rug that used to be in your parents' kitchen."

"Amanda?"

"Don't worry. We were tidy."

"Amanda."

I catch my breath and say, "Carrie."

She takes my hand and pulls it into her lap. "When you and Gabe left for New York, and I couldn't stop crying into a dish towel that smelled like Nina's spit-up . . ."

"Uh-huh," I say, as if familiar with the dish towel. And maybe I am.

Carrie is messing with a metal ring on my middle finger. "My mom made me promise I would never apologize to you. She hated your guts. And I kept defending you, saying, 'No, no, Amanda and I are even now; we broke each other's hearts.' Rosalind thought that was bullshit though, because having a crush on someone and having a baby with someone aren't the same thing. But now you guys have Jack. So, I'm calling it." Carrie squeezes my hand. She looks at me. "We're even, and I'm sorry."

I nod, understanding both the range and the limits of her apology. She's sorry for hurting me, but she's not sorry for having Gabe's baby. That's the thing about babies: after you have one, all imagined alternatives to the past become tragedies.

"I don't want Gabe to keep us separate," I say. "We'd be like one of those families whose pets don't get along. Like, there's a cat in the garage and a dog in the kitchen, and if you forget to shut the door between the two, murderous mayhem ensues."

"I don't want that either," Carrie says.

Through the window of the guest room we hear crying. So rarely has Jack woken up without bursting into tears. The problem, it seems, is that he never consented to falling asleep in the first place. He never consented to any of it—the car seat, the insatiable hunger, the separation from his mom. His life is a series of injustices inflicted upon him. I close my eyes, hoping it occurred to Gabe to thaw the milk preemptively. Hoping he doesn't give up and emerge from the house carrying our son in front of his body as a shield against my own frustration.

I drop my chin, press my cheek into my shoulder, and wait.

Gabe stays inside.

Carrie catches me staring at the tattoos on her left arm, some of which I know she did herself, contorting her body and straining the muscles in her neck to make it possible. The colors are muted, the designs soft but intricate, like illustrations from a picture book.

"Let me tattoo you," she says.

"What would you give me?" I ask.

"Whatever you want."

"The state of Ohio with a heart in it."

"No."

"The word *mom* in old-timey cursive, surrounded by those little blue birds who help Cinderella get dressed."

Carrie rolls her eyes.

"What about that girl everyone always wants?" I ask. "From your portfolio?"

"That girl is *you*."

"She's teenage me."

"You want me to tattoo teenage you on your grownup body?"

"She's not really me," I say. "She's the way you saw me."

Now Nina is pushing through the screen door, letting it slam behind her. "Mom!" she shouts with so much urgency that for a second I worry she's injured.

"Yes?" Carrie answers, tranquil.

"Where's the peanut butter?"

Carrie closes her eyes. "There's a new jar next to the microwave."

Before going back inside, Nina frowns at me. "Your baby's crying."

"Take it up with your dad," I counter.

For whatever reason, Nina slinks back inside as if I've reprimanded her.

"She'll be your stepdaughter now," Carrie says.

"What does that make you and me?"

Leaning over her knees like a person experiencing vertigo, Carrie smiles at the grass and says, "There's no word."

* * *

Carrie does not tattoo teenage me on my grown-up body. I never wanted her to, really; I only wanted her to admit that the most popular piece from her portfolio is me, the direct result of all the hours we spent arched over matching sketchpads. "Put your head back the way it was," I would say, "you're ruining my drawing."

"Stop talking," she would say, "you're ruining mine."

If I had known Carrie would monetize my scowl, maybe I would have written that admissions essay, *The Night My Best Friend Gave Birth*. I was afraid writing it would feel like stripping our friendship for parts, and I was hurt when it appeared that

Carrie had, with her tattoos, done exactly that. But maybe she never saw it that way. Maybe to her those sketches were always a means to an end—practice for some better life.

Maybe our whole friendship was practice.

The night before Gabe and I leave Ohio, I tell Carrie to sketch me an idea. The only instruction I'm willing to give her is "something for Jack." Undaunted by the task of paying homage to someone too small to have a personality, Carrie finishes the drawing in five minutes flat.

"For your shoulder," she says, presenting me with her sketchpad. "So you can still hide it from your mom."

For the rest of my life, I will blush while explaining to strangers that I have a tattoo of a jackrabbit in honor of my son named Jack. Carrie's idea is sappy and embarrassing and I love it. One day, Jack will love it too. (And then hate it. And then love it again.)

We leave the kids with Gabe, and Carrie drives me to Mansfield. Her studio is on Main Street, wedged between a Greek diner and a children's bookstore. In the front window is a framed *New York Times* profile, published the same year I heard Carrie interviewed on NPR. Inside, her studio has brick walls and a clean glass reception desk.

In a back room, Carrie tells me to lie down on what appears to be a massage table wrapped in plastic. The sight of the table immobilizes me. Fear makes a desert of my throat. Maybe I can't do this.

Carrie touches me. "You okay?"

"Are you sure this is safe? Like, for breastfeeding?"

"The ink won't get into your milk, if that's what you're asking."

"And I won't get an infection?"

"No. I'll show you how to take care of it."

Maybe I don't want another body-based chore. Maybe I don't

want my body to be the subject of anyone's dispassionate scrutiny ever again.

"Will it hurt?" I ask, stalling.

"Compared to pushing a baby out of your vagina? The pain won't even register."

Carrie shows me the stencil she has made of the jackrabbit drawing. Suddenly I want the rabbit on my shoulder more than anything. I want a tattoo for the same reason I wanted to have sex with Gabe when I was seven weeks postpartum. So rarely in the past year has my body been under my authority.

I climb onto the table and lie with my face in a pillow that smells vaguely medicinal. My nursing tank top gives Carrie full access to the canvas of my shoulder blade. With gentle confidence she transfers the stencil to my skin.

"Tell me if you feel yourself freaking out, okay?" she says, and the needle begins to vibrate.

Carrie's wrong. The pain registers, but it's the kind of pain I can breathe through. It's the sting of a hot shower on a fresh sunburn or a cube of ice clutched tightly in my palm. It's a pain I can forget and then remember and then choose to live with. It never swallows me whole.

After finishing the rabbit's outline, Carrie switches to a bigger needle for the shading, which hurts a little more.

"How much do I owe you for this?" I ask.

She laughs at me.

CHAPTER FOURTEEN

Angela Beatty, recently promoted to staff writer for *The Atlantic*, sends me an email after Gabe and I get back to New York. Her name in my inbox rings only a distant bell. I click, and the photo of Jared Jenkins's funeral procession loads within the body of the message. Having only ever glanced at it over Nina's shoulder, I'm impressed by the image enlarged on my laptop's screen. For the first time, I appreciate how much the picture reveals: not only the casket draped in the confederate flag or the pro-Trump banner or the blue backdrop of Deerling's cloudless sky, but the self-righteous sneer on the driver's face. His confidence that he is honoring his friend, that there's a version of America—long gone or still to come—that could have prevented the death of a teenage kid who didn't want to wear a seatbelt.

"Did you take this photo," Angela Beatty wants to know, "on Sunday, June 26, 2016, in the town of Deerling, Ohio?"

That she doesn't ask me to supply the family's name is a relief. I write back, "Yes. Why?" and receive an immediate response.

"Do I have your permission to publish it alongside a piece I'm writing about Trump supporters in the rural Midwest? It's a striking photo of an ugly thing. I think it needs to be seen. Where I live, people don't realize how passionate his fans have become."

Jack is asleep in his vibrating chair on the coffee table. I'm deep within the embrace of our broken yellow couch, basking in the comfort of my own apartment, which Gabe scrubbed spotless before he met us in Cleveland.

Jack will never claim to be from New York. He won't remember the M train barreling past the kitchen window, the bedroom door that never fully shut, the pipe in the bathroom that stays so hot we have to warn our guests not to touch it. (Of course, they touch it.) He will belong to Ohio. To his dad and to me and to Nina and to Carrie. Remembering that this was not part of the plan when I was round with him, pulsing and aching and sick with him, makes my blood run cold. I feel as if I've seized the wheel and swerved at the last moment, narrowly missing the sharp slope of the ravine to my right.

Was Deerling everything you wanted it to be? Gabe asked over the phone, exasperated, pretending what I wanted was lost on him.

Yes. Unequivocally.

"Publish the photo," I tell Angela, because Nina should get what she wants too. Nina should get everything. "Put Deerling on the map. But for the record, we don't live there anymore."

* * *

What Gabe says, when I've drunkenly demanded answers, is that he didn't immediately know I was interested. When we found him reading poetry alone in the woods, it was Carrie who greeted him, who struck up the aggressive back-and-forth that passes for conversation when you're seventeen. She was the one who asked for his screen name, and who, during those last weeks of summer, sought opportunities to touch obscure parts of his body: she pressed his anklebone and said, "Skinny." She pulled on his earlobe and asked, "Did you sterilize the needle, at least?"

Meanwhile, what was I doing? I was laughing at Gabe's jokes—disconcertingly hard, he claims, as if maybe *he* was the joke—and speaking to Carrie in an alienating shorthand, forever reeling her back to the shore of our friendship. Gabe had no way of knowing that in one year he would ask me to give her up for him. Or that I would do it.

I don't believe he was ever oblivious to my longing, which wasn't subtle. But I don't blame him for choosing Carrie, for assuming it made no difference which girl he kissed that year. Deerling was supposed to be like Vegas. (High school was supposed to be like Vegas.) Our lives were allegedly spread out before us, as immaculate as the layer of snow that blanketed the dump each January, concealing its creeks and trails.

The three of us were babies.

"My mom will be at work until at least seven," Carrie promised. "We can rustle up some adult beverages and chill until then."

At her house, Carrie promptly left Gabe and me alone in the yard while she pillaged the garage for the promised hard lemonade—which Mr. and Mrs. Hart, both of them abstinent and devout, stocked for their less disciplined guests. Gabe collapsed cartoonishly into an old hammock that Carrie and I hadn't gone near in years. The hammock sagged almost to the ground and Gabe wore an expression of good-natured regret.

The silence between us was so strained it was intolerable. I stared at the weeds of Mrs. Hart's long-abandoned garden, hoping to appear lost in a thought that had nothing to do with Gabe, one so deep and complicated he would have trouble comprehending it, even if I were to let him try.

"So, who are you?" he said at last. "The wordless sidekick?"

I suspected Gabe had misinterpreted the way I'd climbed voluntarily into the back of the truck, where a shallow bench seat gave me an unobstructed view of his left shoulder as he rode shotgun.

"Not a sidekick. The best friend."

"Ah. So, I guess I should expect to see a lot of you?"

"Carrie hasn't managed to shake me yet."

"Has she tried?"

"Of course. But I'm all she's got."

Carrie reappeared, ducking beneath the partially closed garage door. She had two bottles of lemonade wedged between the fingers of her left hand, a third bottle clutched in her right. "Let's drink these fast," she said, "and then find something to do."

"What do you mean *something*?" Gabe was lying in the hammock with one arm bent above his head. I could see down the sleeve of his T-shirt, where clumps of deodorant clung to a nest of dark hair. "Isn't this enough?"

Carrie and I looked askance at each other. This, so far, was nothing.

"We'll need a change of scenery," I said.

"Some food," Carrie added.

"Drugs," I proposed.

"At least one *dear diary* moment."

"Oh, at least."

Gabe twisted the cap from his drink and said, "I think I've made a mistake, following you people home."

Correctly, Carrie predicted, "Too late now."

ACKNOWLEDGMENTS

Love and gratitude to my agent, Susan Ginsburg, whose guidance over the past decade has meant everything. I'm also grateful to Stacy Testa for her comments on an early draft and to Catherine Bradshaw for her help at every stage.

Thank you to Peggy Hageman, whose sharp editorial eye and sense of humor made revising a dream.

Thank you to the entire team at Blackstone Publishing, including Ember Hood, Josie Woodbridge, Rick Bleiweiss, Jeff Yamaguchi, Greg Boguslawski, Lauren Maturo, Megan Wahrenbrock, and Mandy Earles.

Thank you to my writer friends and first readers, including Kerry Winfrey, Liz Zaretsky, Lauren Rochford, and Carolyn Eyre.

Thanks, finally, to the three loves of my life: Dan, Wes, and Hank. Let's get back in the car.